Death Knock

A Noshes Up North Culinary Mystery

Book 2

Mary Grace Murphy

Category: Cozy Mystery

Editor: Brittiany Koren/Written Dreams
Cover art design and page layout: Ed Vincent/ENC Graphic Services
Cover photographs © Shutterstock

Published in the United States of America

0 1 2 3 4 5 6 7 8 9

Dedication

This book is dedicated to the memory of Maxine and Robert Vial, my mom and dad. They instilled the love of reading in me, which carried over into my enthusiasm for writing. I miss you both every day.

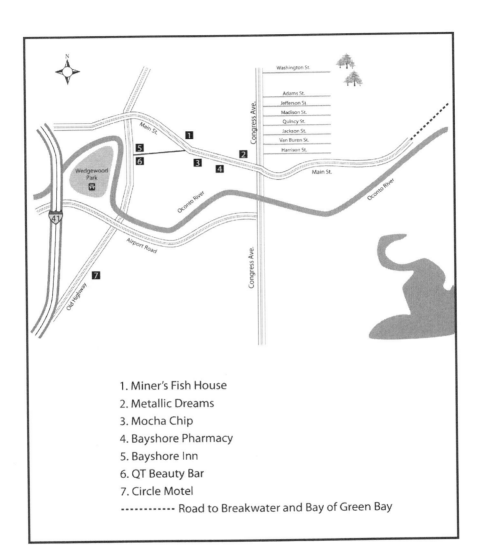

1. Miner's Fish House
2. Metallic Dreams
3. Mocha Chip
4. Bayshore Pharmacy
5. Bayshore Inn
6. QT Beauty Bar
7. Circle Motel
----------- Road to Breakwater and Bay of Green Bay

Chapter 1

The pounding on the front door of her Bayshore, Wisconsin home startled Nell right out of a daydream. This was no polite little knock. The racket drilled into her eardrums and woke her dogs from a sound sleep. "What the heck?" she mumbled, as she hurried to the door amidst a flurry of small barking canines.

Looking through the side panel, Nell observed an unfamiliar rugged looking man as he alternately rang the doorbell and pounded on the door, almost like a cartoon character. She hesitated, wondering if it was safe to open the door. Living with only her dogs since her husband, Drew, died, she was more wary of potential dangers. During that momentary hesitation, the thunderous noise stopped. Nell peeked through the window in the dining room, hoping she'd see him leaving. All she noticed was an older vehicle parked in her driveway. There was no sign of the man getting into the car.

Nell turned and jumped, taken by surprise, as she looked toward the kitchen and saw the tall stranger looking in at her from the big window. Her boys, a Schnauzer, George, and Maltese, Newman, noticed the man at the same time and tore off toward him barking.

"Boys, stay," Nell commanded as she knew the dogs would head straight for the doggie door. They obediently stayed put as she went to talk to the stranger. No getting out of it now.

"Can I help you?" Nell inquired through the screen door.

"I hope so." The man met her at the door. "I'm looking for Annie Marshall and my information tells me she lives here, 924 Adams Street. Could I speak to her, please?"

"You have the wrong house." Nell told the intruder, for that was how she now felt about the man. Coming around the house into her backyard was unacceptable to Nell. "And the wrong street. She lives on Jefferson, the next block over. Also, I don't appreciate you coming onto my property like this."

"I'm sorry, ma'am," he apologized. "But it's crucial I see her as soon as possible. Thank you so much for your help." The man was already moving as he spoke and was soon on his way.

"Ma'am," Nell snorted. "He didn't look that much younger than I am." She coaxed the boys over for belly rubs and then walked with them outside in the backyard. "What's up with that? What do you two think?" Nell asked them. Their only responses were hopeful looks at the ball. After tossing it to them a few times, Nell took the dogs back in the house.

Perhaps she shouldn't have been so quick to give this character the name of Annie's street. A former student of hers, Annie was going through a bit of a rough patch. From what Nell had heard, she divorced her husband several years ago and recently returned to the area. She was raising her two kids alone. Nell remembered her as being a good student and nice girl as a seventh grader. But that was years ago. Annie sure didn't need any added trouble now.

Nell pulled her phonebook out of a drawer. "I wonder if her address is 924 Jefferson or a different house number. Darn. She's not listed. Probably only has a cell phone. Next time I'm out and about I'll drive past her house to check on her."

***

No matter how hard Nell tried to focus, distractions overwhelmed her. The dogs needed to be walked, the bills needed to be paid, and Facebook needed her comments. After taking care of those important items, she brought up her blog, Noshes up North. For the life of her, Nell couldn't think of a topic to write about today. As was her schedule, she had posted a new recipe on Tuesday and wrote a restaurant review on Thursday. At least one other day of the week, Nell blogged about this or that, but now nothing seemed to strike her fancy.

After all the excitement a couple months ago of having a murderer after her, she'd had plenty of topics to keep her going. Noshes Up North had followers from all over the state, from the Midwest, and even a steadily increasing number from other parts of the United States. With so many followers, Nell felt compelled to keep them updated with the happenings of the case. The suspect pleaded guilty to the murders of two women and the attempted murder of Nell. Life in prison was the expected sentence. Nell was more than ready to move on, but lately keeping up the blog felt a little more like work and a little less like fun.

Her thoughts wandered to Sam Ryan, who she had been seeing since the two of them helped the police find the cyber stalker and solve the murder. She spent a fair amount of time at his restaurant, Sam's Slam, Home of the Grand Slamburger, just so she could see him. Being the owner and operator of that establishment sure put a crimp in his free time. But thinking about Sam made her smile, and she'd been smiling a lot lately. She'd gotten to know him well and realized there was a whole lot more to Sam than him reminding her of a chubby Mark Harmon with a deep, sexy voice.

Sam was four years older than she, had warm chocolate brown eyes, and a lopsided smile that made her want to smile back every time. He was a single father and had raised his daughter, Benita, into a respectful and caring young woman. Nell had gotten to know and care about her, too. She admired the loving relationship father and daughter had for each other.

Nell appreciated Sam's efforts to spend time playing with her dogs, and even going on walks with her occasionally. It was exciting to think about where their relationship might lead. There had been teasing back and forth about starting some flames in the fire pit in her back yard, but the heat was already starting to build between them.

An angry outburst emanated from her stomach. How long ago was it that she had last eaten anything? Nell marched straight into the kitchen, thinking about what was in the fridge. She knew she had the makings for a nice healthy salad, crisp lettuce, juicy cherry tomatoes, and cucumber slices for crunch. She could add fresh mushrooms, a chopped green onion, orange pepper slices, and maybe even a small scattering of shredded cheddar cheese. Then she'd top it all off with a bit of ranch dressing. Mmmhmm.

As she made the salad, she kept telling herself how good it was for her. Eating in this manner had helped her take a few pounds off her more than generous frame. While she had always been pleasantly plump, her figure had definitely blossomed over the years. Writing her blog was keeping her more stationary as she sat in front of the computer. She was not as active as when she was a teacher. Nell knew it was time she worked on a new and healthy lifestyle. Especially with her hair turning to silver and her glasses getting thicker over her light blue eyes, she hardly recognized herself anymore. In her mind she'd still be that young girl in high school, but her outward appearance revealed the truth. To help her get into better shape, Nell had recently joined the Bayshore Fitness Center. The facility was not far from her house and offered all the usual exercise machines, a weight room, and a pool. She had gone a few times, just walking the track. She planned to tackle one of the machines soon.

When she finished the preparation, Nell took her salad and went out on the patio. George and Newman followed her, most likely hoping for scraps. The salad, so colorful and brimming with fresh vegetables, was delightful, but Nell couldn't help thinking it would have made a nice side dish to something more substantial, like one of Sam's Slam burgers. The boys were crestfallen as they didn't receive the last bites of a sandwich.

"No crusty bread and meat today. Sorry, guys," Nell said, bending down to pat George's head.

A glimmer of a thought of ice cream crept into Nell's head. Initially only occupying a tiny dot of the space in her brain, the longing spread and soon had her in a vice grip. The image of a luscious, dripping, and enormous ice cream sundae would not let her mind shake free. A great big gob of a creamy French vanilla covered in rich gooey caramel and warm chocolate fudge topping sprinkled with pecans and crowned with thick whipped cream would fill the bill.

Nell swallowed hard, willing the tempting dessert to appear in her mouth. Somehow the salad just didn't compare.

Nell would have to make it compare. She didn't have any of those items in the house and she refused to go to the store to purchase food she didn't need and would undoubtedly make her feel worse in the long run. Instead she looked over at her boys. "George! Newmie! Wanna go for a walk?"

The boys answered in the affirmative with a round of spirited barking and jumping. Nell left the house with her boys, who she knew planned to check for any recent pee-mail.

In the back of Nell's mind, she was hoping to walk over to Jefferson Street and stop in at Annie's house. She not only wanted to let her know that someone was looking for her, but also to check that she was okay. Something about that guy just rubbed Nell the wrong way.

Annie's house showed no sign of life as the three approached. "Boys, let's just walk up and ring the doorbell. We'll give it our best shot." Nell waited after ringing the bell and then rang it once more.

Again no response.

As they walked toward home, Nell couldn't shake her bad feeling about that man who pounded on her door. Annie would receive a call from her tomorrow. She hoped it wouldn't be too late.

Chapter 1.5

Beautiful red hair falling to the floor. Gently touching the lovely head that no longer bore the weight of such long locks. A wooden box with green silk inside to form a comfortable resting place. A heavy wooden cover so she cannot escape. Such loveliness needs to be contained and kept pristine.

Chapter 2

Nell opened the door of the huge three-story building that was formerly a warehouse. She had stopped at her good friend, Leigh Jackson's, for a drink. After catching up, the two of them were going to the new pub in town for a plate of fish.

"Hello, Nell. What kind of trouble are the two of you going to get into tonight?" Ed, Leigh's husband, was working on an exhibit for their decorative metal shop, Metallic Dreams, but had turned to greet her with a twinkle in his eye.

"I hope a lot," chuckled Nell. "I could use a little excitement."

"Be careful what you wish for," Ed said, flicking a hand through his short gray hair. Nell watched him a moment as he got down on his hands and knees and crawled around the backside of the display pieces. His lean body had no difficulty stretching to do the job. "Go on up. Leigh's been on pins and needles all day waiting to see you."

"Well then, it looks like I'm not the only one who needs something new and different."

Ed guffawed and went on with his work.

When Nell reached the top of the stairs, she called out to Leigh.

"Come on in, I'm in the kitchen. Want a beer?" Leigh's voice was almost giddy with excitement.

Nell closed the door behind her and inhaled the spicy warmth of autumn leaves and cinnamon apples emanating from the large candle on the dining table. She made her way into the kitchen as Prada, one of Leigh's three Siamese cats twined between her legs. As Nell bent to pet the cat, she called to Leigh, "Sure. How long has it been since you've had a drink? It must be quite a while because you sound…."

Nell stopped dead in her tracks. Before her stood Leigh, the wavy auburn hair that normally flowed past her waist was gone. Instead she sported the most fabulous version of a pixie haircut Nell had ever seen.

"I love it!" Nell grabbed Leigh and twirled her around. "How did you make the decision to get it cut so short? We've been friends for thirty odd years and the shortest I've ever seen your hair was in a Farrah Fawcett style when we first met. Goodness, you look so much younger!"

Leigh grinned. "I needed a change. Do you really like it?"

"You better believe I do. You and Ed should be going out tonight, though. People would think he was cheating on you." Nell readily accepted the mug of beer Leigh handed her.

"Let's chat in the living room." Leigh put bowls of pretzels and spiced nuts on a tray along with plates and napkins. A few kitty treats were also on the tray in a separate kitty bowl.

As Prada accepted her treat, Coco Chanel came running. Finally Louis Vuitton came lumbering out from the bedroom. "Here's one for you, Coco, and, yes, you get a treat, too, Fat Louis," Leigh said.

Nell, as usual, marveled at Leigh and Ed's creativity as she admired the eclectic room. Their whole house, which was the middle floor of the old building, displayed their unique take on decorating. Most of the items were pieces they had designed and made themselves. Customers from all over the Midwest came to their studio.

"We've been so busy at the shop that Ed and I are debating whether or not to have a website," Leigh said, "but we can hardly keep up with the custom orders we have now."

"Business is brisk. That's good news." Helping herself to snacks, Nell admitted, "Leigh, I had stopped even trying to imagine you with short hair. I thought it would never happen."

"I've actually been toying with the idea for months, but never mentioned it. I was afraid I'd chicken out. I just had it done today so you're the first person other than Ed to see my new look." Leigh beamed.

"I'm so proud of you. It must have been a gigantic decision."

"Oh, it was. As a new venture, I've been designing and making jewelry, but the earrings I worked so hard on couldn't even be seen under all my hair. I decided I no longer wanted to be defined as the woman with the long red hair." Leigh took a sip of beer. "I've been trying on jewelry all afternoon. It's been so much fun!"

"I can see your pretty face and your emerald eyes just sparkle. I bet you feel a lot lighter, too. You're so tiny that your hair must have been half of your weight."

"You're right, Nell. I do feel lighter. Even driving home from the salon was different. I didn't need to adjust my hair so I could avoid sitting on it."

"Your outfit is also new, isn't it?" Nell examined the tailored white blouse and crisp dark jeans with a careful eye. "No skirt tonight?"

"Another change I'm making. Tomorrow I want to finish packing up the types of clothes I've been wearing for the last thirty years and have Ed take them to Goodwill in Marinette the next time he goes to Menards." Leigh's lips curled. "I've actually been interested in fashion for quite a few years, but I had so much of the Mother Earth type clothing I didn't want to be wasteful."

"So all those issues of Elle, Marie Claire, and Vogue that you've bought over the years have finally worked their magic."

"Now it's out with the old and in with the new."

"I hope you don't take that attitude with your friends," Nell laughed.

"Never. Maybe we can go on a shopping excursion soon."

"Love to on a Saturday sometime. And you know how shopping makes me hungry, so we'll need to hit a lunch place to take a break from shopping that day, too."

"That goes without saying!" Leigh grinned.

"I love planning lunch for a different day even before we've been out to a new place for supper." Nell waved a pretzel in the air. "It's so much fun writing a food blog."

Leigh reached over to the coffee table to scoop out some spiced nuts on her plate. Prada was ready to pounce on the table so Leigh threw her a treat and slid the pretzels closer to Nell.

Taking that opportunity for a closer look at Leigh's jewelry, Nell was quite impressed. As usual several fingers were adorned with eye-catching rings of various sizes. Leigh had a single, large silver bracelet spiraling up her left forearm. The true standout, though, were her earrings. Part of the reason being how they stood out because of her short hair, but the beauty of the intricate metal work was exquisite.

"I think you could make your whole business jewelry now. I love all your pieces." Nell took her friend's hands and had a closer look at the rings.

"Thanks. That's exactly what I'm thinking about doing. I could give my home décor items a rest and delve into body art. Of course I'd still do special order pieces as they came, but it'd give me the chance to focus my creativity in a different direction. And perhaps Ed would take over more of the home decorating aspect of our business."

After enjoying the snacks and some serious catching up, the friends left Leigh's home and walked down Main Street to a new establishment for a meal. Miner's Fish House had recently opened and Nell couldn't wait to try it. She planned to write a review for her blog, Noshes Up North. An ad had been placed in the local weekly paper toting their authentic British fish and chips and Cornish pasty. Nell, who was from the southwestern part of Wisconsin, thought she was the only citizen of Bayshore who was descended from the sturdy miners of Cornwall, England. Even if she hadn't planned to review Miner's Fish House she would still be eager to taste its offerings.

As they neared the establishment, Leigh and Nell took note of the new British style pub sign hanging above the door. Below the name it had a picture of a miner holding a fishing pole on one side and a large fish with a pickax on the other.

"That sign certainly makes a statement," Leigh said.

"Too bad I don't know what the statement is." Nell winked at her friend. "Let's go in and check it out."

When the two friends entered, they were delighted by the sight of comfy couches in the bar area. "This is just like the pubs in Ireland and England I saw when I visited," Leigh squealed.

"I'm so impressed," agreed Nell. "When Drew and I took our trip there ten years ago, we so enjoyed the homey atmosphere of the pubs. They were a spot where town folk went to mingle with their neighbors and relax in good companionship. We were struck by the number of families at the pubs. They weren't places for heavy drinking, but a bit of a social event. Bayshore can use a place like this." Nell's thoughts lingered for a bit on her late husband. She missed Drew every day, but had decided after five years to go on with her life. She had to admit that her friend, Sam, had motivated her to come to that decision.

There were two stools available right at the end of the bar and the ladies sidled over. As they took their seats, Nell continued to look around the new establishment.

"I love the look of this place. It's so cozy and quaint."

"So far, so good," agreed Nell. "It'll be interesting to see if the dining area has the same feel. Also the newspaper article mentioned there was a separate room for darts and board games. From the size of the place the owners signed themselves up for quite an undertaking."

The handsome thirty something male bartender approached them with a charming smile. "What's your pleasure, ladies?" He smelled good. It was a familiar scent, but Nell couldn't put her finger on it. Maybe sandalwood?

"What British beers do you have on tap?"

"We have a great assortment. There's Newcastle Brown Ale, Dragon Slayer IPA, and Young's Double Chocolate Stout. A couple Irish beers, too. Guinness and Harp. And of course we have Bud and Bud light."

"I'll try the IPA," Nell decided.

Leigh piped up with, "I'll go with Guinness."

"Super. Would you ladies like it in a pilsner or a 20 ounce British pint?"

After they agreed on the pint, the bartender left to get their brews. "I'm surprised there aren't more people here," Leigh commented. "This is a beautiful new pub and it's Friday night in Bayshore. The place should be packed."

"I was thinking the same thing, but it's early yet. And maybe because it's new, people are tentative, waiting to hear if it has good food or not."

"I think it's been open for three weeks. I'm keeping my fingers crossed it'll be wonderful food. Then you can give it a True Nosh on your blog," Leigh said with a smile.

"Another thing, the bar being so huge is deceptive." Nell turned and looked around the room. "There are a number of empty stools, but if you took the number of customers and put them in one of the other places in town their bar areas might look close to full."

"That's a good point."

"Here are your pints." The bartender set the drinks down. "And for your viewing pleasure, here is our list of bottled beer for future reference. If you need anything else, my name is Will. Just give me a holler."

"Thanks, Will," Leigh and Nell rang out together.

"I think Will is gonna be a draw," Leigh whispered. "With his dark wavy hair and dreamy brown eyes, he'll soon have the available women down here in droves."

"He's a charmer," Nell agreed. "I think this will be the only beer I'll order tonight though," she said. "After having one at your place I probably should have ordered the smaller size."

"Me, too," agreed Leigh. "But somehow I bet we'll manage to choke it down."

Nell and Leigh tried their own beers and then sampled each other's. Luckily they each liked their own choice better than their friend's.

Coming in from the dining area were three Bayshore couples who navigated toward them. "Oh, Leigh, your hair," squealed one of the women. "I almost didn't recognize you. I love it."

"Thanks. It's quite a change."

"Change is an understatement," another woman chirped. "You look thirty years old."

The others also complimented Leigh, greeted Nell, and then ambled out the door. This was going to be Leigh's night and she deserved it.

"Darn," Nell grumbled. "I should have asked them what they ordered and how they liked it."

"Let's ask for menus," Leigh suggested. "Then we can peruse the selections while we sip and chat. Since it's a new place, it may take us some time to make a decision."

At Nell's signal, Will brought menus right over. "There's no hurry, ladies. Take your time."

"Thanks, we will," answered Nell.

On the cover of the menu was the picture of the sign above the door—the miner with the fishing pole and the fish with the pickax. Opening up the menu, Leigh and Nell were greeted with a wonderful array of British and American food.

"This takes my breath away. Nell, look at all the British choices."

Pasty…Fish and chips…Shepherd's pie (lamb and beef)…Bangers and mash…Steak and kidney pie…Scotch eggs…Ploughman's lunch…Cottage pie…Welsh Rarebit…Yorkshire pudding…

"Good grief! There's a lot of selections," Nell exclaimed. "I don't suppose I should order and sample them all in one night."

"I don't suppose," laughed Leigh.

"Then in the American section is the listing of different burgers and other sandwiches, along with steak, chicken, pork, and seafood entrees," Nell rubbed her hands together in glee. "The food descriptions are so tempting it's almost sinful."

"They also have a pasta and salad section."

"I'm not ordering a salad here until I've sampled every other dish I want to try." Nell shot Leigh a sinister look. "And that's that!"

Nell glanced over at the door as several more people walked into the bar. The women came right up to Leigh to compliment her on her new do. Leigh's customers, Nell realized. Nell shared some pleasantries and then excused herself to check out the ladies room.

Furbished elegantly, even displaying fresh flowers and scented potpourri on the counter, the ladies room was a pleasure to walk in because of the smell alone. How unique!

She peeked into the game room as she passed on her way back to the bar. The huge stone fireplace caught her attention. The sound of the crackling wood made Nell look forward to cooler weather. On one side of the large area several young men played darts. There were empty tables for chess, checkers, and other board games that had been stacked in a cabinet. There were even trivia cards on the tables. *This room will find a lot of use I'll bet.*

Nell stopped in midstep as she approached the bar and looked at the area from a different angle. There, across the bar was the man who had come to her house earlier that day banging on her door. A chill ran up her spine.

He was focused at something or someone in a different direction—so intently his eyes appeared to be drilling a hole. Nell slowly turned her head, already knowing that the object of his interest would be Annie Marshall. It was, and she was talking to Leigh. Nell pulled herself together and walked over to join them. They were in the middle of a conversation, but when they finished Nell blurted out, "Annie, did that fellow find your house today?"

"Who do you mean, Mrs. Bailey?" Annie questioned while finger combing her brown hair.

"It's Nell, please. I'm no longer Mrs. Bailey to you. That guy over there." Nell tilted her head to point him out and then turned to look at the man.

To her surprise and chagrin, a woman was sitting down on the stool that the man had previously occupied. Nell checked all around the room. "He's disappeared. A man came to my house today looking for you. I told him you lived on Jefferson. Did he contact you?"

"No, but I was at work all day," Annie said. "What did he want?"

"I don't know, but he seemed very agitated and in a hurry. Then as I came back into the bar I noticed the same man staring at you."

"Are you sure it was the same guy?" At Nell's nod, Annie asked, "What did he look like?"

"Probably in his late forties, rugged, with dark hair and eyes. I'd guess around six feet with a good build like he lifts weights."

"That's a good description, Nell," Leigh interjected. "Do you know who it could be, Annie?"

"Not a clue. But I'm not going to let it ruin my night. Thanks for the heads up, Mrs. Bailey." At the tilt of Nell's head, she added, "Nell."

Annie walked back over to where her friends were sitting. They soon were all laughing and joking around with the handsome bartender.

"I don't like this at all," whispered Nell. "Something isn't right. Why was it so crucial for him to talk to her this afternoon when he came to my house and now he leaves without saying a word? It doesn't make sense."

"I know when those blue eyes of yours are this focused you have something on your mind. I doubt he's a rapist or murderer waiting to attack Annie."

"How do you know?" Nell shot back. "He could be. Why was he staring at her like that? He had to have followed her here. What's on his mind?"

"Perhaps he's an old boyfriend who wants to talk to her, but doesn't want any trouble," suggested Leigh. "Annie is surrounded by friends."

"Oh, no. She's so sweet with a perfect figure. He was too rough-looking and too old to ever have been with Annie." Nell stuck her head back in the menu.

"I thought you said this guy was in his late forties," Leigh challenged. "Just how old is Annie, do you think?"

"Well, I can figure it out pretty darn quick. I taught her when seventh grade was still being called junior high and not middle school. That was during my first few years of teaching. I'd say she's in her mid-forties."

"And everyone knows it's unheard of to date someone three, maybe even *four* years older. Isn't that about the age difference between you and Sam?"

"Point taken," Nell conceded. "But he didn't look like an old boyfriend to me."

"I was just giving an example, Nell. There are plenty of other reasonable explanations of why he was checking her out across the room. Maybe he even was gazing at me and admiring my haircut," Leigh laughed.

"I suppose." Nell glanced back at her menu.

"By the way, Annie mentioned she has been here three times already."

"Really? How does she like it?"

"She said it's great. Friendly staff, great atmosphere, and yummy food."

"Glad to hear it."

Leigh set down her menu. "I've made my decision."

"What are you going to have?"

"One of their Friday night specials, the Walleye Platter," Leigh said. "How about you?"

"Even though British Fish and Chips are on the menu every day and not just on Fridays, I really want to try them, so that's my choice." Nell signaled Will and told him they were ready for a waitress.

"Annie was a former student of mine. How do you know her?"

"She's been in the shop several times. She's made quite an impression on Ed. Annie seems to have an eye for interesting pieces. She's bought quite a bit of his handcrafted garden art."

As Leigh continued to describe Ed's pieces, Nell watched Annie and her friends, who appeared to be having a great time, out of the corner of her eye. *If she isn't concerned, I guess I can let it go, too.*

Leigh's voice drew Nell back to their conversation. "Have you come up with it?"

"Come up with what? What are you talking about?"

"The item that isn't here that's in most bars. Have you spotted it or I guess I should say not spotted it?"

Looking around the bar, Nell noticed the usual décor, plus the Union Jack, and other British embellishments. Finally it came to her. "A TV! They don't have a TV."

"Bingo. What could be their reasoning? Every sports bar has several," Leigh wondered. "With the way bars are packed around here for football games, they might miss out on a lot of business."

"Or they may be *fishing* for a different kind of clientele," Nell chuckled.

The waitress, who introduced herself as Lynn, appeared to take their order. "You can't go wrong with ordering fish at Miner's Fish House," she proclaimed as she wrote down their selections. With assurances that it wouldn't be long until they could go to their table, Lynn returned to the kitchen.

After Lynn left, Leigh teased, "You do realize that you're going to get mushy peas with the fish and chips? That was the only part of the meal I didn't devour when I was in England."

Nell sighed and nodded her head. "Maybe they have some sort of secret recipe for them here."

"If they do and the peas are good, we'll know they aren't authentic. Not that I'd complain."

"We both visited the UK a long time ago. Our tastes may have changed," replied Nell. "I'm going to try them with an open mind."

"I don't know if you read the article in the paper or not, but it told how the owners, one from Mineral Point, Wisconsin and one from the Upper Peninsula of Michigan met through their mutual love of pasty, married, and decided to make it their career. I hope I love this place because it would make a great entry for my blog." Nell looked up as the waitress reappeared to take them to their table.

The dining room gave off a homey feel with oak tables and cloth napkins. The old pictures in the room were large oak-framed depictions of miners and fishermen. On one wall were miners from Mineral Point, Linden, and Lead Mine, Wisconsin and others from the Upper Peninsula of Michigan. On another wall were fishing photographs taken off the bridge in Bayshore and out on the bay.

"Now I sure can see how they came up with the name Miner's Fish House," Leigh commented.

Trays were coming in and out of the kitchen as the dining room filled up. From what she could tell, orders were equally divided between the Bayshore standards of walleye and perch, and the new British Fish and Chips.

They didn't have to wait long for their order. As the waitress set it on the table in front of them, Nell's nose almost whistled with glee as she breathed in the tantalizing aroma. The fish and chips, delivered in true British form, arrived in a basket. The three large pieces of steaming deep fried cod were a crispy golden brown and piled high on one side with sizzling hot fries next to them. The requisite mushy peas were served in a separate container along with creamy coleslaw in a nod to Americans.

The waitress set a heaping plate before Leigh of a long filet of pan-fried walleye, her requested baked potato, and coleslaw. "I'll be right back with the malt vinegar and ketchup. Would you like anything else?"

"Tartar sauce and lemon?" Leigh asked.

"Absolutely." Lynn went in and came out of the kitchen in one smooth move. She delivered the condiments and moved on to more hungry diners.

Even though the friends were savoring their meals and enjoying their time together, Nell couldn't shake her uneasiness relating to the man watching Annie. Had they seen the last of him?

Chapter 2.5

The man heard the door open, but was too busy to turn his head to see the new arrival. Handing Bud a beer and making a quick joke, the bartender noticed he no longer held his friend's attention. He turned in the direction Bud was looking with an unexplainable feeling of dread.

Was it just in his head or had the entire room gone silent? Everyone was staring at the door. A force of nature was coming toward the bartender, step by step almost in slow motion with the sleek moves of a panther.

How could it be? She hadn't changed in twenty years—or could she have gotten even lovelier? Long and luxurious, her shiny black hair accentuated her flawless olive skin. Her body—soft and round in all the right places—was sheathed in a provocative, yet tasteful black dress. Each step she took brought flames of heat and passion to his core and probably every other man in the place. Had he been able to take his eyes off her, a quick scan of the room would've undoubtedly shown disapproval on the face of every woman.

His heart pounded in rhythm to each step she took. Ears ringing and bile rising from his throat, he found himself unable to move.

Walking right up to the bar, she leaned over to him, breasts peeking out of her dress. "Do you still love me, Sam?" she whispered.

Chapter 3

Nell rose early with the dogs on Saturday morning, and took them out for a long walk down the presidents—the streets named for the early presidents of the United States on Nell's side of town. That gave her a chance to check Annie Marshall's house number on Jefferson Street. It wasn't the same as hers. Annie lived at 942 Jefferson. Nell's place was 924 Adams. The man was off one street and had transposed the last two numbers.

Nothing appeared to be amiss as she walked the boys past Annie's house, although one never knew what went on inside. She thought about knocking, but there wasn't a car in the driveway so she suspected Annie was out. Besides she had already given Annie the message that someone was looking for her.

The leaves could be seen falling already after a beautiful color show in early September. Nell thought this year's display was even more breathtaking than usual. Part of the reason may have been that she was appreciating being alive after the scare she experienced in the summer. That had been too close of a call for her. She was very blessed and thanked God every day.

Back at the house she set down clean water and food before George and Newman. Nell picked up her notes and considered how to write her review of Miner's Fish House. Nothing came to mind. Looking for more ideas, she checked her blog for comments from her followers.

One Broke Girl

I've started my first job after college and my parents are visiting from Fond du Lac in a few weeks. Do you know of a place in my area (Coleman) that is reasonable, but still nice? My parents like good food and cocktails. I want this to be my treat. Is there a supper club nearby that a first-year teacher could afford?

Helen47

Thanks for the heads up about the Wisconsin beer cheese soup at the Riverfront in Peshtigo. A friend and I both ordered it for lunch recently and couldn't have been more pleased. Keep up the helpful and interesting reviews, Nell. I'll make it a point to always check here before I go out to a new place.

Nell was delighted to see she was being taken seriously and her reviews were beneficial to people. She was doing what she loved. Of course, she wasn't making any money at it, but that would come later. Possibly. Hopefully...

She had a couple potential places to consider before answering One Broke Girl. She wanted to look through her files first. Luckily, she had time to come up with the perfect spot.

But she needed to get her thoughts together about Miner's Fish House. Maybe if she talked to Sam about it first she'd clear her mind. She wondered if he'd be back in the Slam this early. *One way to find out.* She punched in his number. After several rings there was a gruff, "Sam's Slam."

"Sam. What's wrong?" Nell's skin prickled. She had never heard him speak in that tone before.

"Ah, Nell. It was a rough night," Sam grumbled. "I didn't do all the work I usually attend to before I left last night. I have all that work and my regular jobs to get done before we open up today. I'm a little out of sorts."

"How about if I come up and help?" Nell volunteered. "I can clean and probably do a bunch of other things, too."

"Nah, I don't think so."

"Sam, what else is wrong? You don't sound like yourself."

After a long pause Sam came out with it. "The Bean's mother came back last night." Then in a rush, "Look, Nell, I have a lot of work to do and a lot on my mind. I need to get off the phone and get busy."

They said their goodbyes, leaving Nell standing in her kitchen with a hundred possible scenarios going through her mind. *Does this woman want money? Did she cause a scene in the bar? What was Benita's reaction? Was Sam happy to see her? Had he been carrying a torch all these years?*

As much time as the two of them had spent together these last few months, Sam had hardly spoken a word about his ex-wife. Nell didn't even know her name. Perhaps this woman wants to become part of Benita's life. And Sam's.

Nell's heart beat faster as she absorbed the idea. The pleasant relationship she had going with Sam may be over. It had just started to develop, too. She didn't want to form an attachment and have it end this way, but it seemed quite possible now. Sam sure didn't want her to come up there, or even waste time talking to her.

To take her mind off her depressing thoughts, she'd eat something to make her feel better. She dug around in her refrigerator and cupboards, but found nothing to her liking. She decided to go to the marvelous new coffeehouse/dessert shop in town, The Mocha Chip. There was a little angel voice in her head whispering, "No, no, no." But a much louder and more powerful devil voice shouting, "YES, YES, YES!"

She wanted to change from her walking clothes into something a bit nicer.

Going to her closet, she pulled out a pair of tan pants and a burnt orange cotton sweater. She added her dangling leaf earrings and the gold necklace Drew gave her for their first anniversary. Nell petted the boys, promising she would be back soon, and hopped into her car.

Parking on Main Street, she walked the few steps to the shop's door. The enticing aroma of strong coffee enveloped her in a cloak of warmth as she entered. Nell scrutinized the delicacies in the dessert case with an appreciative eye. Each item looked better than the one before it. How she had missed dessert!

"I'd like a piece of the flourless chocolate cake and a large Mocha Chip Mocha, please."

"Would you like that for here or to go?" the teenage girl behind the counter asked.

"For here. I'll be over there by the window." Nell paid the cashier and went to her table. She hadn't been seated long when her cake and coffee were delivered.

The rich denseness of the cake reminded her of a cross between a truffle and thick Door County fudge. The smooth texture of it on her tongue was such a delight, shivers ran up her spine. Her mocha was the perfect blend of espresso, hot milk, and chocolate. *One can never have too much chocolate.*

Nell reveled in her bit of bad behavior, savoring the flavor of her choices for as long as possible. She'd pay for it on the scale tomorrow.

From her vantage point in the shop, she could see quite a large section of Main Street. As she lingered, she noticed friends and acquaintances going here and there. Then she noticed someone who put her on alert. It was that man who was following Annie. He was soon out of range. Nell knew once she finished her treat, she would take a stroll down the street to investigate. *What was this guy going to do?*

In an additional blow to her healthy eating plan, Nell stopped back at the counter and ordered a dozen Mocha Chocolate Chip cookies to go. She might need them later.

Dropping off the cookies in the car, Nell proceeded down the street looking in all the store windows. No sign of the stranger. She walked a little farther down Main Street and stopped in to see Leigh for a minute.

Leigh was working on an earring at a table in her studio when Nell walked through the door. "Hi, Leigh. Recover from last night?" Nell asked.

"No problem. Ed had to go to Green Bay so I'm taking care of the place myself today. What are you doing downtown?"

"I've had a temporary setback on my road to good health. I hit The Mocha Chip—hard. Flourless chocolate cake and a large mocha."

"That's not so bad. You'll burn that right off," encouraged Leigh.

"There's also a dozen Mocha Chocolate Chip cookies in my car," confessed Nell.

"Oh. Well, freeze them. Get them out of your sight. Put them out of your mind. Think of other things." Leigh set her tools aside and looked up at Nell.

"Anything wrong? You were doing so well avoiding desserts."

"Possibly. I'm trying to stay busy to keep my mind off Sam."

"Sam? Did something happen?" Leigh questioned.

"I'm not sure. I talked to him this morning, but he doesn't want to see or talk to me," Nell said with a quivering lip.

"Did he give you a reason?"

"His ex-wife came back." Nell rubbed at her eyebrow.

"So that's it? He told you she's back and he never wants to see you again?"

"Not exactly," Nell admitted. "I called him and he said he was really busy, something about having a hard night last night and was behind on his work. I offered to help him and he said no, that Benita's mother came back last night and he had to get off the phone."

"That big Irish guy wasn't giving you the brush off. He'd have to deal with me if he tried that." Leigh got up to give Nell a hug. "Why are you imagining such things?"

"It makes me wonder what he was doing that he had a hard night and couldn't get his work done."

"Nell!" Leigh shook her head.

"I know I'm exaggerating, but this makes me uncomfortable." She twisted her necklace around her index finger.

"Just give him some time. He's probably worried about his daughter and how she's going to interact with her mother. Don't make yourself one more problem that Sam needs to solve."

"Good advice, Leigh," Nell said as she squeezed herself into a chair used for customers at the shop. "I hope you're right."

"I am right. So, change of subject. Something happened a few minutes ago that's interesting," Leigh said as she walked toward her workbench. "A man came in the studio, he said 'just looking around' but he was very interested in every aspect of our business. He asked if we would think about selling. It caught me totally off guard."

Immediately Nell's suspicions were aroused. "What did he look like?"

"Rather handsome in a rugged kind of way. I'd say around six feet, dark hair and eyes, good build, maybe late forties."

"Anything about that description sound familiar?" Nell stood back up and walked over to Leigh.

"Oh," Leigh gasped. "Could he be the man who was following Annie last night?"

"While I was at The Mocha Chip, I looked out the window and saw him walking down Main Street in your direction. That's why I came down here."

"Oh, so you didn't come in just to see me?" Leigh laughed. "Well, he was just as nice as could be. I don't think he's up to anything suspicious."

"Did he give you his card? We could use it to see who he is or who he says he is anyway."

"No."

"Hmm. If he was serious about buying your place, he would have left his card or at least given you his name. How does he expect you to let him know if you *do* decide to sell?" Nell shook her head. "I still think this guy is bad news."

"He said he was going to contact me in a few days," explained Leigh.

"You aren't seriously thinking of selling, are you?" Nell frowned at the thought.

"Oh, I doubt it. We've never considered it before. Of course, I'll let Ed know about this guy's inquiry. But we've always been happy here, and the business is starting to take off."

"Is this fellow an artist? What's he want to do with the building?" Nell started to rub her left eyebrow again.

"I have no idea. He didn't say."

"What exactly did he say, Leigh?"

"If you must know, he commented on my hair. He said it really looks nice and he liked it short better." Leigh rose, turned away from Nell, and moved to a cabinet across the room.

"Who is this guy? He liked it short better?" Nell shrieked. "When has he ever seen it long? I can't believe this. Do you ever remember meeting him before?"

"As far as I know today is the first time I've ever seen him."

"Last night at Miner's Fish House he was staring a hole through Annie Marshall and you were talking to her, so he could've seen you. But your hair was already short then." Nell paused in thought. "Oh, no, Leigh, maybe you're the one he's following!"

Chapter 4

When Nell stepped into her kitchen with her bag from The Mocha Chip, she knew she was in trouble. She wanted to eat the whole dozen cookies immediately. She realized it was her emotions running away from her, but knowing that didn't squelch the feeling. George and Newman greeted her with their usual enthusiasm. *She could eat a cookie and give them a tiny part of it.*

"Hello, George. Hi, Newmie. Should we have some cookies?"

Hearing one of their favorite words, they answered by doing their version of the happy dance. Amid the yipping and jumping, Nell managed to bring two cookies out of the bag and a couple of dog treats from their bowl. The trio made their way out to the patio where Nell almost inhaled the two sweet treats while the boys gobbled their dog treat with just a few crumbs of the cookie on top.

"You two don't know how lucky you are. A bakery cookie is a pretty expensive t-r-e-a-t," Nell said spelling out another one of their favorite words. She didn't want to get them excited all over again. She also knew that she shouldn't give them any more of the cookie with chocolate, which isn't good for dogs.

Nell refrained from eating more cookies as she muttered, "Bad things come in threes. First, this stranger following either Annie or Leigh, second, Sam's ex-wife returning, and third, this sugar kick I need to fight. The trio of bad things are done. I couldn't handle a fourth." The boys' tilted heads showed her they were trying to understand and would help if they could. They were so sweet, always there for her. Being alone after her husband passed on had been tough, and the boys filled a void for her. George and Newman gave her a reason to get up in the morning.

"Well, boys, I'm at a loss. I just don't know what to do with my day. Maybe that means playtime for you. Where's the ball? Let's find the ball."

Nell managed to find enough energy to chase the boys around the yard to their great delight. But when she finished, she was the only one tired.

The day turned to evening as Nell pondered her situation with Sam. She'd been hoping he would call her, but the phone had been eerily silent. How she wished she knew more about this woman—Sam's ex-wife. Sam had never brought her into their conversations and Nell refused to pry. She wished she would have inquired, or at least shown an interest. Did Sam dislike this woman, still love her, or have no feelings about her at all? The not knowing was driving her insane.

The phone rang as Nell was leafing through food magazines while sitting on the loveseat. She had to get up carefully so as not to disturb the boys laid out on each side of her, sawing logs.

Glancing at the caller ID, she saw it wasn't Sam, but her good friend, Elena Walker. Nell hadn't spoken to her for several days and was happy to have a chance to hear what was happening in Elena's life.

"Hello, Elena. How are things at work?"

"Just fine, no changes here. Anything new and exciting going on with you?" Elena was such a good friend and always so encouraging that soon Nell's insecurities about Sam came pouring out like molten chocolate out of a lava cake.

"I don't think you should get too concerned about this situation yet," Elena cautioned. "Didn't this woman come back last night? You don't know that it even has anything to do with Sam. Perhaps she still has parents in town or she's here on business, or she wants to see her daughter."

"If she tries to take Benita away, it'll break Sam's heart," Nell moaned.

"What are you talking about, Nell? Isn't his daughter in her twenties?"

"Yes, but she and Sam have a wonderful relationship. I don't want anything or anyone to change that." Nell walked out to the kitchen and absently pulled another cookie out of the bag, broke it into pieces, and started to munch.

"Don't worry about events that may never happen. Sam will call you soon and everything will be just fine."

"Thanks for the encouragement, Elena. I should make supper now. Talk to you again soon."

Nell looked down at the two little rascals at her feet. Even though they had been sleeping, they knew she had a cookie. She gave them each a doggie treat then pulled out ingredients to make supper.

Tonight was going to be a chicken night—Mediterranean Chicken Pasta to be exact. Nell took two boneless breasts out of the refrigerator and cut them into bite size pieces. She then sautéed them in olive oil. Once the chicken was golden, she removed the pieces from the skillet and set them aside.

Next, Nell sautéed onion and garlic in the pan drippings. She poured in some white wine to help loosen the chicken crumbs in the pan. She then added a can of diced tomatoes and brought it to a boil. Once boiling, Nell lowered the heat, poured in some more white wine, and let it simmer. She so enjoyed cooking, it almost took her mind off all of her worries. Almost.

Retreating to the living room, Nell turned on the local news. Nothing too exciting happening in Green Bay and Bayshore wasn't mentioned at all—which wasn't uncommon. She pondered the events of the day, wishing she had never called Sam. Ignorance would have been bliss. But she had called him and now she couldn't get herself to think about anything else. What if she never heard from him again?

Nell returned to the kitchen and put a pot of water on to boil for the pasta. She also added ribbons of fresh basil, ground Italian seasoning, and some cayenne for heat to the chicken and sauce. While cutting up some pitted Kalamata olives, Nell nicked her finger enough to draw blood.

Darn! She knew better. *Keep your mind on the task at hand.* She wrapped a band aid around her finger and dropped the penne into the pot.

"George. Newmie. Want some food?" Nell called to the boys as she dumped food into their bowls. They were already in the kitchen while Nell prepared her meal, ever hopeful something yummy would fall to the floor.

Nell checked the pasta. Almost ready. She put the olives into the sauce. She positioned the TV tray in front of her chair and then got her plate ready. The aroma in the kitchen was heavenly as she ladled a large helping of the chicken and sauce over the pasta. Her final touch was sprinkling feta cheese and more basil on top. Beautiful!

As she watched the Food Network, she devoured her meal. The TV chef hadn't completed his presentation yet, so Nell decided to get another helping. She scooped out a second serving just as large as her first. Wow, this was tasty! She'd be sure to put this recipe on her blog. She thought of all the ingredients she had in the fridge for a healthy salad—what she originally had intended to go with one medium serving of chicken and pasta. What a giant step backward she had taken on her road to good health today! The flourless chocolate cake, the mocha, the cookies, and now two gigantic helpings for supper. Her "portion control" was out of control. To say nothing of activating the launch of sugar into her system.

After giving the last two bites of chicken to her boys, Nell carried her empty plate out to the dishwasher. She tidied up the kitchen, put the leftovers in the fridge, and moved the bakery bag of cookies out of sight. But not out of mind.

She had just settled back into her chair, switched TV channels and found a NCIS marathon. Mark Harmon—Sam. He reminded her so much of Gibbs on the popular show. The same look, but Sam was brawny with warm brown eyes. What is he doing right now?

Her anxiety caused the usual reaction. The waistband on her pants were screaming for mercy, but those mocha chip cookies still found their way into her mouth.

Feeling full enough to pop, Nell was putting on her comfy pajama bottoms when the phone rang. Sam!

Nell allowed Sam to take the lead in the conversation. He related the events of the day that didn't seem much different than his usual days. Likewise, Nell shared the antics of George and Newman. She purposely avoided asking about his ex-wife.

Finally Sam broke the ice. "Sorry I haven't called you sooner, but with some of the stuff going on, it's been a madhouse here." Sam's heavy sigh spoke volumes.

"Do you want to tell me about it? I'm a good listener," Nell offered.

"I know you are," Sam said. "And I will tell you, but not tonight. I need to take a shower and go to bed."

"Okay, Sam. Tomorrow?"

"I sure hope so, Nell. I'd love to get away and talk to you for a few hours. I'll try to work it out."

Chapter 5

Nell turned off her phone as she entered church the next morning. She hadn't heard from Sam this morning, and tried hard to keep her mind on the pastor's sermon rather than her relationship. On the way out, Nell chatted with other members of the congregation about a future Bible study, then made her way home. Her cellphone didn't show any missed calls, but her answering machine was blinking when she entered the house.

"Nell, this is Sam." *Finally he called back. I'm like a seventh grade girl waiting for my latest crush to call.* "I was wondering if today around one would be a good time to get together. I'll come down to your house. I really need to get away from here for a time. Let me know."

She called back right away, but also got a machine. Nell left a message saying that one o'clock worked for her and she'd see him then.

The Sunday paper called to her, so after picking up the house, Nell sat down to read it. The world and state news annoyed more than enlightened, but the sports section had updates on the Packers' players—who was healthy and who couldn't play for a few weeks. There was no game this week, or Sam wouldn't have been able to get away from the bar—even in Marinette.

The Life and Family section had an intriguing recipe. Nell found her scissors and realized it was almost noon. She cut out the recipe, fixed herself a salad, and had finished eating when she heard Sam's car pull in the driveway.

The boys ran to the door, barking like they'd never laid eyes on him before. Nell let him in with a big hug, and then Sam bent down to play with the boys. George and Newman showed their approval with yips and licks as the two of them crawled over each other to get to him.

They walked into the living room and Nell sat down on the loveseat.

"Sit down, Sam." Nell gestured toward the recliner. "Boys! George. Newman. Settle down!"

"You and your little dogs are a sight for sore eyes, Nell," Sam confessed. "I love how you named them after characters from Seinfeld."

"It was my favorite sitcom for a lot of years." She patted the seat next to her and the boys jumped up to lie down. "Are you okay?"

"I tell ya' I've never been so happy to get away from my bar."

"What's going on, Sam? I'm worried about you," Nell said, leaning forward as she listened.

"I'm becoming reacquainted with the embodiment of evil. A person I thought I was shed of years ago–Benita's mother—is back in town and turning our lives upside down." Sam wiped his hand down his face as he shook his head.

"Tell me everything," Nell encouraged. When Sam furrowed his brow, Nell added, "Or as much as you feel comfortable sharing."

"To tell you the truth, I've never been comfortable talking about the Bean's mother. The time we were together was the most horrendous period in my life and I've been through some pretty rough stuff. I've tried to put her out of my mind as much as I could. Thinking about her was just too damn painful. But I'm willing to give you the short version."

"Thanks for your trust in me. Sam, you keep referring to her as the Bean's mother. Does this woman have a name?"

"Jessica. Jessie. Jess. By the end I thought of her as Jezebel." Sam rubbed his eyes with his hand. "I didn't realize talking about her would be this hard. I've worked on erasing her memory for the last twenty years and now, after being with you, it's finally happening."

"I thought maybe you still loved her," Nell admitted, her voice barely above a whisper.

"Love her? Hell, no. More like loathe her. She has the face of an angel and a heart colder than the frozen tundra of Lambeau Field. I can handle it, though. She's already chewed me up and spit me out. But Benita, my little Bean—she's the one affected. She's lived her life without a mother. I know a girl needs her mother."

Nell thought about her own life and how she lost her mother in a car accident when she was still in college. There were countless times when she would have liked her mom's sage advice or her warm embrace. Benita had missed out on so much if she hadn't seen her mother in twenty years. "You've done a wonderful job raising her. Benita is bright, funny, and has a good work ethic. You have an amazing daughter."

"Thanks. It hasn't been easy. I don't want Jess to change that. I don't want her to spew her venom and have a negative effect on the Bean. I don't want my little girl to hurt the way Jess hurt me. And hurting is all her mother knows how to do."

Sam's hands were clenched into fists. It was clear he was angry about this woman's presence.

"I can see how much pain she's caused you. Do you want to continue talking about her?" Nell wanted to know the whole story, but wanted to be sure that Sam wanted to share this story with her.

"Yup. I've got to get this out. It's embarrassing, but I want you to know." He took a deep breath. "I was managing a bar at a resort in Door County when the most beautiful woman I had ever laid eyes on, walked in the door. Her silken ebony hair flowed like a river down to her waist. Shimmering skin the color of a healthy tan. Flawless, so smooth… Damn it, Nell. I don't even have the words in my vocabulary to adequately describe her loveliness."

Nell swallowed hard as she was somewhat taken aback by Sam's description.

"She and her mother, Rose, were up from Chicago on vacation while her father was working. They planned to enjoy the peninsula for the summer. I was hot on her trail, as was every other man in the area. She flirted with all of us. Until the day she walked in, I'd been focused on my work and trying to get ahead. I'd saved a pretty good chunk of change, hoping to buy a place of my own in Door County. All of that changed the day I met Jessica and my savings went out the window. I spent a huge portion of my nest egg wining and dining her, trying to impress her."

Sam glanced over at Nell sitting on the loveseat.

"I wanted her to fall in love with me—to see me for the dependable and hardworking, yet fun guy that I was. I didn't want it to matter that I didn't have money, but I couldn't bear the thought of losing her, so I didn't share my true financial status. The way I was spending money led her to believe I was loaded. I never said outright I had money, but I sure acted as though I did. I bought fancy duds and even purchased a flashy sports car. I figured I'd never be in the running if she knew I was a poor working stiff. I was positive she'd soon love me if she just got to know me. And I knew the place I planned to buy in Door County had great potential. I'd be a rich man and we'd have it all."

"Oh, Sam, no."

"I was so blinded by her beauty that I couldn't see any of her faults. I had visions of the two of us working together to rebuild my bank roll. I mentioned my desire to work hard, buy a place and make it on our own, but not with family money. I was trying to gently give her clues I wasn't interested in her money, just in her. We had a fantastic summer and at the end of August, she agreed to marry me. I was the happiest man on earth. She said we had to elope because she didn't want to tell her parents. I went along with it. I gave her whatever she desired. She told her mother by phone that we wed and then we had a blissful weekend. The only joy we ever experienced as a married couple."

"What did her rich parents do? Were they livid that she married you?"

"Rich parents? That's a laugh. She and her mother had rubbed as many nickels together as they could to stay in that resort for the summer. There was no father anywhere in the picture." Sam rose out of his chair and looked out the sliding glass doors to the backyard. "They were a couple of con artists, grifters planning to make a huge score off the sap that Jess married. And I was said sap. The real reason Jess wanted to elope was so my *rich* family wouldn't stop the engagement. She wanted a ring on her finger and cash in her pocket. But I didn't even care initially about what she had done. I was never drawn to her for money. Believe it or not, even after I realized what she was doing I still loved her and wanted to live my life with her."

"Oh, Sam. I'm so sorry." Nell rose, then went over to stand next to him and gave him a hug. "You must have been devastated."

He held her tight, but continued. "Jess went on to say that she'd never intended to stay married to anyone as old as I was and the only reason she culled me out of the herd was she figured I would already have made a lot of money. She figured my parents would die soon and I'd inherit their fortune. Then she'd take off with the lion's share of the money."

"How old were you, Sam?"

"I hate to admit this, but thirty-six." At Nell's gasp, Sam dropped his arms from around her and hung his head. Finally he looked up. "Certainly old enough to know better. I had a good head for business and was about ready to put a down payment on a place when I met Jess. After she was done with me the money was gone. All I had left was a huge car payment and bad memories. The place I was going to buy is one of the biggest resorts in Door County now. The owner is a millionaire just as I would have been if I hadn't blown it."

"How old was Jessica?"

After a long pause Sam exhaled. "Almost twenty-one."

"She was twenty? Sam!"

"I know. But she told me she was twenty-eight. She looked and acted much older. I should've known better. I was thinking with the wrong head." Sam turned away and didn't see Nell roll her eyes.

"The age factor is a concern. How old is Jessica now, Sam?"

"Well, the Bean is almost twenty-six, so I guess that would make her forty-seven. When she walked into The Slam Friday night she still looked twenty-eight."

Clearing her throat, Nell said, "Go on, Sam. What happened? How did you end up with Benita?"

"Jess and her mother had done similar scams before. She had already been married once and was paid handsomely for a quick divorce. Another time she was given a huge sum of money from parents who wanted her out of their son's life. The problem was how fast she and her mom could go through cash. Every time they ran out of dough, they looked for another sucker. Jessica would lure him in and soon his money was gone." Sam rubbed his temples as he paused for breath. "I found out she was no stranger to the sheets."

Nell shook her head and waited for him to continue.

"Rose had a voice like a fishwife and wanted to make sure her daughter was able to suck me dry even of the little I had left. I can still hear that harpy screeching."

"Chances are, Sam," Nell pointed out, "that harpy was closer to your age than you were to her daughter's."

"Turns out you're right. Rose was thirty-eight when I met her. Anyway, they had gone through all of their money trying to look rich enough to snag a wealthy husband. Irate is putting mildly the feeling they had upon realizing I had no money. The three of us lived in my apartment, mother and daughter in one bedroom, me in the other, just long enough for Rose to figure out the best deal for the two of them. During that time Jess discovered she was pregnant from our one weekend together. That wasn't in the plan." Sam shrugged.

"Rose's shrill voice still rings in my ears hollering about birth control pills not being one hundred percent accurate. Rose's first thought was abortion." Sam looked at Nell with tears streaking down his cheeks. "Can you imagine my life without ever having the Bean?"

Nell patted Sam's back as her mind whirled with all the information he had just shared. What else was there about Sam that she didn't know?

***

"Are you up for taking the boys for a w-a-l-k?"

"Great idea," Sam agreed. "I need to shake off this feeling of hopelessness I'm experiencing right now."

Nell grabbed the leashes from the hook in the laundry room. "Don't feel defeated, Sam. Whatever is going on, I'll help you through it. I don't see how your ex-wife could have any influence on Benita now. When was the last time Jessica was in the area?"

Stepping outside, Nell again appreciated that the heat of summer was gone and autumn was in full bloom. She could smell wood burning through a chimney; the change of seasons was in the air. George and Newman were excited to be out and acted as though they had never been on a walk before.

"It's been twenty years since I've laid eyes on her in Marinette or anywhere else, but she looks exactly the same. It's like Jess is taking some sort of youth potion or something." Sam squeezed Nell's hand as they continued to walk down her driveway. Sam painted quite an unpleasant picture of his former wife's personality which he said was the total opposite of her outward appearance.

Finally wanting to get Sam's mind off of the woman for a while, Nell chose to walk the Presidents. They saw lots of people out in their yards decorating for fall and Halloween. They stopped to visit with a few and enjoyed the small town feeling of friends and neighbors nearby. And it was good exercise, something Nell was making an effort to do more often. Finally walking back in the house, Nell wanted to hear the rest of the story. The boys went right to their water bowls, leaving her and Sam alone.

"This has been a much needed break for me, Nell, but I'd better get back to the bar."

"We haven't finished talking about your situation." She picked up Sam's hand and held it. "What harm can Jessica cause now? Does she want money?"

"Money?" Sam laughed with a scowl. "No, she bled me dry until the Bean hit eighteen. I paid her so she wouldn't sue for custody. She's not getting any more cash out of me ever again."

"Then what?"

"She plans to live here. She wants to be a part of our lives. Lord, help us... Jess said she wants me back!"

"What?" Nell almost shrieked.

33

Chapter 6

As Nell drove to the Dairy Dome after Sam left, she conjured up mental pictures of a raven-haired goddess (the most beautiful woman Sam had ever seen) next to images of herself gobbling the jumbo Turtle Top Sundae she was going to consume. *Gee, I wonder who is more appealing.*

At one time Sam loved this woman. She's the mother of his child. That's a connection that would always remain. Sam's sun rose and set with his daughter whose genes are half Jessica's. Nell twisted the necklace she always wore back and forth. She'd never have that special bond with Sam.

He said Jessica was an evil, manipulative shrew who would do anything to get what she wanted. Nell had zero experience with that sort of person. Sam warned her that Jess could come after her, so maybe she would want to stay away from him and the bar for a time. She couldn't do that, though. After years of being alone, Nell was sharing her life with someone again. She had strong feelings toward him. It could even be love. She wasn't about to hide from someone Sam didn't care about in the least. Surely once this Jess got the picture she'd leave Sam alone.

On the other hand, the information Sam revealed about himself turned out to be more than a little upsetting. Just knowing that Sam, at thirty-six, could be so smitten by outward appearances gave Nell pause. He wasn't at all like that now. *Or was he? She'd only known him a few months. Could there be something more Sam was keeping from her?*

And shouldn't someone be able to tell the difference between a twenty-one year old and a twenty-eight year old? Or does all reason go out the window for men when they do their thinking with that "other head?"

Nell released her gold necklace as she pulled up to the Dairy Dome drive-thru and placed her order.

The rich fudge sauce and thick caramel on the Turtle Top Sundae enticed Nell as it draped the heaping mound of ice cream. She balanced the treat in the drink holder and refrained from having a taste until she drove the short distance back home.

George and Newmie were happy to see Nell as she entered the house, or was it the ice cream that piqued their interest? "Boys, go potty outside. Then you can have some ice cream." Seeing no movement toward the door, Nell walked out with them.

When their business was accomplished—two pairs of eyes never leaving the ice cream treat—the three came back in the house. Putting all negative thoughts out of her mind, Nell concentrated on devouring her sundae. A few spoonfuls of vanilla ice cream were doled out to the boys and soon all that was left was a large plastic cup.

The devastating feeling of failure engulfed Nell as she threw away the cup. She had been doing so well changing her eating habits that her recent setbacks took their toll. Her sugar tooth had been awakened and now her thoughts were of cheesecake, fudge, and rich caramel bars. When she avoided desserts for a time she stopped thinking of them. However, when sugar crept back into her body the need for more increased every day. She must beat the urges back again.

Nell hadn't lost a lot of weight, but it had been steadily coming off. She still had her restaurant reviews to do, so she was eating out regularly. Her new system of immediately wrapping up half of her entrée in a doggie bag for later turned out to be easier than she thought. That strategy combined with eating in a more healthy way at home allowed her to melt off a few pounds without too much pain. Now that she had started at the Bayshore Fitness Center, weight should start dropping off her at a faster pace. She must stay focused on the positives.

The clock showed it was time for supper, but Nell wasn't hungry. She'd just slammed down a huge sundae, though the sugar would make her ravenous soon. Two trains of thought were going through Nell's mind. One—eat something healthy and get back on track. Two—finish the day with something you haven't eaten in a long time. Savor it. Then tomorrow go back to the battle against sugar and other unhealthy foods.

Decisions, decisions.

On the way down to the grocery store, the angel voice whispered in her ear, "Turn the car around. Go back home and eat something healthy. There's that good chicken dish you made yesterday."

The devil voice laughed with glee. "Think what a scrumptious meal you could make. Buy heavy cream, cheese, maybe a big, juicy steak, potatoes— whatever you desire. You deserve it after all you've been through."

As Nell walked through the market she was bombarded with unrequested input espousing different views. "Look at the beautiful vegetables. Swiss chard or kale would make a lovely dish. And the fruit. Don't forget about the fruit. It's not too late. You can cook a wonderful meal that will make you feel strong and proud of yourself rather than bloated and guilty."

Heading to the meat and cheese section an opposing opinion whispered in her ear. "Now, you're in the right spot. Make something you haven't eaten in a while. You've been watching your food intake for months. Live a little. There's plenty of time to diet tomorrow."

Finally she'd had enough of the imaginary voices and decided to make a pizza. She picked up a premade crust, a package of hot Italian sausage, a can of sliced ripe olives, and a package of shredded mozzarella cheese. She strolled through the frozen food department and put a pint of caramel swirl ice cream in her cart. That should be soothing after all the spicy pizza. At the checkout, Nell added a small candy bar with lots of chocolate and caramel at the last minute. She couldn't find the king-sized version.

Nell went right to work on dinner when she returned home. George and Newmie rushed up to her and then stayed underfoot as she prepared her meal. She pulled out onion and garlic from the cupboard, chopped them up, and fried them with the hot sausage. The aroma made her aware of how much she loved pizza and missed eating it. She removed the crust from its wrapping and put it on a cookie sheet. She poured a bit of olive oil on the crust and spread it all over. Next, she found a can of tomato sauce in the pantry and added the contents onto the crust. Spicy Italian seasonings went over the tomato sauce. Then hot crushed red pepper, too. When the meat was browned, she spread it evenly on the crust. The final two ingredients, ripe olives and cheese, topped the pizza. It went in the oven and the timer was set.

Nell couldn't help but lick her lips as she noticed her boys were doing the same. She had saved a little of the cooked sausage for just that reason. The boys swallowed their portions whole and Nell almost did the same. It had been quite some time since she had eaten any herself.

When the timer went off, Nell's mouth watered and she craved the pie just from the intoxicating smell. She took the pizza out of the oven and let it rest for a couple minutes as she opened a bottle of beer.

Unable to wait any longer, she sliced it up. The mozzarella stretched as she pulled apart her first piece. She put three giant slices on her plate and went to the living room to watch TV. Back to another bad habit. She had been eating her meals at the bistro table in the kitchen and concentrating on the food, rather than mindlessly eating in front of the TV. Last night she ate in front of the TV and now tonight. She promised herself she'd be good tomorrow.

The cable movie didn't hold a candle to the taste of that first bite of pizza. The movie only served as background noise that accompanied the pleasure the comforting cheese and spicy sausage offered. The three pieces disappeared and then three more were on her plate. The boys received token pieces of crust and meat, but the eating machine that was Nell, plowed through the pie. Even after she was full, Nell kept eating. She wanted it all gone so she could go back to healthy eating the next day.

Pizza finished, Nell was bloated and feeling guilty just as she knew she would. That didn't stop her from eating the ice cream and candy bar, though. Nell gave the boys a good portion of the ice cream as she couldn't finish it all, but ate the candy herself.

Why didn't I just eat a smaller portion and save the leftovers? Nell chided herself. *Because that would make sense and I wanted to go back to eating with abandon for one day.*

As Nell sat in the recliner watching TV with a dog on each side, her thoughts were drawn to Jessica. Sam's ex-wife wanted him back, but he didn't want anything to do with her. His story was sincere. He made a mistake—one that cost him a lot of money. But he had Benita to show for it and she had turned out to be a real blessing in his life.

Nell's mind wandered to her son, Judson, in Alaska. They weren't close, although they had talked and emailed more often since Nell's close call with a murderer. She hadn't shared the strain between her and her son with Sam. How could she? To tell Sam the truth—that Jud blamed her for his father's death because she was off shopping with friends when Drew had a heart attack—what would he think of her then? Jud believed she should have been home, and if she were, she would have been able to save his dad. Then the kicker—after Jud had needled her one too many times, Nell finally exploded at him, reminding Jud that *he* should have been home that day, as was the original plan. *He* had canceled his trip home so he could go to a football game with college friends.

Five long years had gone by without Drew and the wound was just starting to heal. Thinking of how much she was holding back from Sam, she could hardly blame him for not being an open book when she hadn't been herself. *Oh dear, I can hardly point out the sliver in Sam's eye and overlook the log in my own.*

Then, to top it off, who was that man following Annie and/or Leigh? Does he mean them harm? That concern popped into Nell's head and took its place along with the others. Even a nice romantic comedy on TV didn't help to lift her worries.

Chapter 6.5

The abuser lifted the victim up and slammed her down hard on the floor. Then kicked and stomped on her before he pulled and twisted her arm until it was almost torn off. No love here for the red hair.

Any container would be sufficient. Even if it broke open, she wasn't going anywhere.

Chapter 7

"Good morning, Nell."

Even over the phone the warmth in Sam's voice was a healing balm for Nell's overactive imagination. She'd experienced a restless night, and just hearing his greeting let her know everything would be okay between them.

"I've been so worried about you."

"Don't spend your time worrying about me. I'm fine. I can take care of myself," Sam assured. "I'm concerned about you. I unloaded a lot on you yesterday."

"You did, and I have to admit I spent my night thinking everything over." Nell started to pace her living room. "I'm not letting you go without a fight, Sam."

"Whoa, Nellie. Who said I was going anywhere?" Sam paused. "I didn't mean for you to think Jess was serious when she said she wanted me back. Hell, no. She didn't want me twenty-seven years ago and she doesn't want me now. She's up to something."

"What do you mean?" Nell's heart beat faster.

"My mind isn't as devious as hers. I have no idea what she wants, just that she'll fight like a tiger to get it. And anyone who stands in her way runs the risk of being destroyed," Sam cautioned. "That's why I mentioned you might want to stay away from me and The Slam until I find out what she's planning."

"How long will that be?"

"I don't think it'll be long before I have some idea what she's plotting. Jess said she was moving back here, but she has a room at the Best Western. I'll bet she doesn't look for an apartment." The sound of a door slamming on the other end of the call startled Nell. "Beer truck is here. I'll talk to you later."

Their conversation had put things in a different light for Nell. The sun was shining brighter and the birds were chirping louder than moments ago. Sam wasn't overwhelmed by Jessica's beauty, and that made Nell feel better. Maybe the situation would be an inconvenience, but not a disaster.

She decided to stop thinking about Jessica and start working on her review of Miner's Fish House. She grabbed her mini iPad, read over the notes she wrote when she came home Friday night, and began to put them in some sort of order.

Mary Grace Murphy

Nell's Noshes Up North

Miner's Fish House—Bayshore, WI

Wonderful memories flooded through me when I entered Miner's Fish House with a friend the other evening. She and I had both been visitors to Great Britain years ago, so we were quite impressed with the décor in the three remodeled buildings that now house this large, British style pub. The bar area offered tables, booths, and comfortable couches for families. The couches are a nice touch and something I had seen often in England. The middle building is used for the dining room, with the third turned into a game room for board games, trivia, and darts. That room has a magnificent fireplace. The remodelers did such a fine job it appears the pub was originally one large building instead of three combined.

Many years ago when I had the opportunity to travel to England and enjoy their history, scenery, and food, some of their dishes were bland to my taste. Except two items—the pasty and fish and chips. The night I checked out the new establishment in Bayshore was a Friday, so it was the perfect time to try their fish fry. My friend ordered the walleye and I had the "traditional fish and chips" which featured cod. We were both extremely pleased with our choices. The breading was light, yet golden brown and crispy. The chips (French fries) were crunchy on the outside and soft on the inside. The perfect texture. Malt vinegar was a standard on the tabletops as a condiment for the fries. But Wisconsinites beware! Mushy peas are served along with the fish and chips. I didn't care for them in England and I didn't care for them here, either. I may someday make a suggestion that they only be put on the plate if the patron wants them. Otherwise it's a waste.

The walleye was pan fried, served with a delicious baked potato and we both had creamy coleslaw that delivered a spicy bite to be savored. A memorable evening.

After writing about her fish and chips plate, Nell decided to wait until she'd eaten lunch at the pub before she published it. She'd return soon to try the pasty. Having experienced two meals there would make for a better review.

"George! Newmie! Wanna go for a walk?"

Another beautiful autumn day. Nell attached their collars to leashes amid great fanfare. She promised herself she'd treasure these days as all too soon winter would be here. Winter was no joke in Northeastern Wisconsin. This year the weatherman predicted even more snow than last year and Nell wasn't looking forward to it.

George and Newman walked with good manners until they spotted a

40

squirrel. Then the gyrations began. Nell was barely able to keep their pulling and twisting little bodies under control. The squirrel darted over to Madison Street and the dogs tried to follow. But Nell had a different plan, and herded the dogs down Jefferson.

How she would love to knock on Annie Marshall's door and talk to her about that strange man! Now that he also was watching Leigh made it more important than ever that she find out who he was and what he wanted.

She paused in front of Annie's house. The house looked quiet, but it was the middle of the day. Nell chose not to bother her, especially since she had the dogs. Most likely no one was home anyway.

The boys and Nell continued with their walk, all three enjoying the everyday noises common in the neighborhood, and being out in the fresh air. Returning home, the boys made figure eights around her feet as Nell made a healthy salad for lunch. Sitting down finally, she gave Leigh a call.

"Hello."

"Hi, Leigh. What's new with you?"

"Nell, I'm so glad you called," Leigh whispered. "Would you come over?"

"Of course I will. What's wrong?"

"I'm not sure anything is, but I need your opinion. And please don't say anything to Ed when you get here. Just come on upstairs."

"Sure, whatever you say. I'll be right there."

***

Leigh's shaking hands told Nell that something was very wrong indeed. Nell immediately gave her a comforting hug. "Tell me, Leigh. What is it?"

Leigh lifted up the lid of a wooden box and handed it to Nell. She looked inside and then back at Leigh. "A child's doll. Where did you get it?"

"It was in front of the back door this morning. I was in the shop and heard a gentle knock at the back door. I walked to the rear of the store to open the door. No one was there." Leigh clasped her hands together and nodded toward the box Nell was holding. "I looked down and found the box with this doll."

"That's weird. Does the doll hold any particular meaning for you?"

"Take a good look at it." Leigh reached over, pulled it out of the box, and handed the doll to Nell. "Doesn't she look familiar to you? I had one of these dolls growing up."

"With those freckles it looks like Pippi Longstocking, only with short hair…"

"That's my point. It *is* a Pippi Longstocking doll only the red hair has been cut. It wasn't purchased that way. Someone cut the braids into this cute style." Leigh's eyes narrowed. "Why would someone put this on my doorstep?"

"Maybe to say they like your new haircut?" Nell suggested. "Your hair is auburn instead of bright red, but the cut you received Friday is drop dead gorgeous. The doll's cut is adorable, too. It takes away Pippi's little girl look." Nell furrowed her brow.

"I can tell by your face that some idea just came to you," Leigh challenged Nell. "Tell me the truth. What are you thinking?"

"To be perfectly blunt, I think it has something to do with that guy that came to my house last week asking about Annie. The same man who came into your shop and complimented your haircut," Nell confessed. "Something isn't right about him."

"I don't know why he would do this," shivered Leigh. "It reminds me of a scary movie when the doll is all hacked up to threaten someone. Do you think that's what this is about?"

Nell shrugged. "I'm not sure. The thing is, the doll *isn't* all hacked up," Nell said handing it back to Leigh. "Look how carefully the hair was cut. And the doll's body is in perfect shape as if it's been treated with love."

"What do you think is really going on, Nell?"

"Right now I think you've got a secret admirer. It may be that he has no intention of hurting you, but he isn't showing his admiration in a normal way. If you don't respond the way he wants, who knows what he'll do."

"I don't like the sound of that." The cat, Prada, jumped up on Leigh's lap and she absently stroked her fur.

"Are Pippi Longstocking dolls even sold anywhere anymore?" Nell pondered and then pulled her iPad out of her gigantic sand-colored purse that could almost be used as an overnight bag. "One way to find out." Her fingers flew and soon she had an answer. "Here we go. There are many offerings on Amazon and ebay."

"But would there even be time for the doll to ship?" Prada jumped off Leigh's lap as she bounced to her feet. "And it would take time to cut and style the hair. I had my hair cut on Friday. Today's Monday and I found the doll about ten o'clock this morning."

"This...stalker, for lack of a better term, might have already had the doll and planned to give it to you with long hair. Getting your hair cut may have put a monkey wrench into his plans." Nell took a better look at the box in which Pippi had been placed. "The box looks nondescript. It reminds me of the boxes Drew had Judson build when he was first learning how to use tools."

"What do you think of that luxurious green silk in the box? Is it meant to cushion the doll?" Leigh asked as she bent over to pick up the cat. Prada wanted no part of being carried and jumped right back down again.

"I'm only using my common sense and thousands of hours reading mysteries and watching crime shows, but I think this guy has a major crush on you and protecting the doll is very important to him." Nell looked Leigh in the eye. "I gather you haven't mentioned this to Ed."

Leigh shook her head.

"Why not?"

"I didn't want to worry him for no reason. I wanted to get your opinion

42

first and was just going to call you when you called me." Leigh walked over to her refrigerator, looked in, and closed the door again. "You think I need to tell Ed?"

"Yes, I do. I don't know why you're so hesitant," Nell said. "Ed may have an idea or two about what to do. And maybe you should talk to the police. It's possible this guy could be dangerous."

"What could the police possibly do about this doll?" Leigh shrieked. "It isn't even mutilated. They wouldn't have anything to go on to find out who did it."

"Just to let them know. Then they're aware there could be someone in Bayshore that has these tendencies. There's no harm in letting the police in on the situation," Nell assured. "I imagine they'd appreciate it."

"I'll discuss that idea with Ed. Why don't you stay for supper and you can help me tell him about the doll," Leigh wheedled.

"Hmmm, I don't think so," Nell shook her head. "You can handle that on your own. Time for me to head home."

"Okay, thanks for coming over, Nell. I'll call you after I tell Ed."

"Good." Nell gave Leigh a hug. "I'm serious about going down to the police station and talking to someone. It couldn't hurt."

***

On the drive home, as Nell was thinking about the Pippi Longstocking doll, she darted up Jefferson Street just to see if there was any movement around Annie Marshall's house. The garage door was up, so Nell took a chance and pulled into her driveway.

She knocked on the front door and waited. Annie glared out the window before she opened the door.

"Oh Nell, it's a good thing it's you," Annie raged, hazel eyes flashing. "If it would've been another false alarm and *shoebox*, I'd be on the phone right now."

"What is it, Annie? What's wrong?"

"Take a look at this." Annie led the way into the kitchen. She motioned toward a beat up old shoebox on the table. Inside the box was a mutilated doll. An arm was almost completely ripped off hanging on by threads, there were cuts on the face and body of the doll, and it was filthy.

"When did you find this?" Nell asked.

"Just now when I came home from work. I'd barely gotten into the house when there was a loud knock on the back door. I thought that was odd, but went to answer it. No one was out there. Just this horrible box." Annie's lips pursed, then she spouted, "I've a good mind to call a couple mothers and let them know the truth about their 'sweet' daughters."

"Whose daughters? What are you talking about?" Nell didn't think she and Annie were on the same page.

"Girls at the high school. Lori was chosen to be on Homecoming Court and she told me last night how jealous some of the other girls were. She didn't seem worried about it, though and I'm sure she never dreamed any of them would take it this far." Annie paused. "I was glad to see you at the door, Nell. Maybe you can help me figure out how to tell Lori about how her so-called friends are treating her."

Annie ran her hand through her hair. "You know when someone goes after your kid, it's worse than if it happened to you. And every high school has its share of mean girls."

"Hold on a minute there, Annie. I don't think high school girls did this."

"But the boys don't care who's on court. This would be much more like snippy girls."

"No, I mean I don't think this doll has anything to do with Lori or Homecoming."

At Annie's questioning look, Nell continued. "I'm on my way home from Leigh Jackson's, where she showed me a similar doll—a Pippi Longstocking—she found in a box outside her back door this morning. Only her doll was in perfect shape, except for the hair."

"The hair was destroyed? This is too bizarre."

"Pippi's red braids were cut and the hair was styled beautifully," Nell explained. "Not an inch of that doll was harmed."

"Oh. I don't like this situation, either." Annie sat down on a kitchen chair, putting her head in her hands. "What a weird coincidence that you stopped over here after being at Leigh's. Why are you here anyway?" Annie paused and looked up at Nell. "You thought I'd have a doll, didn't you?"

Nell leaned over and touched her arm. "Not a doll necessarily, but I think that guy I was telling you about Friday night has something to do with this. Have you seen or heard from him?"

"No. What connection would he have to Leigh? I don't understand this at all."

"He came to my house looking for you Friday, the same guy I saw staring at you and Leigh at Miner's Fish House Friday night. Then, he stopped in at Leigh's shop Saturday." Nell rubbed her left eyebrow. "He told Leigh that he liked her hair better short. Leigh doesn't remember ever seeing him before. We know he saw her Friday night, but her hair was already cut. When could he have seen her hair long?"

"I don't know, Nell. This is so weird. So you're saying he cut and styled the doll's hair and gave it to Leigh because he likes her. And then," Annie gasped. "He mutilated the other doll because he doesn't like me!"

"I don't know anything for sure, Annie." Nell squeezed her hand.

"But Leigh's red hair is just like Pippi Longstocking. This doll has red hair, too. I don't. My hair isn't anything like this doll."

"You must recognize the doll, though. It's Midwest Annie."

Chapter 8

"A beat-up Midwest Annie doll given to Annie," Nell talked to herself as she drove the short block home from Annie's. "That's a regional doll that is not well known in other states. But this guy knows about it. Then there's the well-known red-haired doll with a short hairstyle given to Leigh who just had her auburn hair cut. What does it all mean?"

As soon as she got in the door, Nell got right down on the floor and played with the dogs to de-stress. They basked in her attention. *Life is too short. Hold your loved ones close.*

She pulled herself up off the floor and walked outside with George and Newman while considering her options. None of this was any of her business, but she cared about the women involved. She had advised Annie to talk to the police. Her doll was more threatening than Leigh's, but she hoped Leigh would contact the authorities, too. She had a gut feeling that guy from Friday had something to do with all this…drama.

She and the boys went in the house and she started making a salad for supper. Yes, a nice, healthy salad after last night's food fest would be good. Then she'd reheat some of her Mediterranean Chicken Pasta. Just one normal-sized portion would do. After she'd eaten and cleaned up, she'd try to put the dolls out of her mind.

The phone rang after Nell finished her supper. She put her plate on the kitchen counter and saw that it was Benita.

"Hello, Benita."

"Hi, Nell. Am I disturbing you? I can call back later."

"Not at all. How can I help?"

"I'm sure Dad told you that my mother came back Friday night. He did, didn't he?" Benita asked.

"Yes." Nell, hearing the strain in Benita's voice, was unsure where the conversation was headed. "Didn't you want him to tell me?"

"Oh, it's okay that he told you. That doesn't bother me. I need to ask you something, but I wanted to be sure Dad told you about my mother first."

"What is it, Benita?" Nell's curiosity was piqued.

"I haven't seen her since I was six years old. Now she wants to spend time with me. And, Nell, I want to spend time with her, too. I've always wanted to understand why my mother left us, but I have a sinking feeling I'm being disloyal to my dad. What do you think I should do?"

Nell went into the living room and sat down, the phone still firmly clutched next to her ear. "Talk to him. He's a reasonable man. He'll appreciate that a girl needs to know her mother."

"You don't know how he's been acting lately. He's a different person. Everything sets him off."

"Hmmm… My guess is that Sam thinks you'll want to spend a lot of time with your mother and maybe he could lose you."

"That's partially right. I do want to spend time with her. But Dad could never lose me. We've gone through too much together. I'm just worried about hurting his feelings."

"Unfortunately you won't be able to avoid that, Benita. Talk to him. Tell him what you've told me. Give him a chance to understand what you're feeling."

"That's what I hoped you'd tell me," she admitted. "Just giving you the heads up that Dad might need to talk to you tonight or tomorrow. It all depends on when I get my nerve up."

"I'll be ready. Good luck, dear."

Nell smiled, realizing Benita wanted her opinion. Her smile faded as she thought about how concerned, and even heartsick, Sam was going to be. He didn't want his daughter anywhere near his ex-wife's clutches. But she was Jessica's daughter, too, as much as Nell knew Sam hated to acknowledge it.

Even though Benita was a petite little thing, she was twenty-six years old and thoroughly capable of making her own intelligent decisions. Sam was just going to have to suck it up.

Nell heaped another portion of the pasta dish onto her plate and stuck it in the microwave without thinking. She was too busy wondering what she'd say to Sam when he called. The food was reheated and eaten before she came to terms with what she had done.

"Good grief! I scarfed that down without even enjoying it. All those carbs and calories. And I had a salad, too!" George and Newmie looked up at her as if to say, "What about us?"

"Anybody want a treat?"

The boys climbed over each other as Nell put her dishes in the dishwasher. She dug into the treat bowl which was filled with spoon-sized wheat cereal. She used the cereal as treats so George and Newmie didn't gain too much weight. Too bad a bite-sized piece of wheat cereal didn't make her as happy as it did her boys.

Then she settled into her recliner in the living room with the dogs snuggled in, one on each side, as she found a cooking show on TV. With her iPad in hand, she read over the first part of her review of Miner's Fish House. Everything looked good. Soon she would try lunch there and have another entry for Noshes Up North.

With that chore out of the way, Nell couldn't help but think about Sam. What would his reaction be to his little Bean wanting to spend a lot of time with her mother?

***

"I knew that woman was after the Bean. I just knew it."

Sam's call had saved Nell from watching yet another TV chef make a chocolate cake with bacon sprinkles. "Did Benita tell you that she called me?"

"She did," snapped Sam.

"I hope you aren't upset that I was honest with her. I know you don't want Benita to have anything to do with her mother, but be realistic, Sam…"

"I *am* being realistic," Sam cut in. "Jess will lay on the charm with her like you can't believe. She'll have the Bean wondering how she ever was able to tie her shoes without her mother there."

"I don't think you're giving your daughter enough credit. What I was going to say before was a girl needs her mother. It's only natural that Benita wants to get to know her. Give her that chance. I think you'll fare better if you tell Benita it's okay, rather than if you fight her on it."

"I don't know if I can do that. I'd be sacrificing her to the devil."

Nell took a slow, deep breath. She needed to have patience with Sam. This was a delicate subject. "Benita wants to spend time with her mother, but she doesn't want to hurt you. She told me you'll never lose her." Nell waited for Sam's response.

After a long pause Sam grumbled, "I'm fighting a battle I can't win. I tell the Bean to see her mother, she may never come back. I tell her not to go, she'll hate me for it and go anyway."

"Neither of those things will happen, Sam, you know that."

"That's easy for you to say." A heavy sigh. "Ah, look I need to get off the phone."

"I'm sorry if you didn't like what I said to Benita. She called me for an honest answer and I gave it to her."

"I know, Nell."

As soon as Sam was off the line, Nell remembered she hadn't told him about Leigh, Annie Marshall, and the dolls. But then again he had enough on his mind. What would Sam decide to do?

Chapter 9

Nell woke up to the realization that Leigh had never called her last night to tell her what Ed thought of the Pippi Longstocking doll. After feeding and walking the boys and waiting a reasonable amount of time, Nell called her.

"I know I didn't call you last night," admitted Leigh. "I was trying to find just the right moment to bring it up to Ed and the longer I waited, the more foolish I felt for waiting at all. I should have told him immediately. It was too late to call you after Ed and I talked."

"What did he say, Leigh?"

"He's concerned there's some foul play brewing and agrees with you that I should talk to the police."

"Thank goodness." Nell took a deep breath. "I have a little more fuel to add to the fire."

"What do you mean?"

"On my way home from your house yesterday afternoon, I stopped at Annie Marshall's. I wanted to see how she was doing."

"And how is she?" Leigh prompted. "Evidently something is amiss."

"She's rattled. Annie found a mutilated doll in a shoe box outside her back door yesterday."

Leigh gasped, "Was it Pippi?"

"It wasn't Pippi, but it did have red hair. It was a Midwest Annie doll."

"No!"

"Annie initially thought it was from a high school girl who was jealous of her daughter, Lori," Nell explained. "I gave her my theory, so now she's taking it more seriously."

"And your theory being the strange guy is behind both incidents?"

"Well, yes. Doesn't that make sense to you?"

"As much as I like to kid you about exaggerating, my friend, I think you're right. I'll give Annie a call and compare notes."

"Good idea," Nell agreed. "Maybe you could even talk to the police together."

"Maybe. I'll let you know something by the end of the day, I promise."

A shiver went up Nell's spine. "Leigh?"

"Yes."

"In the meantime, be careful."

***

Nell thought about the hours ahead of her but didn't see there was anything she could do about the problems her friends were experiencing. She'd given advice to Benita and Sam about Jessica, and she'd given her opinion to Leigh and Annie about the stranger. Now it was a waiting game.

While she waited to hear word from Leigh, Nell called her friend, Elena, to see if Elena was interested in checking out the pasty at Miner's Fish House for lunch. Thankfully Elena had time, and they agreed to meet in two hours. Nell was hungry already just thinking of the tasty dishes at the pub.

Instead of eating a snack, she kept herself busy as she vacuumed the kitchen and living room. Then she promised herself she would vacuum the rest of the house when she came home. She applied make-up, changed into fresh black jeans and a red Badgers sweatshirt, grabbed her purse, then jumped in her car to drive toward Main Street.

Parking close to Miner's Fish House didn't appear to be a possibility. Business must be picking up. Finally, she found a spot several blocks away. She told herself the exercise would be good for her as she puffed to keep up a brisk pace. The smell of burning leaves filled the air. *Someone is getting a head start on their raking.*

The tables in the bar area were filled, but Nell didn't see Elena. Either she wasn't here yet, or was in the dining area. Walking out of the bar area, she went past the dining room in order to peek into the game room. The beauty and aroma of the wood fireplace added to the coziness of the room as did the sound of wood crackling. A lone man was practicing darts. Nell doubled back to the dining room and spotted Elena at a corner table with a glass of soda. A few of the other tables were occupied, too. Not a bad crowd for a Tuesday lunch.

"Howdy, stranger," Elena greeted. "Seems like forever since we've been out together."

"I know," Nell agreed, sliding into the chair across from Elena. A pang of guilt gnawed at her as she thought of all the time she spent with Sam. "We need to catch up."

Nell ordered a diet Sprite as Elena shared news about her family and her store, The Dining Room, while Nell gave Elena the tiny bit of information she had from her short phone calls with Jud. Nell appreciated the help Elena had given her when she was being stalked just a few months ago. Maybe her friend could look at this doll disaster with a fresh eye and see something Nell couldn't. She'd start by explaining Sam's situation first, though. "Sam called a few days ago and said his ex-wife came back."

Elena set her glass on the table without the intended sip. "Nell, this is huge! Details, I need details. I should have ordered a beer."

"Well...he explained some of their background to me, but I want to talk to him about it more. Let's just say they both behaved badly," Nell hedged, fumbling with her napkin and unsure now about opening the subject matter to Elena's curiosity. "But according to Sam, this Jessica is a real piece of work. She says she wants Sam back, but he doesn't believe her."

"He doesn't believe her? Is he saying if he believed her, he'd go back to her?"

"No. Nothing like that. Sam despises Jessica," Nell explained. "His first thought was that she had something up her sleeve. He initially thought she wanted to make trouble for him."

"What does he think now?"

Their waitress, Lynn, came for their order and they both chose a pasty. Being from southwest Wisconsin originally, Nell had high pasty standards. Her mom and both her grandmothers made a delicious pasty, as did most women in the area. During her childhood, the school cooks even made it for hot lunch. She hoped the pasty here hit the mark.

"Getting back to Sam, his concern is that she wants to turn Benita against him."

"Would that even be possible?" Elena questioned. "Don't they have a great relationship?"

"They do, but I think Sam forgets his daughter is twenty-six, not eight. He claims his ex-wife is so evil she'll be able to turn her against him. He doesn't want Benita even talking to her."

"Have you met this woman?"

"No, and Sam doesn't think meeting her would be a good idea. He said Jessica might try to hurt me."

"Well, I'm with Sam," Elena cautioned, meeting Nell's eyes. "You just got out of a dangerous situation; don't put yourself in another one."

"Don't worry, I'll be careful."

As she was talking to Elena, a thought nagged at Nell. There was something familiar about the man throwing darts, although she had only seen him from the back. Could he be the strange man stalking Leigh and Annie, who she now thought of as the "doll man?" She'd wonder about it all day if she didn't find out.

She excused herself to the bathroom, but instead walked over to the game room and carefully edged her head into the doorway. The man, whoever he was, was gone. The game room was totally empty. She went back to her seat with more on her mind now than a pasty.

Lynn appeared a few minutes later with a sturdy tray holding two large, steaming, crusty pasties at the same time Nell's nose detected incoming food. The aroma took her to a higher place.

"Here you go," the waitress said, setting their plates down in front of them and a bottle of ketchup on the table. "Is there anything else I can get you right away?"

"No, thanks. This looks wonderful," Nell replied. "Oh, wait. Would you happen to know who that man was in the game room throwing darts a few minutes ago?"

"Sorry. I didn't even realize anyone was in there," she said, and hurried back to the kitchen.

Nell tucked into her pasty while wondering if they always had a wood fireplace burning unattended. She knew, as she looked at Elena's questioning eyes, that she had some explaining to do.

***

As Nell and Elena relaxed after their delicious pasties, they chewed over the facts of the doll dilemma. With so much to discuss, she and Elena opted for dessert.

"I'm going to try one of their specialties, the Sea Salty Caramel Guinness Brownie," Nell said.

"Oh, that sounds good! Shall we split one?" Elena suggested.

Nell felt her mouth drop open in horror at the thought. "Sorry, Elena. If I don't eat it all, I'll take it home for later along with the other half of my pasty." Nell shuffled in her seat. "Unless you'll only order dessert if we split it."

"No, it's fine Nell. I'll order the same and take part of it home, too." Elena waved the waitress over and they ordered their decadent treats.

"I know this was a lot to tell you all at once, Elena, but do you have any thoughts about Leigh, Annie, and the dolls? I'm stumped."

"My initial thought is the whole thing is unsettling. In my opinion, the dolls being involved is the product of a sick mind. I don't like the idea of some creep like this guy even being in Bayshore, much less being involved with friends of mine."

"My thoughts exactly," Nell agreed. "I hope both Leigh and Annie take my advice and go to the police. Even though the police may not be able to do anything, they need to know about what is happening."

"Nell, please tell me you aren't going to get involved. It hasn't been but a couple months since you were being stalked."

"I know. Believe me, I wish there wasn't anything going on that would give me cause to get involved. But this is Leigh—and Annie. If something is amiss, I must help them in any way I can."

Elena nodded. "That being said, I want to help, too. Julie's working at the store more often now that the kids are back in school and she's asked for additional hours. The new dining room tables have been delivered and the new fall tablecloths and napkins are on display. I'll be able to get away more often now. So, don't go running off on your own like you did before. Okay? Call me," Elena pressed. "I mean it."

"Okay, okay," Nell acknowledged. "I promise I'll try."

"I suppose I need to be satisfied with that." Elena's eyes opened wide as Lynn returned to their table with gigantic brownies oozing with salty caramel. "I'll let you know now that I'll need a to go box."

The waitress set the dishes down and smiled. "Sure."

"You probably can make that two boxes," Nell said with a lick of her lips.

51

Chapter 10

After greeting George and Newmie when she entered her house, Nell went right to her answering machine. No messages. She was hoping for something from Leigh, but it was only midafternoon and Leigh promised she would contact her by the end of the day. No call from Sam, either. Not knowing what was happening set her on edge.

To keep her mind occupied—or at least her body active after eating such a filling meal—Nell changed into her work clothes, took the boys outside and played fetch in the backyard. After tiring them out, it was time to finish the vacuuming and the other cleaning in the house. Using a little elbow grease would keep her busy for a couple hours. *To work!*

However, cleaning didn't keep her mind off her other pressing matters as she hoped it would. Nell stewed about Sam. How upset was he about the advice she gave Benita? Would it affect their relationship? Benita had every right to a relationship with her mother. Nell had to admit what was really bothering her—how beautiful was Jessica? Would she agree with Sam that she's the most beautiful woman Nell had ever seen? She sure hoped not. She couldn't compare in this body. No hourglass figure or long flowing hair here. She needed answers.

The afternoon morphed into evening as Nell finished her chores without a single phone call interrupting her. At least she had her supper ready to go. The other half of her pasty and brownie would fill the bill nicely. She made fresh coleslaw while the pasty warmed up in the oven. A pasty was too precious to be microwaved. The Miner's Fish House made pasty just like home. No better compliment could be given. The knowledge that she could have the flaky homemade pasty whenever she wanted both thrilled and worried Nell. The three main ingredients of pasty—crust, potatoes, and beef weren't the healthiest options for her. But if she had it occasionally…

The oven buzzer went off causing Newmie to yip and George to sit at alert. The boys recognized the sound of the oven going off and associated it with food. She'd save a small portion for them.

Her pasty and coleslaw ready to go, Nell sat at her bistro table with the two little pups at her feet sporting big eyes and licking lips. They sat quietly, not begging, but being available if any morsels were to drop.

The pasty was every bit as delectable as it had been at lunchtime. The coleslaw was a good accompaniment and was the standard side dish for pasty in southwest Wisconsin. And as the good Cornish girl she was, she used ketchup to accent the pasty rather than gravy as some people did in the Upper Peninsula.

Nell gave a chunk of round steak to each of her boys and put her dish in the dishwasher. She then turned to the Sea Salty Caramel Guinness Brownie. Such a decadent blend of flavors! Caramel and chocolate went well together, as did the Guinness and chocolate. The salty and sweet in the sea salt and caramel were a taste sensation. Putting it all together was pure genius. Oh, yes. Miner's Fish House would soon become a staple in Bayshore and undoubtedly for the neighboring communities as well. Nell planned to finish her review tonight.

A clean house and a full belly. Life was good.

Nell settled into her favorite chair and turned on the TV. NCIS was about to start which only brought her thoughts back to Sam. She was tempted to call him, but decided against it. She wanted to wait until he had something he chose to share with her, not badger him into telling her more before he was ready. Anyway, she wanted the phone free for when Leigh called.

Finally the long awaited ring of the phone. Nell set her dvr to record the remainder of the episode and almost pounced on the phone.

"Leigh?"

"Hello, Nell. I told you I'd call you by the end of the day and here I am."

"Thanks, you've been on my mind." Nell paced in the living room as she talked to her friend. "Did anything happen?"

"Yes. I invited Annie over here when she finished work. We had a good conversation and then went to the police station and shared our concerns with Officer Wunderlin."

"Oh, I'm so relieved," Nell gushed. "What did the officer say?"

"Just what we thought he would say. That there was nothing they could do, but thanked us for letting the police department know. He said to be careful and contact him if anything out of the ordinary happened. Annie and I both felt better after we left."

"What are you two going to do?" Nell asked.

"What can we do?"

"I don't know. Certainly be on the lookout for anything unusual. I guess just what the officer said," Nell conceded. "Did Ed go with you?"

"No, but I assure you, neither one of us will take any chances. It's been a long day, so I'll call you if anything else happens, okay?"

"Of course, and thanks for calling." Nell put the landline phone back in its base with trepidation.

There had to be something that could be done about this doll man before he did something to hurt one of her friends. Realistically, Nell understood the police had their hands tied, but she didn't. Who was this character? Where was he staying in Bayshore? She'd have to do a little investigating of her own.

Chapter 11

Elena climbed into Nell's car the next morning, and handed her a bag. "This is for you." The grin on Elena's face was a dead giveaway she had something up her sleeve.

"Alright, what's in here?" Nell opened up the sack and pulled out a deerstalker hat and a pipe, then laughed, "Well, I guess that makes you Watson."

"It does, Sherlock, and I'm so happy you called me," Elena smiled. "I'm ready for an adventure."

"Where is this from?" Then it dawned on Nell. These items belonged to Elena's late husband. "Was this part of Tom's costume from when he played a detective in the Machickanee Players production?" Nell put the hat on and posed with the pipe.

"Exactly right. Yes, Tom bought these items for the play. I thought you'd appreciate the sentiment more. I suppose I should donate some of that stuff to Goodwill one of these days."

"I don't know," Nell laughed. "They might come in handy." Then more seriously she said, "If you want to get them out of the house, why don't you give them to the play group?" She handed the hat and pipe back to Elena. "They might need them for another mystery production."

"Good idea. Are you ever going to do another play with the Machickanee Players?"

"I've thought about it, but I bet it wouldn't be as easy to remember my lines now." Nell gave Elena a smile. "Also, I'd miss doing the plays with Tom."

"I admit that I had an extra fondness for the plays you and Tom were in together. I would sit and laugh at the two of you." Elena chuckled, and then asked, "What's our line of attack today?"

"We'll drive past the Bayshore Inn and the Circle Motel and see if I can recognize the doll man's car. When he was at my house I was focused on him and wasn't really paying attention to his vehicle. I know it was an older car and had a dark color. I think maybe blue or black. We'll figure out what to do next from there."

It didn't take long to reach Bayshore Inn, located on the old highway that still ran through the edge of town. Several pickups were parked in the lot, and a couple midsize cars. Nell drove around to the back and only found a dump truck and the dumpster. They continued down the highway heading out of town toward Green Bay and to the Circle Motel. Even fewer vehicles were parked there. No large dark cars at either location.

"Not seeing his car could be a good thing, Nell. Maybe he's gone."

Nell pulled up in front of the office and stopped the car. "Maybe not for good. For all we know he could be doing something to Leigh right now. I'm going in there. I'll describe the man to them, see if he's registered or has been registered." She got out of the car and went in the motel.

Within five minutes Nell came back to the car with a frown. "Nothing here. Let's go back to the Bayshore Inn and I'll ask there, too."

"What will we do if he's registered?" Elena took a piece of gum out of her purse and put it in her mouth. "Gum?"

"No, thanks." Nell shook her head. "If we know where he's staying, we'll be able to keep an eye on him. If we do find him, do you think I should confront him?"

"No!" Elena shouted, catching her gum as it flew out of her mouth. "This man is obviously deranged. Don't draw attention to yourself."

"You're right. I'll be careful."

Nell parked in the lot of the Bayshore Inn and hoped for better luck. "Be right back."

After close to ten minutes, Nell returned with a smile on her face. When she opened the car door, Elena asked, "What did you find out? Is this where he's staying?"

"No, but Cassy Rundle was at the desk. Did you know she worked here?"

"I don't know Cassy Rundle. Was she one of your former students?"

"Yes, and he isn't registered here," Nell answered. "However, she knew who I was talking about from my description. She said she saw the guy at Miner's Fish House Saturday night."

"How does that help us?"

"Elementary, my dear Elena. I saw him there Friday night, Cassy saw him there Saturday night, and I think I saw him there yesterday at lunch. We know a place he likes to go. That's progress."

"Something tells me we're headed toward Main Street to look for a dark-colored older car parked somewhere near Miner's Fish House. Am I correct in my thinking?"

Nell turned to Elena with a grin. "It's the next logical step."

While still several blocks from the pub, Nell said, "Let's start looking for the car. Yesterday I had to park this far away."

"I know you said it was a dark color. There's a deep burgundy Buick," Elena pointed to the corner of a side street. "Would that be a possibility?"

"Yes, and over here is a dark blue sedan. It could be either one. Let's go in."

"Oh, Nell. Do you think that's wise?"

Nell found a spot on a side street and parked. "I don't know if it's wise or not, but if he's in there I want to know. Don't worry, Elena, I won't speak to him." She gave her friend a wink. "We could have lunch and keep an eye on him."

As soon as Nell and Elena walked in, they spotted their suspect sitting at the bar. "There's an empty table right here." Elena pointed as she sat down with her back toward the man. "I guess you'd want to sit so you could look at him."

"Thanks." Nell picked up a menu. "We'll have to order lunch."

"I think I'm too nervous to eat," Elena admitted in a whisper. "If this guy is the one that left the dolls, there's no telling what else he is capable of."

"The operative word there is 'if', Elena. We don't know for sure that he did anything. That's why we're scouting him out."

"Could I get another round here, Will?" The man pushed his empty mug toward the bartender.

"Sure thing, Ian."

"Ian. His name is Ian," Elena said under her breath. "That's something we didn't know before."

"If that really is his name. It sounds made up to me." Nell grumbled.

"There's nothing made up about Ian." Elena challenged. "That's my cousin's name."

Nell shrugged her shoulders as Lynn came to their table, took their diet soda orders, and left. She and Elena continued to read over the menu. "Since this is an investigation, not a culinary excursion, I'm ordering something basic that would be easy to pack up or even leave if we need to exit suddenly," Nell whispered.

"Need to exit *suddenly?* You mean we're going to follow him?"

"Well, yeah," Nell began. "I'm going to, but you don't have to come. Actually it might be risky, so maybe you better not." She started to laugh. "You might break a nail."

"For your information, Nell Bailey, my manicurist is on speed dial," retorted Elena. "But if you're going to follow him, so am I. I asked to be involved and I meant it, but I had hoped to stop you from getting into a dangerous situation."

"You'll stop me from getting in over my head, if that's what you mean. But we haven't even gotten our ankles wet yet. You know, Elena, you might want to be careful about what you ask for in the future."

Lynn returned with the sodas, and the duo requested a large order of homemade chips and salsa. "I'll be back in a jiffy," Lynn said as she turned to go back in the direction of the kitchen.

"Those chips are only going to accentuate my hunger," Nell said taking a sip of her diet Sprite. "But if there's a chance we can follow *Ian* to his lair it'll be worth it."

"I know this morning I was excited to go on an adventure, but now I'm not sure how much excitement I can handle," Elena confessed.

Lynn came back with their order and as Nell and Elena began to nibble on chips and salsa, Nell paid close attention to where Ian was at the bar. Will was standing by him and they were chatting quietly.

"I wish I could hear what the two of them are saying," Nell whispered. "I wonder how well Will knows this Ian." She made a mental note to talk to Will at a later time.

"Chances are the bartender only knows him because he's a customer."

"That's kinda what I'm thinking, too. Miner's Fish House hasn't been open long enough for them to know each other well." Nell lowered her head and sighed.

Elena caught Lynn's attention for another soda and their bill.

They paid the bill and sat listening for any conversation they could hear from the bar. Now they were free to pick up and leave when the need arose.

"Looks like he's getting ready to leave," Nell murmured. Once Ian was just out the door, Nell stood up and Elena followed suit. They moved to the door as rapidly as they could without drawing attention to themselves and left.

Much to their dismay, Ian was only halfway down the block, smoking a cigarette. Since he was just standing there, Nell guessed Ian probably planned to return to Miner's Fish House when he finished smoking. There'd been a ban effected and no smoking was allowed in restaurants across the state of Wisconsin, so smokers needed to go outside if they wanted to indulge in the habit. But now Nell and Elena were outside with no excuse to go back in the building.

"Rats!" Elena hissed.

"Why don't we walk across the street and go down to the coffeehouse? I think we can see this place from there if we look out the big front windows."

"Good idea." Elena glanced at Nell.

When they entered The Mocha Chip, Elena sat at one of the tables by the window while Nell went to the counter. Nell came to the table with two peanut butter cookies and two regular coffees in to go cups. "We're prepared for whenever he comes out," she said.

"Thanks."

"I don't see Ian outside. We can't be positive that he went back in the bar," Nell frowned. "He could have his cigarette and decide to leave, and we may not even see him go. We could sit here for hours not knowing. How much coffee can we drink?"

Elena's shoulders slumped as she took a small bite of her cookie. "And I sat down with my back to the window. I should have been watching him."

"That's okay. We'll come up with another plan."

"I know what to do, Nell. I'll go outside and check to see if that burgundy car is still there."

"And the dark blue one? Even if they're still parked there, it means nothing. Maybe neither of them is his car. You stay here and I'll go back to the Fish House looking for something…my cellphone that may have fallen out of my purse. If he isn't there, I'll ask Will about him. See what he knows."

"Great idea. I'll wait for you here."

***

Nell saw Ian sitting at the same barstool he had been when she came through the door. She walked over to the table where she and Elena had been seated and made a big show of searching for something. She then approached the bar.

"Will, I've misplaced my phone and think it might have dropped out of my purse when I was in here earlier. If anyone turns it in, could you let me know? Here's my card with my landline number."

"Sure," he said as he read the card. "Nell."

She left the pub, crossed the street, and was almost to the Mocha Chip when Elena came rushing out. "Ian's out the door and heading toward the corner where the burgundy car is parked. We have to hurry."

Elena walked at a pretty good clip while Nell tried to keep up. They were almost to the corner when Ian, driving the dark burgundy car, turned on to Main Street and proceeded in the opposite direction.

Trying to catch her breath, Nell rasped, "Now we know he says his name is Ian, he drives an old dark burgundy Buick, and he likes to hang out at Miner's Fish House. That's pretty good for a few hours' work. Could you read his license plate?"

"No, we should have taken it down when we were still trying to figure out which car was his. But what would you do with that information?"

"Give it to Leigh or Annie to give to the police." By the time Nell and Elena returned to the car any chance of following Ian was long gone, but they decided to ride around town on the off chance they might catch a glimpse of his car. After going past every commercial building on Main Street and the businesses on the highway, Nell drove through the local neighborhoods as well.

"This is a lost cause, Nell," Elena said as she continued looking on both sides of the street. "He probably went home."

"Possibly," Nell acknowledged, "but where's home? If he's not staying at either of the motels in town, where? He could be staying in Marinette or Green Bay, but I don't think he'd spend so much time at Miner's Fish House if he was so far away."

"Maybe he's staying with a friend or relative."

"Well, that's why I'm driving down the residential streets. Since we're not having any luck I suppose we could call it a day. What do you think?"

"That's fine with me, as long as you're really done for the day." Elena gave Nell the fish eye. "I don't want to find out you took me home and kept on investigating."

"You won't find out." Nell turned with a smile, but noticed Elena frowning. "I was just joking."

"Ha, ha."

They rode the rest of the way to Elena's house in silence. Nell reached over and touched Elena's arm as she got out of the car. "I think we're off to a good start. I need to think things through. Maybe tonight I can come up with our next move."

"I don't want to see you in the path of a killer again. I'm just trying to help you stay safe."

"I know, Elena. I appreciate what a wonderful friend you have always been. But I also don't want to put you in danger. And, of course, Leigh or Annie wouldn't want to see either of us hurt trying to keep them out of a precarious situation."

"True. Good luck thinking about what we should do next, Cagney."

Nell emitted a deep belly laugh. "Something will come to me, Lacey."

Chapter 11.5

The reds, yellows, oranges, and deep purples, the captivating colors of autumn flowers set in an elegant vase. A note of admiration secured to the old wooden door with a dart. What a clever idea!

Chapter 12

Nell began her day irritated. She hadn't come up with a miraculous plan to find where Ian was staying. Ian. He didn't look like an Ian. That still sounded like a made-up name to her.

After mulling over the facts that were known and questions she didn't have the answers to, Nell was discouraged. She checked over the review she had finished writing last night for Miner's Fish House and added it to the first part of her review about the fish and chips.

My second trip for a meal at Miner's Fish House was just as tasty as the first. My lunch companion and I both ordered a pasty. Pasty is a meat pie invented by the miners in Cornwall, England years ago. A crust was laid out in a circle and then potatoes, beef, and onions were spread on one side and the crust was brought over and pinched at the edges. It was then baked and the miners were able to take it down into the mines with them. At lunch time, they could hold the pasty in their hand and eat it without any dishes to worry about. There have been many variations throughout the years. It could be made with different types of meat, vegetables baked inside or served on the side, or drizzled with ketchup or gravy.

When our waitress brought out the pasties, my friend and I were pleased. They were piping hot and the familiar smell almost made me swoon. I don't often make pasties myself so I may be able to satisfy my need here. One bite made me a believer! The beef used was round steak rather than hamburger. The potatoes were cooked through, which sometimes is an issue. The right amount of onions and light spices were packed into the pasty. Good flavor all around. The restaurant offered both ketchup and gravy. Gravy is more of an Upper Peninsula thing, so I took the ketchup. The same delicious coleslaw that comes with the fish and chips also accented the pasty. Yum!

As readers of my blog know, I have a sweet tooth. Let me correct that sentence. I have a mouthful of sweet teeth. On the dessert menu at Miner's Fish House was a Sea Salty Caramel Guinness Brownie. It sounded too tantalizing to pass up. I'm so glad I didn't. The portion served was so gigantic I took half of it home. Its elegance and perfection were breathtaking. A brownie covered in dark chocolate ganache and topped with salted caramel dripping down the sides was almost too good to be true. When I took my first bite my mouth cried with delight. No, that was drool.

Most of us have experienced the ecstasy of sea salt and caramel. And chocolate and caramel are an old favorite, as most of us have enjoyed in a Snickers bar. Blending the ingredients all together made it a tasty sensation. But the addition of Guinness beer in the brownie gives the dish a flavor punch. It doesn't taste anything like beer, but delivers a tang enhancing the other ingredients. A definite winner!
My two meals here were delightful. This pub deserves the name—Miner's Fish House.

A true nosh or truly nauseous?—You Decide!

Now that two British favorites had been sampled and approved, Nell wanted to get the word out that the new place was serving great food. She hit publish.

The boys were anxious to go for a walk and Nell knew it would do her good to get outside. She hooked up the leashes to their collars and off they went.

There was a nip in the air. Nell hoped winter wouldn't arrive too early this year. The threesome walked a couple of the President streets and then George and Newman completely flipped out. Two squirrels chased each other across the street. The boys registered their opinion with barks and pulling. The squirrels found a safe haven up a tree and Nell coaxed her dogs to continue walking. She and Drew probably should have taken them to obedience school when they were puppies.

Thinking of Drew brought on a whole new set of feelings. Anger. Sadness. Regrets. She had a few. But she'd look to the future, not the past. She missed her husband, but she was starting a new life with Sam. She hoped so, anyway.

Returning home, Nell filled the boys' food and water bowls and chose a juicy peach for her breakfast. She had just finished the luscious fruit when her phone rang.

Unknown name registered on her caller ID. There was an unfamiliar number underneath it. Before Nell could decide whether to pick it up or not, the answering machine responded. Then a voice lashed out with such venom it made the hair on the back of Nell's neck stand on end.

"If you know what's good for you, you'll stop cavorting with my husband. Sam has always loved me and he still does. And my daughter doesn't need your advice about anything, either. Leave her alone. We're going to be a family again. Just stay in your little Podunk town and don't interfere. I hope I have made myself clear. If I need to draw you a picture, that can be arranged. But believe me, if you don't stop hooking up with my husband, you'll be sorry."

Nell stood looking at the phone. *Cavorting? Hooking up? Good grief, what's wrong with this woman? Does being exceptionally beautiful allow you to get away with saying anything you want?* After listening to her voice,

Nell could only envision Jessica's ugliness.

She picked up the phone, then put it back down. Her need to talk to Sam was waging a battle with her fear of Jessica's threats. He had warned her that Jess might try something. She had to talk to Sam. Needed to hear his comforting voice. As she stretched her arm to reach the phone, it rang. Sam's Slam and the familiar number shone on the screen.

"Thank goodness it's you, Sam. I…"

"Oh, thank goodness," Jessica mocked. "Look who's sitting at the Slam using Sam's phone. It isn't you, Grandma!"

The phone disconnected.

"Grandma!" What's that all about? True, she hadn't heard from Sam in a while, but things couldn't have changed that much. She hit his cell phone number.

"Hi Nell, it's good to hear your voice. You bring a sense of calm to my hectic life, which right now is in complete shambles."

"Where are you, Sam?"

"Over at the car shop for an oil change. Why?"

"I just received a couple of phone calls from Jess. They were less than friendly."

"I'm so sorry, Nell. I didn't want you involved," Sam sighed. "I can't wait until she realizes that I don't have any money or anything else she wants and goes back to the big city. Marinette is way too small for her to actually settle down here. What did she say to you?"

After she told Sam the gist of the conversation, he bellowed, "The nerve of that woman to use my phone at the bar like it belonged to her. I'm going right over there and order her out of my restaurant. The Bean's in charge while I'm gone and unfortunately she would have welcomed her mother into the Slam. I was afraid this sort of crap would happen."

"What sort of tactics is Jess capable of?"

"Anything low and despicable," he responded. "Nothing physical, though. I don't want to worry you. Jess isn't a murderer. But it wouldn't be out of character for her to spread vicious rumors or even slash your tires. That's why I didn't want her to know you were a part of my life."

"I wonder how she found out about me."

"The Bean must have mentioned you in passing. She truly doesn't understand the depth of her mother's maliciousness."

"Oh Sam, my heart goes out to Benita. She wants to love her mother so much. I understand that."

"I know she's missed out on a lot, not having her mother around." Sam paused as Nell heard the sound of someone talking in the background. "Oh, it looks like my car is finished. I'm going back to the Slam to get things straightened out. I'll call you later." Sam coughed then softly admitted, "I miss you, Nell. I'm not the same person without you."

"I'll be waiting for your call," Nell said with a smile in her voice and hung up the phone.

With those thoughts occupying her brain, she needed a lot more than a peach to carry her through the day. She searched her refrigerator for something tasty that would hit the spot.

Aha! Nell pulled out blue cheese, Portobello mushrooms, and ground round. Black and Blue Burgers with mushrooms—yum!

First, Nell chopped up some onion and garlic, and started them sautéing in a mixture of olive oil and butter. A few pieces of garlic were held back from the pan to put into the raw beef patties.

Next, she stuffed the remaining pieces of garlic into the three patties that she formed from her pound of meat. The intoxicating aroma of the sautéing onion and garlic mixture filled Nell's whole being with anticipation for the delightful taste that was to come. She turned down the heat and let the onions continue to caramelize. Then Nell sliced the baby bellas and sautéed them in butter. After they began to soften, she poured a little red wine into the pan, deglazing it, as she listened to the sizzle, then turned the heat on low.

Nell removed the onions and mushrooms from the pan, covering them with a plate to keep them warm. After seasoning each burger with salt and pepper, she placed the patties in the skillet.

As the burgers fried, Nell made a crisp lettuce salad. Not that she wanted a salad as she had eaten so many of them lately. French fries would have been a scrumptious side dish, but she tried not to keep potatoes in the house. She knew she'd feel less guilty if she had a salad anyway.

After turning the burgers over and just a little before they were done, she put a generous helping of bleu cheese over just one of them. The other two would be going into the fridge for another time and she would blanket them with cheese when she reheated them.

She put the cover over the pan for the last bit of time. Two slices of wholegrain bread went in the toaster. A pretzel roll would have hit the spot, but the bread was healthier.

Showtime! Nell put a slice of thick toast on a plate. She spooned some of her homemade sauce with chipotle peppers and mayonnaise on top of the toast and a third of her onion and mushroom combination. The blue cheeseburger was set on top and the burger was crowned with more of the mushrooms, onions, and garlic. Mmmhmm… She slanted the other piece of toast against the sandwich at an angle and took a picture. The burger would go on her blog as one of her favorite homemade recipes.

She was satisfied with the look of her sandwich. The cheese draped down the sides of the burger, but didn't have that over-the-top look of being overwhelmed with the taste of cheese. Nell liked cheese—after all she was from Wisconsin—but she wanted to be able to taste her burger and mushrooms.

Now the moment of truth. Nell sank her teeth into the sandwich with a combination of anticipation and craving. Want and need—she was hungry and hoping for a delicious meal to fill the void. The garlic flavor melded with the blue cheese, which was accented by the mushrooms and onions… Juicy, but not too messy—in other words, perfect. If she was eating at a restaurant, this burger would be a true nosh.

She finished her lunch quickly, too quickly.

"George! Newmie!" She hardly needed to say the dogs' names as they were already at her feet. She gave them each a piece of burger and crust of bread. All was once again right in their little worlds.

Now she needed to take care of her little world. The thoughts fighting for space in her brain gave her no respite. How would Sam's discussion go with his ex-wife? Would Jess, as Sam predicted, tire of the small city and go on to bigger pastures? And if she did, how would Benita fare? She and Nell were just beginning to have a natural relationship. Would that be ruined?

And then there was Ian. Was he the doll man? Were Leigh and Annie in danger, or was he just playing some sick practical joke? How would she find out the truth?

Nell picked up her phone and hit Elena's number.

"The Dining Room, Elena speaking."

"You always answer so professionally, even when you know I'm on the other end."

"Answering like that sounds good to customers who are in the store—even though no one's here at the moment," Elena admitted. "What's up? Any new leads? I don't think Julie is busy this afternoon, so I can probably get away."

"Sorry. No new leads, but I did receive a nasty phone call a couple hours ago." Nell then filled Elena in on Jessica's call and what Sam planned to do.

"I don't think this Jessica is anyone to take lightly," Elena warned. "Don't get in her way or have anything to do with her. Just stay out of it."

"I know, I know. I'm not looking for trouble, but how can I stay out of it if Sam needs my help?"

"Chances are you staying out of it is the best way you *can* help Sam," Elena replied. "He doesn't want to involve you in any of this ugliness."

"You may be right. I just feel so useless."

"A customer is coming in the door, Nell. Talk to you later."

"Sure. Good bye."

Nell hated waiting for Sam to call. She was nervous and somewhat lost on what to do with her time. The house was relatively clean, her review for Miner's Fish House was written, and the boys were sawing logs in the living room. She knew she should try a new restaurant soon for a review, but that wasn't something she could do this instant. Instead she decided to work on the New Recipes part of her blog and wrote up her Black and Blue Burger and uploaded the picture she had taken at lunch. Just as she had finished with the post, the phone rang.

Sam. Finally!

"Sam. What happened? I've been so worried."

"How about if I come down there? It's a pleasant autumn day. We could take a drive and look at the colors, or maybe go out by the Breakwater. Is half an hour too soon?" There was tension in his voice.

"What's the matter?"

"I have to talk to you. Please, Nell. Half an hour?"

"Okay. I'll be ready. Drive carefully."

***

What was on Sam's mind? Nell worried as she waited by the front window for him to come up her driveway. When he pulled in, she hurried out to the car without waiting for him to come in the house. After giving him a quick side hug in the car, Nell sat back in her seat and asked Sam point blank, "What's going on?"

"I can see I'll never be able to hide anything from you." Sam's attempt at a laugh fell flat. "Did you want to bring the dogs? We could take them for a walk out by the water."

"No, I just want to talk to you."

"Okay." Sam backed out of the driveway and headed out of town. "I went back to the Slam to confront Jess about her phone calls. She didn't take it well. Our discussion turned into a huge scream fest in the kitchen. Thankfully there were only a few customers and I don't think they heard much. That woman pushed so many buttons. She still brings out the worst in me. The Bean started to cry. It was a mess."

"Do you think Benita understands why you have those feelings toward her mother?"

"Oh, yeah. And she's starting to have some of the same thoughts, but she still wants to spend time with her. We're different in that way." Sam rubbed his hand over his face. "Personally, I don't want to spend any time with that woman."

"Just try to stay out of Jessica's way as much as you can until she moves on. You've been pretty sure that she'll leave soon." Nell gave him a tentative smile. "Wait it out."

"Yeah. That's where we have a problem." Sam paused.

Nell looked at him, wanting to allow him to tell her in his own way.

Sam parked his car at the Breakwater and they scanned the docked boats and the ones out on the bay from the car.

"Jess wants the Bean to go to Chicago with her for a few days. She says her mother is sick and has requested to see her granddaughter. One last time." Sam opened the car door and got out.

"Would that be so bad?" Nell slammed the car door as she walked toward the water. "It would give Benita a chance to be around her mother without feeling like she is betraying you at every turn. She'd come back and possibly have some of her *mom hunger* satisfied. If she doesn't go, she may always feel guilty for not seeing her grandmother before she died."

"I'm going, too."

"*You?*" Nell's voice rose louder than she intended. "Why would you go with them?"

At Sam's silence Nell asked, "Does that woman have some kind of hold on you?"

"No, damn it! I think I need to go—for the Bean's sake. Who knows what would happen to her if she was alone with her mother and grandmother. I don't believe for a minute that Rose is on her deathbed. She's just a couple years older than I am. They're up to something. I can smell it."

"Sam! What do you think could happen to Benita? Are the two of them running a human trafficking network? She's twenty-six years old! She can take care of herself with her mother. Or do you secretly want to have a few days with Jessica?"

Sam shot Nell a disgusted look. "Don't be ridiculous."

"You know what, Sam? I don't understand this whole dynamic. The relationship between you and your ex-wife. Her relationship to Benita. The grandmother. This is way out of my comfort zone. It all seems to be coming out of a bad reality series." Nell walked a few steps away from Sam and sat down on a bench. Sam followed and sat next to her.

"We've made no commitments to each other. Actually we're still in the getting to know each other phase," Nell said.

"What are you saying, Nell? If I go to Chicago you want nothing more to do with me?"

"I'm not saying that." Nell took a deep breath, then let it out slowly. "It's just that you say you don't want to spend any time with Jess, but you're willing to go away with her to Chicago. She could hurt you again like she did so many years ago. I don't want to see that happen to you."

"That will never happen again," Sam sneered. "She means nothing to me. I loathe the woman."

"I almost think you protest too much," Nell murmured. "Hate is very close to love."

"Part of the reason I'm even considering going to Chicago is that I think the Bean will be more willing to go if I'm along. Jess won't leave here unless the Bean goes with her. I know I have to get Jess out of Marinette and her proximity to everything and everyone I hold dear. Including you. If her mother really is ill, the Bean and I will have a chance to say goodbye.

But if this is some sort of elaborate hoax and Jess *is* up to no good, I can help my daughter work through her disappointment in her mother." Sam reached for Nell's hand. "I know very well how old she is, but I also remember I was thirty-six when Jess made a fool out of me. I'll always protect my child no matter her age."

"I understand, Sam, and I respect that. You have to do what you think is best for Benita." Nell rubbed her eyebrow. "When will you leave?"

"I have several bartenders lined up, but Polly will be in charge in our absence. I'll be going over everything with her tonight." Nell stood up and started walking toward the car.

Sam followed in the same direction. "We plan to leave early tomorrow morning and I'm not sure when we'll be back. Just staying one night would be my choice, but I don't suppose I'll be that lucky. It would be worth staying down there a few more nights if it would assure that the Bean and I could return without Jess."

"Then I guess you better head home. You have a couple stressful days ahead." They settled into the car and soon stopped in front of Nell's house. Sam leaned over to give her a kiss. "Keep us in your thoughts."

"And in my prayers."

***

Nell could hardly wait for Sam to back out of her driveway. Her head felt like it would explode. She needed to talk to someone about this new turn of events. She quickly went outside with her excited pups and let them release their pent-up energy. Afterwards, she headed to her car, and to The Dining Room to have a chat with Elena in person.

She could understand Sam's reasoning, but the idea of staying as far away from Jess as possible had a lot of merit, too. She was anxious to get Elena's take on it.

Nell was driving down Main Street past Miner's Fish House when a car suddenly peeled out in front of her. She stepped on the brakes hard to avoid hitting it. She should have leaned on the horn, but noticed it was a large, *burgundy* car.

Ian! And she was right behind him. Now was her chance to see what he was going to do.

Nell slowed down, hoping Ian would not look back and see who was behind him. He'd gone all the way down Main and turned left on the highway.

It had been a long time since Nell had tailed someone. Back in high school, her friends followed certain good-looking upperclassmen. Those excursions always ended in giggles and French fries at the drive-in. This was a whole different kettle of fish. She didn't dare let herself be spotted. She had to keep her speed at a steady pace and not draw any attention to her vehicle.

Ian's right turn signal was on. Could he be going to the small municipal airport? Her imagination went wild. Perhaps he's a pilot getting ready to take off in his own small plane.

As she traveled down Airport Road, Nell wasn't sure how much longer she could remain inconspicuous.

Wait! His right blinker was on again. He was turning on to Wedgewood Way. Was he going to Wedgewood Park? Had he been camping? Was that why he wasn't registered at a motel?

Nell slowed her car way down. She couldn't take the chance of Ian seeing her if she continued through the campground. She turned around and headed back toward Airport Road.

By the time Nell arrived at The Dining Room, Elena was getting ready to lock up. Nell quickly brought her up to date with the Ian sighting.

"Why don't we go over to the Jump 'N Jaunt and see if we can spot his car at the campsite?" Elena suggested. "Just give me one minute here and I'll be ready to go."

"Brilliant! I knew there was a reason you're my partner." She gave Elena a wink. "Would you mind driving? I don't want Ian to recognize my car in case he spotted me before."

Within a few minutes she and Elena were sitting in Elena's parked car next to the gas station/convenience store looking toward Wedgewood Park. The Oconto River flowed right in between the station and the campground. Campers could see across the river to the station, and travelers had a prime view of the river and a good chunk of the campsites.

"Look, Elena! Isn't that Ian's car way down on the left next to that blue Winnebago?"

"It sure is," Elena answered, glancing at Nell. "So what's our next move?"

"I'm not sure. Right now I'm just happy we know where he's staying. We'll be able to drive by here and see if he's home or not. And we'll know when he leaves town because his camper will be gone."

"That RV can't be gone soon enough for me," Elena sighed. "I want everything back to normal."

"I don't think I even know what's normal anymore." Nell turned to Elena. "It looks like we're done here for the night. Let's go back to the store and fill you in on what's new with Sam."

Chapter 12.5

A note.
    And a dart!
That should make short work of her.

Chapter 13

Nell paced her kitchen with a nervousness that made the dogs skittish. They weren't accustomed to her moving around so fast. She was usually of the slow and steady variety. This morning, however, Nell had Sam on her mind as she pulled the few ingredients out to make corn muffins. She wasn't making them from scratch, though. Nell stopped doing that years ago. She had found a mix that actually tasted better than her homemade muffins. It was humbling, but she soon learned to accept it for the convenience. She often served the muffins when she had overnight guests and it was always a hit.

Sam had called her last night before bedtime and softly whispered words that let her know he really cared. Of course, he was still going to Chicago with the woman who had caused him so much pain. Nell just had to trust Sam to use good judgment, and maybe he could shed Jessica's negativity and influence on Benita, too.

Occupying her time while worrying about Sam had turned out to be a task Nell was ill-suited for doing. At least making muffins would keep her hands busy. She made up the mix adding in chopped jalapenos and powered chipotle seasoning. Partially filling each muffin cup of the pan with the corn bread mixture, Nell then added her secret weapon—orange marmalade. She'd made it with peach and apricot preserves, but orange marmalade was her favorite. She put a dollop in each cup and more corn bread batter on the top. She had set the oven to bake according to the mix directions and when she bit into one later she knew it'd be the combination of spicy and sweet she loved.

Muffins in the oven, Nell grabbed her paper from the porch and sat down in the living room with a cup of coffee. Not many minutes passed before a bouncy Maltese was on her lap. George looked disapprovingly at Newmie, but soon the stout Schnauzer had also joined them. There would be no reading the paper this time.

"Alright, boys. I give," she sighed. Nell gave her boys some undivided loving attention which made her feel better, too.

However, the sound of the buzzer moved her back into action. The aroma coming from the kitchen was divine. Nell could actually smell their sweet heat. What could be better than food right out of the oven? Now she just needed to allow the muffins a few minutes to cool.

To take all three of their minds away from the muffins, Nell took the boys outside and threw the ball around. All of them needed a little exercise—much more than what could be accomplished today. It was a start, though.

Nell had put a little batter without spices in two muffin cups at one end of the tin. She divided out chunks of those two muffins now so they would last for George and Newman as long as the other muffins lasted for her.

This time she sat at her bistro table to enjoy a muffin and more coffee. Delicious! When she finished, she put the chunks of muffin in the dog dishes and started to plot out the rest of her day.

Before Nell was too heavy into thought, the phone rang and Annie Marshall's name and number appeared on the caller ID. "Hello."

"Thank goodness you're home, Nell," Annie blurted out. "Will you go with me down to the police station?"

"Of course. What happened?"

"I found a note and I think it's from the same guy," Annie said. "It said, 'Get out of town. You're not wanted here. Watch yourself.' So I'm going to watch myself—watch myself march right down to the police."

"I'll go with you, Annie. I wonder if Leigh received a note, too."

"I thought of that and called her, but Ed said she isn't home. How soon can you be ready? I'll pick you up."

"I'm ready now. I'll watch for your car."

Annie pulled in the driveway almost before Nell could grab her purse. Once she was in the car, she couldn't help but notice Annie's quivering lip and red eyes. "You're doing the right thing by reporting this to the police. Just explain it all to them, Annie."

"This whole situation is unnerving. That mutilated doll and now...this." Annie backed out of the driveway and handed Nell a plastic storage bag with a dart and a note attached to it.

Nell read the yellow sticky note and shivered, "Did it come with this dart? To me that's extra creepy. Strange that it's printed with a red marker. For crying out loud! First a doll, then this juvenile note—what's wrong with this guy?"

"The dart held the note to my wooden 'Welcome' sign on my metal back door. I'm not just worried for me, Nell. But I have kids. What if this nutcase got ahold of Lori or Eric?" Annie stopped her car in front of the police station. "This has to come to an end. I can't live this way."

As Nell walked into the station, she put her arm around Annie. "We'll figure this out, and soon."

They were able to meet with Officer Paul Carson. A former student, Nell had worked with him before when she had had problems. He directed them back to his office where he listened to Annie's story.

After Annie related what had happened to her, she gestured toward the door. "Paul, Leigh Jackson and I told Officer Wunderlin a couple days ago about receiving the dolls. He'd have a record of that conversation."

"I'm sure he does," Officer Carson nodded his head. "Rich Wunderlin's new on the force here. A good man. I'll speak to him."

"I came with Annie for moral support, Paul. And you know what good friends Leigh and I are." Nell explained what she'd learned about Ian and his whereabouts and then gave him her best teacher stare. "What's going on?"

"Yeah, after what you went through a couple months ago, I bet this is too much action for you." At Nell's nod, Paul continued, "I'm not sure what's going on, but the warning to Annie to get out of town is of concern. I'll confer with Rich and the chief and be back in a few minutes."

"Thank you," Annie said.

As soon as Officer Paul Carson left the room, Annie said, "I wonder how long this will take."

"Chances are the chief and this new officer aren't both on duty right now—I didn't see anyone else when we came in except the receptionist—so I don't know." Nell stood up to stretch her legs.

The sound of footsteps drew Nell's attention to the doorway. "Unfortunately the chief was called out a few minutes ago and Rich isn't on duty today, so I'll speak with them as soon as I see them," Paul confirmed as he walked back in the office. "What I suggest for now is that you keep all your doors and windows locked and be very careful when you go anywhere. Report anything that seems odd behavior."

"So there's nothing you can do?" Annie asked, shoulders slumped.

"I'm sorry. We have a small force."

"Could you stay at your mom's house?" Nell suggested. "Or could the kids stay with friends?"

"We could stay with Mom for a few days, but that's no long-term solution."

"Rest assured I'll go out to the campground tonight and have a look around. I'll chat up this Ian and see what his business is in our town. We'll know all about him by tomorrow." Officer Paul Carson stood up as the fire alarm bellowed.

The Bayshore Fire Department was connected to the Bayshore Police Station so the area was bustling. Nell knew they should make their exit immediately.

As they were getting into Annie's car, two fire trucks were leaving the station and she could see Paul heading down the street in a squad car.

"I hate to say it, Annie," Nell said, her lips pursed, "but I don't think anyone will talk to Ian tonight."

Chapter 14

When Annie let Nell out at her house, the two made plans to meet at Miner's Fish House that evening after supper to talk things over. Nell promised to contact Leigh and see if she could meet them. She also decided to tell Elena about the note and ask her to come, too. The four of them working together should be able to generate ideas. There was also the possibility that Ian would show up there. Annie wanted to see what he looked like for herself, but she was more comfortable with friends for safety.

Elena locked the door of her Cape Cod style home when Nell pulled up just a few minutes before seven. She opened the car door and said, "Thanks for picking me up, Nell."

"You're welcome. I'm going over to Annie's mother's house to pick her up, too. It's right on the way."

"Good idea." Elena buckled her seatbelt as Nell drove down the street. "I wouldn't want her going alone."

"Ed is walking Leigh down the street to the pub," Nell added. "He might stay. I know he's worried about Leigh."

The pair rode in silence a few blocks. "There's Annie sitting on the swing on her mother's veranda." Elena waved.

Nell pulled the car to a stop as Annie walked down the steps. "I love my mother dearly," she muttered as she got into the car, "but I'm glad we won't be staying at her house very long."

"What's she doing?" Elena prompted.

"We've only been there since the kids got out of school today—just a few hours and she's already hovering, preparing for us to be there for weeks," Annie complained, raising her hands in exasperation. "Since moving back to town I see Mom more often, but in shorter blocks of time. The kids stay with her occasionally, so they don't seem to be annoyed by her antics. Maybe it's just me...that I don't have my own stuff in my own house."

"Or maybe it's because you have an important issue on your mind and you're stressed," Nell suggested.

"I guess that could be a part of it," Annie said as Nell pulled in front of Miner's Fish House and parked. "It doesn't look like they have much business tonight. Do you think that doll man is gonna show, Nell?"

"Ian seems to spend a lot of time here, so maybe." Nell made sure to hit the lock on the car door as they walked toward the pub. "We aren't sure he and the doll guy are the same man."

Annie shivered. "True, but I hope we figure out who it is…and soon."

The three women walked in to an almost empty bar. No sign of Ian.

"Why don't we sit at that table way over there?" Nell walked toward a square oak table almost hidden in the corner. "We can see everyone that comes in, but they won't see us right away."

"Good choice," whispered Annie. "Did you have a chance to call Leigh?"

"Yes. I told her about the note and she'll be here." Nell glanced at the unfamiliar bartender. "Rats. I was hoping Will would be working tonight, then I'd ask him for the scoop on Ian."

"Things aren't going to fall into place that easily for us," Elena said.

A noise at the door caused the women to look in that direction to see Leigh and Ed coming into the building.

"Over here!" Annie waved.

The couple walked over to their table, and Leigh somewhat abruptly, turned to Ed. "You can go now."

"Who said I'm going anywhere? I think I'll sit at the bar and try to get a look at the kinda jerk who sends flowers to my wife!"

A collective gasp was released at the table and Leigh, earrings swinging as she turned to her friends in frustration, said, "I was going to tell all of you tonight." Then she turned to Ed and whispered, "Please, Ed, just go home. I'll be fine."

"All right. I'll go, but you call me when you're ready to leave so I can come get you. Who knows what this deviant would do if he got you alone."

"Ed, I'll give her a lift down the street."

Leigh turned grateful eyes to Nell and mouthed, "Thank you."

"Okay. This nonsense better stop fast, or I'll be the one down at the police station." With those final words a red faced Ed turned and left, showing the giant walleye on the back of his shirt as he went out the door.

"Oh my goodness, Leigh. Is everything alright between you and Ed?" Nell's hands came together as if in prayer. "I've never heard the two of you argue with each other in over thirty years."

"I have to admit, this doll and now the flowers has put a strain on our relationship." Leigh fell silent as the bartender appeared to take their order—a pitcher of beer—and then left.

"What's the story on the flowers? I mean, what gives? I get a threatening note and you get flowers?" Annie fumbled with her purse as she got out a tissue.

"I found the flowers today, shortly after I came home from Green Bay. I walked in after parking the car in the back and the most beautiful autumn flowers were in a vase on the step. An elegant card was fastened to the old wooden door with a dart and it read: *Beautiful delicate flowers for a beautiful delicate flower.* I thought Ed must have ordered them for me and the delivery man left the flowers on the stoop. I picked the bouquet up, full of love from the spicy scent, and went to thank him. He knew nothing about it." Leigh shrugged.

"Ed doesn't think you're seeing someone else, does he?" Annie questioned.

"No. It's not that at all," Leigh assured her. "He's worried because sending items to a married woman who doesn't know you is odd behavior—very stalkerish. Ed thinks this man is as he puts it 'one sandwich short of a picnic'."

"I'm with Ed," Nell said. "What's up with the darts? That's weird. Also, this guy may expect you to reciprocate in some manner, and flip out if you disappoint him. It's so weird that both you and Annie were contacted on the same day again. First the dolls, and now the notes and darts."

"I hadn't thought too much about the dart before," Leigh admitted. "Since there was one with Annie's note, too, it must be the same guy. I think there is cause for alarm."

The bartender brought over a pitcher of beer and a complimentary basket of popcorn. "Thanks, Curt," Leigh smiled.

Nell and the girls munched absently as they continued their speculation about the mystery man.

"Annie, I feel awkward asking this, but can you think of anyone who would want to harm you?" Elena asked.

"Believe me, Elena, I've been racking my brain trying to figure out who this someone is. I'm just a divorced woman with two kids trying to make ends meet. I haven't done anything to anybody. And my ex-husband is living in Arizona. I can't imagine him doing anything like this anyway."

"Well, I think we know who it is, but not who this man actually is, if that makes any sense." Nell put her glass down after taking a sip. "I'd say this Ian who came by my house asking about Annie and then later was staring at Leigh and Annie right down here last Friday night is the only good possibility. He even went to Metallic Dreams to talk to Leigh. He has to have something to do with this, but we don't know enough about him." Nell turned to Leigh. "Did he ever come back to your shop and ask any more questions?"

Leigh shook her head. "Not yet."

"I didn't see him Friday night and can't think of anyone who looks the way you described him," Annie said rubbing her temples. "I'd sure like to see him for myself."

"Elena and I have done a little sleuthing and we know where he's staying." At Leigh's raised eyebrows, Nell continued, "He has a camper at Wedgewood. We saw his car from the gas station."

"Why don't we drive over there right now." Leigh started to get out of her chair.

"Not tonight," Nell countered. "It'll be dark soon. Besides, Leigh, you know what Ian looks like. We have to get Annie a glimpse of him."

"True. Since I'm up, I'm going to run to the rest room." Leigh turned and walked toward the other side of the pub.

"Maybe tomorrow after you're done with work, the four of us could take a drive through the campsite," Nell suggested. "Are you up for it, Annie?"

"Most definitely."

The night wore on and the foursome made plans to put Ian under surveillance. They ordered another pitcher of beer and a pizza from the bar menu. One by one each of them made the short trip to the back of the building "to powder her nose."

They were about ready to call it a night. Nell figured out her bill and went to the back while her three friends figured out the tip. She finished washing her hands and left the rest room. She started to walk right past the game room, but decided to walk in and see if the fire was left unattended as it had been on a previous visit.

The door was almost closed. She knocked on it in case someone was having a private meeting. No answer. Nell tentatively pushed the door open and saw the fire was almost completely out. Maybe the door was nearly shut to keep people out when they let the fire die down.

She glanced around the room, wondering if anyone had even been in here all night.

Looking more closely, the large braided rug that was usually in front of the hearth was gone. Had it been moved somewhere else in the room? Searching every corner, she hit pay dirt. There it was—in an unattractive heap over something lumpy. *Firewood?* Why would that be covered?

Nell walked over, pulled off the rug, and took a peek.

The chilling scream heard emanating from her was shrill enough to make an actress in a horror movie jealous. *What's going on here?*

She backed away to the other side of the room and stood there, not moving a muscle. Her friends rushed in, along with the bartender.

They found Nell standing still, but she raised her arm and pointed in the corner. Four pairs of eyes looked in that direction and saw a man lying face up, almost out of sight. The man's body would have been completely missed under the rug with a brief glance into the room. However, once uncovered, with the fireplace poker stuck in the middle of his chest, darts sticking out of other parts of his body, and covered in blood, he couldn't be overlooked.

"Annie, that's him!" Nell shouted, regaining her composure. "That's Ian!"

Chapter 15

No amount of mystery book reading or crime show watching prepared Nell for actually being the first at the scene of a murder. The police arrived quickly, and upon hearing the sirens, other people practically came out of the woodwork. The waitress, kitchen workers, and Will appeared along with various townsfolk drawn in by the sirens. Ed bounded into the bar, wild-eyed to check on Leigh.

The police controlled the scene keeping the evening's bar patrons separated from onlookers until after being questioned. And questioned they were, together and then separately. Most of the interrogation by Chief Charles Vance was directed at Nell's group as there were few other customers in the pub that evening.

"Look, Chief Vance, you can't possibly think I killed this man, or that any of my friends did either," Nell sputtered when she was alone with him. "We were together all night. Do you think all four of us went off the deep end at once?"

The police chief towered over her and spoke in a hard voice. "I'm not accusing you, Nell. You have to admit, though, the bar was almost empty the whole night and at the time you found him, you four were the only customers. You've all admitted you went to the back of the bar alone at some point during the evening. I'd be derelict in my duty if I didn't look at everyone."

"As the others told you, they just went to use the restroom and came right back. I'm the only one that took a look into the game room." Nell took a deep breath to compose herself. "I appreciate your position. I understand it with my head, but since I know we're innocent, my heart says don't waste your time looking at us. Find the real killer."

"Why *did* you look in the game room?" the chief asked.

"I was just being nosy. I had to walk right past the doorway on the way to and from the facilities. I just stopped and peeked in the room."

"Had you just 'peeked in' you wouldn't have seen the victim tucked away in that corner. You had to go into the room, turn all the way around, and pull off the rug. Why did you do that?" The chief was waiting expectantly for an answer.

Nell wished she had a good one. "I don't know. I like to look at rooms," Nell huffed. "I'm a woman."

"The other women didn't look in the room," Chef Vance pressed. "Why did you?"

Finally the explanation came to Nell. "I write a blog where I comment on the food and appearance of eating establishments. I'm always curious as to how rooms are decorated and maintained every day of the week. I wanted to see if the fireplace was lit."

"And pulling off the rug? What made you do that?"

Nell shrugged. "The rug wasn't in its usual place. When I noticed it, it looked lumpy. I wondered if the owners were covering up the firewood."

"What difference would it have made? If they wanted to cover up the wood, it's hardly an illegal activity." The chief's cold hazel eyes drilled into her.

"Isn't it a good thing that I pulled the rug off?" Nell countered. "Who knows how long that body could have stayed there like that? Or the murderer could have moved it later and no one would have known there had been foul play."

"Enough speculation. I'll accept your answers for now. The medical examiner is taking a look and then I'll call you into the station for more questioning. You're free to go."

Nell walked over to her friends who were waiting for her.

"Are you alright?" Elena gave Nell a hug, as did the others.

"Yes, I'm okay. I didn't like being cross-examined like a common criminal."

"Do you think Chief Vance seriously thinks one of us killed that man?" Leigh whispered as Ed put his arm around her. "That would be ridiculous!"

"As much as I didn't enjoy the grilling, I understand it had to be done," Nell said, walking out the door with the others. "I'm sure the police will figure out soon enough that none of us did it."

"Who did?" Ed pulled Leigh tighter as he spoke. "That's the question. Who was in the pub the same time you were and had the opportunity to kill this guy?"

"You know what?" Annie stood by the back door of Nell's car. "If Ian was the man who has been threatening me, I don't care who did it. Maybe it's good riddance."

"Yes, but why would someone kill him?" Nell posed. "Have all our problems been solved, or have they been multiplied?"

***

Nell woke up early the next morning, cranky from not sleeping well. Her mind had been racing all night, and the boys sensed it. They hadn't been able to settle down, either. Without changing from her Mighty Mouse pajama top, she let George and Newmie out and started the coffee maker.

Sam hadn't called last night, which mildly concerned her, but she'd let it go as she had other matters that needed serious thought.

She put clean water and fresh food in the bowls almost automatically. The boys must have recognized the sound, as they came racing in through the doggie door.

"There you go, Newmie. Have your breakfast, George. You're such good boys. Yes, you are!" she said, petting them.

Nell ate a banana as she waited for the coffee. Then she poured a cup and sat down at the bistro table to consider the murder.

Some points to ponder:

Were the doll man and the flowers/note man the same?

Was Ian that man?

Who wanted Ian dead and why?

How could the murder happen under their noses?

Will the threats/compliments stop now?

What about the darts posted on doors and peppered on Ian's body?

Where should they start looking for answers?

Darn! She had been excited about the lead of the campsite to find out more about Ian. Now it was back to the drawing board.

The phone rang. Sam? No, Elena.

"Hello."

"Hi, Nell. I had a terrible night's sleep last night."

"Me, too," Nell confessed.

"I called Julie and she's going to work at the store for me today. Do you want to get together and discuss last night?"

"Oh, thank goodness, Elena," Nell practically gushed into the phone. "I was wondering if I would go crazy today just talking to myself about it. I'm so worried."

"Is that a yes?"

"YES!" Nell almost screamed into the phone. "I imagine there will be a lot of speculating downtown today, so I don't know that I want to go there. We'd be fielding a thousand questions. There's a place in Oconto Falls I've been wanting to review. We could go there for lunch. It's not too far away."

"Great, I'll pick you up at 11:30."

"Sounds like a plan. See you then."

Nell was right about fielding questions in town. As she took the boys for a walk, she was stopped at four different homes by one of her neighbors running out of the house to get the low down on the murder. The beauty of small town living. She cut their walk short.

Once back in the house, Nell showered and applied as little makeup as she could and still be somewhat presentable. She slipped into her comfortable faded capri jeans and a blue cotton top. Casual was a good look for today.

Elena picked her up right on time.

"Where are we going?" Elena asked. "I forgot to ask."

"Flipper's Cafe. I've been there before and I'm sure you have, too. I've never reviewed it, though."

"That's a good spot. I'm glad we're getting out of town today." Elena was wearing jeans and a beautiful turquoise jeweled top, but her eyes were drawn and didn't have their usual spark.

"Poor Leigh. I bet people will be going into Metallic Dreams purposely to hear her side of the story." Nell sighed. "And I bet everyone at the hospital will want to hear Annie's tale, too."

"Unless they decided to play hooky like I did."

The short twelve mile ride brought them to the Falls in minutes and soon they were parked in front of Flipper's. The restaurant sign sported a large smiling walrus with a bib holding a knife and fork in its front flippers.

"Believe it or not, I'm hungry," Nell said as they walked in the door. "But I certainly don't want anything with red sauce."

"Oh, Nell." Elena gave her a look.

The two of them took a booth in the corner and picked up menus.

"Actually this place is known for baked chicken served daily, so I think I'll order it. I make so much chicken at home that I seldom order it out. But I usually make chicken breasts so this will be a delicious change," Nell said, eyeing the menu.

"That sounds delightful. I'll order it, too."

"Can you imagine one of us last night stabbing Ian, then coming back to the table and eating pizza like nothing had happened? After seeing Ian's dead body, I never could have looked at pizza without vomiting." Nell gave a sour face.

"Why is the chief looking at the four of us anyway?" Elena set the menu aside. "A person would have to have ice water in their veins to either eat and kill or kill and eat. Any one of us would have broken down in tears."

"It's his job. Chief Vance had to question us. I just hope he takes us off the list of possible suspects soon so he can concentrate on the real murderer. I agree. You'd have to be cold-blooded for the eat/kill combination, but we never truly know how we'll act in a stressful situation. Some people do horrible things totally out of character and then proceed to cover them up because it's a matter of self-preservation."

"Are you saying one of us *could have* committed the murder?" Elena asked, incredulous.

"No. That's not what I'm saying at all."

The smiling waitress showed up and took their orders of baked chicken dinners, including two side dishes. After she left, Nell continued, keeping her voice low, "I know none of us killed him, but sometimes things happen that cause people to act way out of their normal pattern. Then they foolishly try to cover it up, rather than come clean. Amateurs are usually caught. And the law goes easier on them, if they admit they committed the crime and called for help immediately."

"You mean if Annie killed him she should have come running out and said that she accidentally picked up the poker and somehow it found its way into Ian's heart? Then she used the darts for decoration? I don't think she would have gotten away with a pat on the head and a thank you for being honest."

"You know just for argument's sake, it couldn't have been Annie anyway. She could have seen him and not even recognized him."

"True."

"But Ian would have recognized Annie." The speed of Nell's voice accelerated. "Suppose he approached her. Annie was taken off guard and grabbed the poker…"

"Nell! You think Annie did it?"

"No! How many times do I have to say it? None of us killed him. My thought is that the perpetrator would have gotten blood on his or her clothing. We were all clean. Making up these scenarios helps my mind churn. Once churning, I may come up with a different idea."

"You're right. Keep that mind churning."

The friends quieted their conversation as the waitress appeared with their chicken. The aroma that enveloped the table would have made her knees buckle had Nell been standing. A giant plate heaped with hot, tender, and succulent chicken, homemade mashed potatoes drenched in butter, and fresh green beans was placed before each of them. She and Elena put their troubles on the back burner, picked up their silverware, and dug in with both hands.

***

Back from lunch, Elena had dropped her off and then Nell had driven downtown a short while later. Now she was in the chair at QT Beauty Bar for a haircut. The salon was situated on the highway within view of the gas station, but on the other side of the street. Just like the Jump 'N Jaunt, it also had a great view of the campground across the Oconto River. Several of the stylists' chairs were placed in front of a large window letting patrons enjoy the beauty of the river and the movement of the townspeople. Nell relaxed in the comfort of the chair while Katrina, the owner who only had a few questions about the murder, washed, cut, and styled her hair.

Nell's eyes, though, were focused on Ian's campsite as she sat in Trina's chair. She was thinking about this bonus view as she drove to the salon, happy that Trina was able to switch her scheduled appointment and squeeze her in today. She realized she was putting herself in a position to be questioned about the murder, but the view of the campsite was worth answering a few harmless inquiries from friends.

Nell moved her eyes to the right and was able to watch as a police cruiser pulled up to Ian's camper. The door to the camper opened and another officer stepped out. The two conferred, and then both went in to the RV.

No more action presented itself to Nell's waiting eyes. She chatted more with Trina and soon her hair was finished. She paid, set up another appointment, and was on her way.

Inside her car, Nell made a phone call on her cell. "Elena, have you heard anything from the police yet?"

"No. Have you?"

"No. I'm outside QT Beauty Bar right now, but during my appointment I saw the police over at Ian's campsite. Do you think I should go over there?"

"Yes, but come and get me!"

"Okay, I'll come pick you up and we'll go to Wedgewood Campground. The chance to speak with the officers is a good opportunity to see if we're in the clear. The thought of being falsely charged with murder and going to trial is unbearable!"

Chapter 15.5

Nothing has turned out as planned. Violence should have been avoided. Why had Ian stuck his nose in where it didn't belong? After he threatened to squeal, there had been no other choice. Especially considering that Ian had been in Miner's Fish House the same night as my red-haired beauty. Did he have the kind of plans for her that I have? Head pounding, a new plot was being hatched. Sometime in the not too distant future an escape needs to be made. It must not cause suspicion, though.

Chapter 16

Nell and Elena pulled up next to the police cruiser once they found Ian's RV at the campground. They had barely gotten out of the car when the camper door opened and Officers Carson and Wunderlin came down the steps.

"Hello ladies," Carson said evenly. "Why are you here?"

"Paul, you know why. Can you tell us anything?" Nell walked over to him. "We want to be cleared of any suspicions as soon as possible."

"The chief is the one to talk to about clearing your names. We're just here looking for evidence."

"Did you find anything?" Elena burst out. "Any clues at all?"

"Please, you must know we can't discuss a case," Officer Wunderlin smiled as he opened the patrol car door. "I'm sure headquarters will get in touch with you soon."

"Okay, thanks," Nell said forcing herself to be polite as the men got in their car. They didn't start the engine, just sat there looking at Nell and Elena.

"Why don't they leave? What are they waiting for?" Elena tilted her head as she looked at Nell.

"Us. They want to make sure we don't stay here poking around." Nell sat down on the car seat. "Paul must have read my mind as that's exactly what I intended to do."

"Darn. A missed opportunity."

"We can come back another time, although I don't know if it would be worth it. There doesn't look like there's anything to see outside. I noticed Paul locked the door so we wouldn't be able to take a look inside, either."

"They might as well have told us to go back to our knitting," Elena grumbled. "They're making me feel old. Besides, Paul isn't very tall. Don't they have height restrictions? He probably shouldn't even be a cop."

"That's sour grapes," Nell smiled. "How about we go see Chief Vance and ask him outright if we're still suspects?"

"Do you think he'll tell us, Nell?"

"Even if he doesn't, we're no worse off than we are right now."

***

No one appeared surprised when Nell and Elena entered the Bayshore Police Station. Nell caught a glimpse of the chief in the hallway and spoke right up. "Chief Vance, could Elena and I have a word with you? We won't take much of your time."

"Yes, as long as it's quick." He directed them through the door to his office and into chairs. "With both a suspected arson and a murder yesterday, the squad has its hands full."

"We just want to know if we're off the suspect list." Nell leaned into his desk. "A simple 'yes' will make us very happy."

"Yes." At her startled look, Vance continued, "Neither one of you, nor your friends, were ever seriously considered to be the killer, for several reasons: no one had a speck of blood on them and the murderer's clothing would have been sprayed. This will be on the news tonight, but the fireplace poker was not the only weapon. Someone stabbed the victim several times with an instrument with a longer blade. I didn't see any evidence that any of you brought a weapon with you. The poker was just the finishing touch. It also was thrust deep through his heart and almost out his back. It would have taken a mighty strong person to have accomplished that move. Time was also a factor. There wasn't enough time for any of you to have completed the murder while pretending to be in the rest room."

"Thank you," Nell and Elena said at the same time.

"That's really all I can tell you, except," Chief Vance turned his head and glared at Nell, "don't get in our way. I know you mean to be helpful, but there is a killer in town and I don't want to have to worry about you getting in his path."

Nell nodded her head and the two thanked him again as they left his office.

***

"What a relief!" Elena's smile lit up the car as Nell drove away from the station.

"Yes, but it was a conclusion he had to come to in the end." Nell rubbed her left eyebrow. "I'm very anxious to watch the news tonight. Interesting about another weapon. That would explain the massive amount of blood. I certainly didn't take a close look at the body, and the blood may have covered up other wounds anyway."

"Are we done with this case, Nell? You know, after what the chief said."

"What do you think?"

"From the look on your face I don't think you're ready to let it go."

"And you'd be right. But you don't have to do this with me. And I'm not going to get in the way of the police. I'm just planning on doing a little research, that's all."

"I'll be right by your side. You know that."

***

At home, Nell was greeted with yips and barks as usual, but also a message from Sam on the machine.

"Sorry to have missed you. I want to talk to you and not a machine, so I'll try again later. I wish I was back at home with you."

"I guess that means you're not home yet, Sam. This may turn out to last longer than you had wanted and certainly more than the one day you would have liked." At the quizzical look on the faces of the two boys, Nell laughed and said, "I should be talking to you, shouldn't I? Wanna go outside?"

Ten feet made their way outside, eight canine and two human. A game of fetch delighted the boys. It wasn't too long before Nell realized how the stress of the last two days had affected her. She was grateful she hadn't polished off all the chicken at lunch and had leftovers for supper. She was just too tired to make a meal from scratch. Nell threw the ball long enough to wear the boys out, then they went back in the house.

She made a few notes on her iPad mini about her lunch at Flipper's Café. As she combined her memories of past meals there, she knew this would be a good time to write up the review for her blog. It didn't take long before she had her entry.

Flipper's Café—Oconto Falls, WI

The hungry walrus on the new sign of this homey family restaurant grabs your attention and draws you into the establishment. I chuckled to myself as I entered, and took a seat at a small table in the dining room.

I was solo dining, which gave me the chance to concentrate on my food and surroundings. Looking at the menu, I was immediately drawn to the wraps. One in particular caught my eye, the Peppered Pecan Wrap. The tortilla was labeled as cracked pepper sun-dried tomato. The fillings were grilled chicken breast, arugula, fontina cheese, red onion, orange pepper strips, and spiced pecans. It was accented with honey and topped with a blue cheese dressing. The combination was so interesting I had to try it.

After the waitress took my order, I glanced around the dining area. Each table boasted a blue and white checkered tablecloth with a small bouquet of cheerful yellow daisies in a canning jar. Every surface sparkled wherever I looked. My instincts told me that the food would be hearty old-fashioned fare.

When my plate appeared I was delighted to see a large wrap carefully divided and stacked at an angle. The fillings inside were artfully arranged and so vibrant I almost didn't want to ruin the effect by taking a bite. I snapped a picture for all of you to see on my blog and then raised half of the wrap to my lips.

After just one taste I knew it was special. The odd combination of ingredients drew me in, but how they blended together made me savor the flavors in my mouth. I tried to identify each ingredient as it rolled over my tongue. The peppery bite of the arugula and the buttery nutty flavor of the fontina cheese matched well with the crunch of pepper strips, onion, and brown sugar and cumin spiced pecans. It all came together with tender chunks of chicken and a dollop of honey, draped with a blue cheese dressing. It was a huge wrap and I relished the flavor combinations until it was all gone. No doggie bag today.

Eventually, I concluded this was not a wrap children would enjoy. It is intended for a more discriminating palate. I hardly know if mine is sophisticated enough, but today I was more enthralled with appreciating the blending of flavors than eating with wild abandon. It may be that this wrap is an acquired taste, but I will order it again. My palate may be destined to acquire that taste.

The next time I went to Flipper's Café was with a friend for lunch. We both chose their daily baked chicken special. A choice of two side dishes was offered, and I chose mashed potatoes and green beans.

When it arrived at our table, the chicken was golden brown and so tender it hardly needed to be chewed. It fell off the bone. Real potatoes had been mashed in their kitchen and we were given a generous portion. The green beans were homegrown and still had snap. I understand why it is a daily special. Their regular customers would probably revolt if it was off the menu, it is so delicious.

Flipper's is a café with two faces. The wrap could have been offered at any trendy bistro in a metropolitan city and the baked chicken tasted as if it came right out of Grandma's kitchen. Such diversity is not often found in a small town eatery, but it is appreciated.

A true nosh or truly nauseous?—You Decide!

Nell was satisfied with her review, but chose not to publish it yet. She'd wait and read it over again in a day or two to see if she wanted to make any changes.

The hands of the clock crawled toward 6:00 and the news. When it finally came on, the murder in Bayshore was the lead story. The telecast showed the outside of Miner's Fish House and the police station where they interviewed Chief Vance. The killer's use of two weapons was mentioned, but nothing that Nell didn't already know.

George and Newmie settled themselves comfortably on Nell's lap. She watched the news mindlessly while petting the boys, thinking about the murder. As she relaxed, memories surfaced from last night. She remembered overhearing the bartender tell the police the last time he had served a drink to the man in back was around 8:30.

She and her friends had met at Miner's at 7:00 so Ian must have already been there. It was 10:00 when she found the body. That means he was dead only an hour and a half at the most when she found him. No one had come from the back wearing a bloody shirt. The killer had to have used the back door.

That put a different spin on it. To her recollection, the few people who were in the bar left by the front door. But then, would she really know? Once her group got their beer and popcorn they were deep in conversation. They were only looking for Ian, and as long as they didn't see him come through the front door they didn't notice anyone else.

Then they got a refill of their pitcher and a pizza, and were happy to be left alone at their mostly hidden corner table. Could there have been someone else in the game room the whole time? The person who killed Ian could have left by the back door in his bloody shirt.

Sam's call came in the middle of Nell's speculations and startled her, until she realized it was him. Then it was much to her relief. "Sam."

"Your voice is like a melody, Nell, and I'm hoping from the sound of your greeting, you feel the same way about mine."

"I do, Sam. Tell me what's going on."

"It's about what I suspected. Rose doesn't look to me to be on her deathbed. She and Jess are working on the Bean to stay down here in Chicago and live with them—permanently. They're working some sort of plan. It's a good thing I came here with her."

Shuffling in her seat when the boys moved, she said, "I hope you get to the bottom of it. Do you have any idea when you'll be able to come home?"

"Not sure yet. I want it to be the Bean's idea to come home, so we'll see. Oh yeah, when I spoke to one of my bartenders today about an order, he mentioned there was a murder in Bayshore last night. And it was at that new place you described to me. Do you know anything about it?"

Nell gulped. She couldn't hide anything from Sam.

Chapter 17

As Nell let the boys out for "last pee of the night" and prepared to go to bed, she reflected on Sam's reaction when he heard she was the one who had found the dead body. He was shocked even more when she filled him in on the incidents concerning the dolls, flowers, and notes. Nell hadn't shared that with him earlier as he had so much on his mind.

Now his first thought was to come back to Bayshore and stay with her so she wouldn't be alone. She liked the idea of his being here—someone caring for her again. Drew had been gone over five years. However, there was no way she wanted Sam to come home before he felt he had matters well in hand. That would only necessitate another trip to Chicago. Nell knew he didn't want to be with Jessica any more than was absolutely crucial to the situation. So, she'd just have to wait a little bit longer to see him.

The dogs hopped up on the bed and Nell joined them with Sam's words still playing in her mind. "Whatever worries you, worries me." It may not be the most romantic comment ever whispered to her, but tonight it struck just the right note.

***

Nell sat straight up in bed, heart pounding.

"Ed." She crept out of bed carefully, trying not to disturb the dogs. Once in the kitchen, Nell looked at the clock on the microwave. It was 3:00 A. M. No one she could talk to yet.

She turned on the stove light and poured a glass of water from the fridge door. Once she settled herself at the bistro table, Nell pondered the information that had ripped her out of a peaceful night's sleep. Sometimes she wished her mind didn't work the way it did. Even asleep it gave her no rest.

After the police reached the restaurant and people congregated at Miner's Fish House, Ed had showed up looking for Leigh along with the rest of the onlookers. The part that made Nell's blood run cold was that he was wearing a different shirt. For whatever reason, she had taken particular notice of Ed's shirt when he walked out the door of the pub earlier in the evening. It was probably because of the size of the fish that it sported. The walleye covered the whole back with a gaping hole for a mouth. The shirt he had on later was a plain tee with no words or pictures. Why would he change clothes between

7:00 and 10:00? She had an answer to that question, but it was one she didn't like.

Eyes wide open and body tingling, Nell knew she would never get back to sleep, so she didn't even try. Instead she made coffee.

Her mind raced as she considered her options now that Ed might be the murderer. Hold it right there, Nell Bailey. This was ridiculous! She didn't believe for a minute Ed killed anyone. However, she knew she would have to find the reason why he had on a different shirt.

The question that bothered her was whether or not she would need to involve the police. If Ed gave her a reasonable explanation why would she take it any further? Yet, shouldn't the authorities be given every small detail to help them find the culprit? She couldn't wait to talk to Elena and Annie to see if they had noticed the different shirts, too.

Or perhaps she should wait until she talked to Leigh. Maybe for whatever weird reason, Ed had a habit of changing shirts after a walk. Maybe if she talked to Ed, he might volunteer to go to the police. There were several ways she could go with this new information.

Nell's mind was churning. Ed would have to have come back down to Miner's Fish House, because she watched him exit through the front door. He could have slipped in the back door of the pub, gone into the game room, confronted Ian, and killed him. That was one possibility.

However, as far as she knew Ed had never met Ian and had no idea what he looked like. Also, Ian, if the doll man was Ian, had only given Leigh a pretty doll and flowers. Was that enough to prompt Ed to stab him repeatedly? In over thirty years Nell had never known Ed to have much of a temper. However, that night was the most irritated she had ever seen him. Still she couldn't imagine him generating enough anger to kill someone.

The boys stirred, ready to begin their little day. Nell walked back into the bedroom and greeted them. "Good morning, George. Good morning, Newmie. Rise and shine in the early morn! Are you ready for an exciting day?"

Newman jumped off the bed right away, but George stretched both his front legs and then back before he was ready to hit the floor.

It was still fairly dark outside, so Nell turned on the patio light and opened the slider for the boys to go outside. They were back in the house within minutes and looking to Nell for their breakfast.

She couldn't shake her thought that Ed was the murderer. She considered taking a ride to the campground to put it out of her mind and kill some time, but decided to stay put. *Ed, what will you do to me if I go to the police?*

***

Nell somehow managed to occupy herself until 7:00 when she cleared her throat and called Elena at her home.

"Hello."

"Elena, I wanted to talk to you before you went to work. You are working today, right?"

"Yes. What's going on? Are you okay, Nell?"

Nell sat down at the bistro table, trying to remain calm. "Yes, yes. I'm fine. I just wanted to talk about the case. We know that the murderer probably has blood splatter all over his shirt, right?"

"Yes, you mentioned that, and so did Chief Vance. Your point?"

"Ed wore a different shirt when he picked Leigh up at 10:00 than he had on at 7:00. Do you remember his shirts?"

"Not offhand. What did they look like?"

Nell closed her eyes, remembering. "One shirt had a huge fish on the back of it and the other was a plain tee. Doesn't that strike you as odd?"

"If this is leading up to you thinking Ed killed that man, I'm not buying it. There are reasons for a person to change shirts. Maybe he spilled mustard on it, or something,"

"I've been coming up with as many scenarios as possible—ever since three o'clock this morning. Of course I don't think Ed killed anyone. But it's creepy that the murderer would have to change shirts if he were to be seen and, coincidentally, Ed changed his shirt."

"You used the right word there, Nell, coincidentally."

"I plan to talk to Leigh and Ed today. If they show me the shirt with mustard or something on it, no problem. But if they can't come up with the shirt I'll need to talk to the police."

"Wait a minute, what makes you think Ed will be okay with needing to prove to you that he isn't a killer? Not trusting him may hurt his feelings. You know he didn't stab Ian. Why would you even consider going to the police?"

"I don't know, Elena. I just think it's the right thing to do. You really think I shouldn't?"

"Go see Leigh. Maybe she can show you the shirt and you won't even need to talk to Ed. Then he won't know you ever had any doubt. Leigh, on the other hand, might be upset."

***

Later that same morning when Nell entered Leigh and Ed's shop, she took an extra good look around. One whole wall was decorated with old implements—farm tools, blacksmithing instruments, and various other devices made into art. A good portion of them were long and sharp, which sent her mind in a spin.

Ed, with his glasses atop his head, was scrutinizing some intricate piecework on his side of the shop, so Nell almost ran over to meet Leigh.

After the usual pleasantries, Leigh gave her a quizzical look and prodded, "What's up?"

"Is there any chance we could go upstairs, to talk? This is going to be hard for me to ask you."

"Sure, I have time. Let's go."

As soon as Leigh opened the door to their private entrance, Prada came twining through her legs. "Now, what is going to be hard to ask me?"

Nell sat down and struggled to find the right words. She waited for Leigh to join her as Coco leisurely walked out of the backroom. The cat sat down on the floor, just out of Nell's reach, staring at her.

"I'll just say it outright. Why did Ed change his shirt from the time he walked you down to the pub and picked you up?"

"What? What are you talking about?" Leigh stood over her, hands on hips.

"When Ed walked you inside the pub, he was wearing a shirt with a big walleye on the back."

"That shirt? I know it well. So?"

"Do you still have it, Leigh? Is it in the bedroom or the wash or something?"

"First, run this past me, Nell," Leigh scowled. "Why do you want to know?"

"This is so hard. Believe me, I trust Ed. But whoever killed Ian would have blood splatter all over his shirt. I noticed that Ed no longer wore the fish shirt when he came down to the pub after the murder."

"Nell! I can't believe you're accusing Ed of being a murderer." Leigh gave Nell a long pained look and then turned away from her.

"But I just said I trust him. We have to get this business of the shirt out of the way, before the police figure it out. It's a loose end that needs to be tied. That's all."

"Fine." Leigh flicked her gaze upward. "I'll grab it from our bedroom and show you."

Leigh's cooperation almost assured her they could get over this awkwardness without lasting hard feelings. She hoped anyway. Nell petted Prada as she waited for Leigh.

"Nell?" Leigh called from the bedroom. "Come in here a minute."

Her first glance when she came in the room was at the bed where the feline giant Louis Vuitton was sprawled looking at her with regal bearing. Turning toward the closet, Nell spotted Leigh pulling clothes out of the hamper.

"I've gone through the hanging clothes twice already. I thought maybe he decided he wanted to wear it somewhere again and took it off right after he came home and hung it back up. You know, sometimes I do that with a pair of jeans when they don't get too dirty." Leigh hit a sock against the lid of the hamper. "But that shirt isn't in there, either. Where could it be?"

Nell shrugged wordlessly, then ventured, "The bathroom?"

"You check the guest bath and I'll check ours."

Nell went to her assigned spot and searched the beautifully decorated and welcoming room. Not a decorator bar of soap was out of place and no clothing inhabited the area at all. She headed toward the other bathroom to see if Leigh found anything.

"I can't believe this. Where *is* that shirt?" Leigh charged out of the master bath almost colliding with Nell.

"I hate to say this, but I think we're going to need to ask Ed about it," sighed Nell.

"No. I just need to look some more on my own," Leigh insisted. "It's here, but I'm nervous and want to clear my mind. If I don't find it, I promise I'll ask Ed."

"I'm so sorry I upset you. There has to be a logical reason." Nell enveloped her in a warm embrace. "Call me."

Concern for Leigh came to the front of her mind as Nell drove home. She may have just left one of her best friends alone with a killer. *Good grief, woman!* Ed hadn't murdered anyone. Why did she even entertain such a notion?

And even if he had, Leigh would be safe. She's the one he's protecting. If it was Ed, they wouldn't need to worry about someone else getting killed. *Mercy!* She didn't like the way these thoughts were going, either.

Her empty stomach was making itself known in no uncertain terms. Nell had a plan for lunch that would give her a comforting meal and leftovers. Elena's Wild Rice Soup was on the menu today. The thought of the deep flavor tucked in the creamy goodness made Nell lick her lips. She almost bounded out of the car and into the kitchen.

She greeted the boys, let them outside, and went to work cutting up onions and bacon, putting them together in a pan to fry. Then she cooked half of a cup of wild rice in a sauce pan. Even though she didn't like using a lot of different pans while cooking, this recipe was worth it.

Nell pulled out her big kettle from under the counter and started adding ingredients. A couple cans of both potato and celery soup went in with three cans of skim milk. She turned the heat on the stove and the mixture cooked. While she waited for it to boil, she cut up some soft, velvety cheese, about a cup's worth, and let it meld with the soup. As the bacon, onion, and rice finished, she combined them with the cheese and put the soup to simmer.

Finally Nell added her own coup de grace—sriracha sauce! The sauce took it from a warm, comforting soup to an explosion in her mouth. The comfort and warmth were still there, but the bite—oh, what a bite!

George and Newmie had come back into the house through the doggie door and were happily waiting for any morsels of food to drop.

As the soup bubbled, Nell made her sandwich with toasted bread, cracked pepper turkey lunch meat, and lettuce. She added a few pickles to her plate, a little of her homemade spread to her sandwich, and she was ready to eat.

Mmmhmm. The thick, luxurious texture of the soup wrapped itself around her tongue and slid down her throat, warming her body from the inside out as it passed. The chewiness of the bacon gave her teeth a purpose and its smoky flavor popped in her mouth. The sensation one receives after a good meal was like no other.

Well, maybe one other.

It had been quite a while since she had made this soup and she needed to thank Elena once again for giving her the recipe. It was wonderful to have good friends.

At the end of lunch, as was her custom, she saved some bread and meat for George and Newman. But she had to chuckle to herself when she bent to give it to them and said, "No soup for you."

The deliciousness of the soup (the sandwich wasn't bad, either) temporarily gave Nell a break from thinking about the murder. How she wished Leigh would call with the good news that she had found the shirt full of mustard, or grease, or anything...but blood.

Just as Nell was finished washing the pans, the phone rang. She crossed her fingers hoping for a shirt full of pickle juice, glanced at the caller ID, and saw it was Sam.

"Hello, Sam."

"I just had to take a walk to get away from those people for a while," Sam huffed. "I figured out Jessica's game."

"Oh, she really had one, huh?"

"I never doubted it for a minute. She has the Bean all set up to go on a con."

"A what?"

"A con, a confidence scheme. Like what she and her mother did to me all those years ago."

"No, Sam," Nell gasped. She couldn't believe this!

"Jess offered the Bean a relaxing morning at a spa. She's never had anything like that before. She jumped at the chance. They just came back and the Bean's all made up and looks so much like Jess I can hardly stand it. It's going to break my little girl's heart when she finds out her mother only came back to get her so she could use her for some money scam."

"How can you be sure of that? Maybe Jess wanted to do something that would make Benita happy."

"I'm sure of it. I know Jessica. I know her for the conniving she-devil she is. I'm going back there and get to the bottom of this swindle right now. I know she's trying to hoodwink somebody, but the Bean can't be a part of it. I'm so frustrated with that woman."

"I know, Sam. Benita will see through it, too."

"In matters of deception, Jess is a master. I'm sure she has it all worked out. The Bean won't know what hit her until she's in too deep. Jessica's one stupid move was giving me the okay to come down here. She should have tried to make me stay home."

"Be careful."

"You don't need to worry about me. Hey, how are you and how's Little Irish?"

"We're both fine." Nell smiled to herself as she thought about the time when Leigh and Sam Ryan met. They took an instant liking to each other which was evident by their constant teasing. They referred to each other as

Little and Big Irish now."

"With everything going on down here I almost forgot about that murder in Bayshore. Anything new?"

"Nothing urgent. I'll fill you in when you come back."

"I hope that's soon. I miss you, Nell."

"Me, too Sam. Me, too."

Chapter 18

As the afternoon turned into evening, Nell's hopeful attitude about Ed's shirt became pessimistic. Had Leigh found it, she would have called immediately. Nell's only thought now was that Leigh was waiting for the right moment to ask Ed about his shirt. How does one ask a loved one for incriminating evidence?

Unfortunately, they were no closer to finding out anything about Ian, either. What connection did he have to Annie? Why did he involve Leigh? They didn't even know if Ian was the doll guy for sure. What if Ian was just an innocent bar patron murdered by mistake? Nell knew first-hand that cases of mistaken identity occurred all the time.

The Food Network was on the screen, the boys on either side of her, as Nell tried to let herself relax when the phone rang.

The moment of truth. Leigh must have talked to Ed. Nell reached for the phone but saw that it was Annie.

"Hello."

"Nell, the police just left my mom's house," croaked Annie. "They came over to ask me some questions about my ex-boyfriend."

"I think that's normal, Annie," Nell said. "They have to look at friends and relatives."

At Annie's silence, Nell continued, "Or is there something specific that has their focus?"

"The police spotted him looking in the window of my house."

"No!" Nell gasped, pinching the skin at her throat.

"It's not as bad as it sounds, but I don't feel comfortable talking on the phone about this…"

"I could come over there or you could come here?"

"Well, I would like to get your opinion. With Mom and the kids here, I'd rather come to your house—if you're sure it's okay with you."

"Absolutely, it's fine, as long as you don't mind a messy house."

"I'll be right over."

Nell jumped into action, knowing she had no more than five minutes to set her house to rights. Magazines, books, newspapers, and dog toys all went into an empty clothes basket. The basket went back into the closet and the house looked a lot cleaner.

She hustled the dogs outside and gave the ball a long throw. George and Newmie both shot off with George in the lead. Before they had even retrieved the ball, Nell heard a car in the driveway. She turned to go in the house, with her two little boys chasing back to follow her every move.

Nell greeted Annie at the door and led her into the living room, closing the front door behind her. "Please sit down. Would you like a drink?"

"No, thanks. I don't want to be gone too long." Annie sat on the love seat. "I just want to tell you my ideas and see what you think."

"I'm all ears," Nell said as she sat in her usual chair. "Use me as a sounding board."

"Officer Paul Carson was driving an extra time past my house and noticed a man looking in a window." Annie pulled out a tissue from her purse. "It was Keith, my ex-boyfriend. He was cooperative with Paul and said he needed to talk to me."

"Did you have any suspicions about Keith before?" Nell sat forward in her recliner.

"No. And I really don't have any suspicions now, either." Annie wiped her nose. "Threats aren't his style. He's a standup guy and we had a lot of good years together. Our only problem was that he didn't want to get married. I thought that since we both had bad first marriages we could make our marriage work."

"Did you live together?" At her nod, Nell continued, "So you finally decided to move away and start over?"

"Initially, I wasn't sure I'd stay away, but coming back to Bayshore was so comfortable and accepting, I knew I was home again."

"You never heard from him after you left?"

"Oh, yes. We talk and text regularly." Annie paused then added, "We were never angry at each other. That's why I didn't give him a thought about being the doll guy. During the last couple months he started to come around to the idea of getting married."

"Is that still what *you* want?" Nell prodded.

Annie looked away, towards the back sliding door. "I think so. But now I wish he'd move up here."

"Where were you living again?"

"Cedarburg, and Keith works in Milwaukee."

"Where's Keith now?"

"Right before I got in the car to come here, he texted me. He's at the Bayshore Inn and wants to talk to me. I'm going over there once I leave here. What do you think, Nell? Could he be mixed up in all this somehow?"

"Honestly, I don't know. The question is, do *you* think he could be involved?"

"I really don't. We were already talking about getting back together."

"Well, he wasn't arrested. That's a good sign. Find out what he needs to talk to you about. See what questions the police asked him. I think that would be interesting."

"Okay, Nell. Please share this with Leigh and Elena. Four heads are better than two. I'll give you a call tomorrow with any more news. And thanks."

Nell and the boys walked Annie to the door. "Take care, Annie."

It wasn't until she heard the jarring tone of the telephone that Nell even thought about Leigh.

"I'm so relieved that you called, Leigh," Nell gushed.

"Well, you're not going to be when I tell you about the shirt."

"What?"

"Ed doesn't have it anymore." At Nell's deep sigh she continued, "He said he was more than a little upset when he came home that night and made himself a Bloody Mary."

Leigh paused. "He spilled tomato juice all down his shirt and was so irritated he got rid of it."

"Got rid of it? Is it in your garbage?"

"He put it in the incinerator downstairs in the shop. Ed burned it up."

The silence was deafening.

Finally Leigh said, "I hope you don't think you have to call the cops. I believe Ed. Occasionally he'll make a drink for himself at the end of a hard day. And that was a particularly hard day."

"Why did he burn it, though? Couldn't he have just thrown it in the wastebasket?"

"I asked him that. He said he was afraid I would find it and spend too much time and effort trying to clean it since it was one of his favorite shirts. It wasn't in the best shape even before the spill, so he just figured he'd toss it and buy a new one."

"I can see that happening," Nell admitted. "But I wonder if the police shouldn't know about it anyway. It would be best if Ed mentioned it to them himself. If I noticed it, maybe someone else did, too. Then later if a person told the police about it, they would already know."

"Ed doesn't think he should give the cops a reason to look at him. Innocent people have been railroaded for lack of anyone else on the scene."

"That's true, too." Nell paused. "Someone else has appeared on the scene, however." Nell shared Annie's information about her ex-boyfriend. "She's going to let me know tomorrow what the police asked him. I wonder if he'll become a suspect, too."

"If he does, that would let Ed off the hook."

"Annie was adamant that Keith wouldn't do anything of that sort. Just as you are with Ed."

"Need I remind you that you know Ed, and the two of you have been friends for over thirty years? Neither of us knows anything about this Keith," Leigh scoffed.

"True. Let's just think about things until tomorrow. After I talk to Annie, we can decide what to do."

Nell ended the conversation, but not to her satisfaction. She knew sleep would not come quickly that night.

Chapter 19

The murder in town was the topic of conversation after church that morning. Nell discussed the information she felt was appropriate to share with her friends. Without speculating too much, Nell drove home.

George and Newman didn't come to the door when she entered her house. She walked to the living room to see if they were hiding. They were snuggled together on the love seat. George lifted his head and looked at her, then plopped it back down again. Her little fellas were just exhausted. Nell knew that when she tossed and turned all night as she had last night, her boys hadn't slept either.

She started the coffee maker and brought the paper in from the stoop. Nell had been considering dropping the print edition and just reading her news online. But she decided she wasn't ready for that just yet. She liked the physical feel of the paper in her hands.

It was evident the Christmas season was approaching because there were already a few ads in the paper advertising fir trees, even though it wasn't even Halloween. Nell picked through the ads, but her mind wasn't on shopping for presents.

The coffee was ready and she poured herself a cup. Why hadn't Annie called? Nell knew it was early, and Annie had a family, but waiting was not one of her favorite things. She willed herself not to make the call first.

After three cups of coffee and some halfhearted watching of the Sunday news shows, her phone finally rang. She grabbed it without looking at the caller ID and said, "I'm so glad you called. I've been on pins and needles."

"Really, Mom? Was I expected to call you earlier?"

It was her son. "Oh, Jud. No. I've been expecting a call."

"Just who were you expecting? A morning-after-the-first-date call?" Jud chuckled.

Nell still hadn't mentioned Sam to him yet so Jud thought he was making a good joke. "Just a former student who is now a friend. Actually there's been a murder in town and I'm doing my part to help her."

"Mother! Your part to help? Really?" Jud snorted. "Here we go again. I don't think the Bayshore Police Department needs your interference. We just went through this a couple months ago. I don't hear any of this nonsense up here in Alaska. You could call, email, or text you know. I'm starting to think I need to come down there and put an end to your meddling."

"Put an end to my meddling? Who do you think you're talking to, some daffy old lady?"

"I know exactly who I'm talking to, Mom. A woman with a will of iron. Now tell me who was murdered and how you have involved yourself."

Nell imaged Jud biting the inside of his cheek, a mannerism he'd displayed since childhood when he was irritated. She decided to share the story.

Jud took a deep breath. "Seriously, Mom. Why haven't you told me about this? The same man that rudely knocked on your door was found murdered. And found by you, no less. That's too much of a coincidence. Didn't you get a big enough scare thrown at you last time?"

"I didn't want to worry you. I'm not the target this time. It's Annie Marshall, and I know I can help her."

"I hate to say the words—small town busybody—but when the shoe fits."

"Judson!" Nell exploded.

"I just want you to take care of yourself, not everyone else in town." His tone was soft, caring.

"I know."

"I worry about you because I love you."

"Thank you, Jud. I love you, too."

"I've always known that, Mom, no matter how I've behaved."

The conversation ended on a high note which delighted Nell. She was so pleased that Jud had called, and he had told her he loved her. And said it first. That hadn't happened since he was a little boy.

Her happiness lasted only a few minutes when Nell realized how upset Jud will be when he finds out about Sam. Not necessarily because she's dating someone, but because she's been keeping it a secret for so long. That fact could destroy all the progress they'd made.

Nell knew she needed to get out and do something. She disliked being idle. "George! Newmie! Let's go for a walk!" It always amazed her how quickly two sleeping dogs could be up and ready to go at the mere mention of the w-a-l-k word. If Annie called while she was out, she could leave a message.

Nell attached their leashes and out the door they went. The three of them walked over to Jefferson Street and strolled past Annie's house. There was no movement there, as her family was still at her mother's house. *Bet Annie's not enjoying that at all.*

The abundance of birds and squirrels made for two happy dogs but gave Nell sore arms.

Good news! Nell noticed a blinking message on the machine when they returned home.

"Annie, here. Give me a call when you can and I'll fill you in on what I know." She left her cell phone number which Nell quickly copied down.

After giving treats to the boys, Nell punched in the number to reach Annie.

"Hello."

"Sorry I missed you earlier; I was walking the dogs."

"No problem. I don't know if anything Keith told me is going to help us."

"Maybe not, but I'm anxious to hear it anyway," Nell said, keeping her notepad close and her pen in hand.

"The reason Keith came up here is he couldn't get ahold of Ian Burke."

"Ian? He knew him? That's huge, Annie."

"Not if you believe his story, and I do," Annie challenged. "Keith said that he's known Ian for a few months and that he mentioned coming up to Bayshore to camp. So Keith asked Ian to check up on me. He admitted that he thought I seemed a little hesitant about getting back together with him and wondered if I was seeing someone else."

"Oh, Annie." Nell put the pad of paper and pen down, and began to pace.

"He showed Ian my picture and said to hit a few nightspots to see if I was going out with someone. He even gave him my address so he could drive past the house."

"This isn't good," Nell worried.

"I know it makes Keith sound controlling, but during all the years we lived together it was never an issue. I believe him when he says he didn't mean any harm, and didn't ask Ian to threaten anyone or do anything other than look. He's a good man, Nell. And Keith said Ian had a keen sense of justice. He always wanted to do the right thing. He doesn't see him coming after me."

"Is this what Keith told the police?"

"Yes. His name and phone number were found in Ian's wallet. I think the police are interested in him, but at least they haven't arrested him yet. Nell, I'm so worried. I know Keith would never kill someone."

"It'll be okay, Annie. But what was this about Keith not being able to contact Ian?"

"He and Ian had talked a couple times on the phone, including right after he knocked on your door. Keith told him to stay in the background, so that's why he didn't approach me. When they spoke the next time, Ian said he saw me out with girlfriends last Friday night and the only man he saw me speak with was the bartender. Keith has been trying to call him since Thursday night with no answer by phone or text. He was concerned and thought he'd take a drive up here to check on him, and also to surprise me."

"Instead Keith got the surprise. Ian is dead and he might be a suspect in his murder. From what you're telling me, Annie, it seems strange Ian would be killed here in Bayshore. He doesn't know anyone. He's camping. Our mayor and city council will be devastated if they think someone is killing tourists."

"Oh, yeah that's right. They're advertising Bayshore as a family friendly travel destination."

After a pause, Nell asked, "If Keith didn't ask Ian to threaten or scare you with the doll, who did? That's the question now. There's another person mixed up in this and maybe that's the one who killed Ian." Nell grabbed her notepad again and wrote down: Another man?

"Couldn't Ian have had some argument with another camper who then saw him at Miner's Fish House and killed him? The murderer might not have anything to do with the doll."

"I suppose it's possible, but that would just add one more person to the mix." This was getting too complicated in Nell's mind. "We'd have the doll guy and a separate murderer. Possible? Sure, but it sounds too coincidental to me."

"You might be right. I better get off the phone. The kids and I are going back to our house today. Keith is taking a couple days off from work to stay with us."

"Okay, Annie. Talk to you soon."

Nell wanted to add "be careful" as she wasn't as sure of Keith's innocence as Annie was, but she bit her tongue.

***

Nell had barely hung up her phone when she heard a car door slam in her driveway, setting the dogs into a tizzy. She looked out the screen door, and to her surprise and delight, saw Sam and Benita.

Opening up the door, George and Newman scampered out to greet Sam, who bent to pet them. Nell's attention turned to Benita and she lost her breath.

In front of her stood a delicate porcelain doll, almost too beautiful to be real. Nell could definitely recognize Benita, but she looked so...different. Nell was used to seeing her in the uniform of Northeast Wisconsin—tee shirt, jeans, and sneakers, but today she sported a short deep purple dress and high heels. Hair that was usually pulled back in a loose pony tail for cooking was set free to her shoulders and shimmered like silk. A face that had a pure natural beauty without cosmetics positively beamed as a bit of product had been applied with a light touch. Nell speculated that new undergarments had been also purchased as the *girls* appeared to be in a higher position and somewhat out and about.

"Benita, you look stunning." Nell gave her and Sam each a warm hug and ushered them into the living room to sit down.

"Thanks, Nell. I can't get used to walking in these heels. I'll be happy when I'm back home and into my comfy clothes again."

"We took off from Chicago this morning. Had to turn our cell phones off on the way home as Jessica couldn't believe we had left. She kept calling and screaming into the phone." Sam turned to Nell and winked so Benita couldn't see him. "I just wanted to stop and let you know we're back."

"Is everything alright?" Nell had to ask even though she knew Sam couldn't go into it.

Benita sat forward on the loveseat. "I don't know how much Dad has told you, Nell, but I'm not meant to live in Chicago...or any other big city. I had a hard time sleeping last night and when I woke up this morning I knew I didn't want to participate in any of my mother's plans. I believe in working for a living and being proud to accomplish what I have honestly."

"Good for you, Benita. I'm glad you're home." Nell turned to Sam with a smile. "Both of you."

"I like the pace of small town living," Sam said with a twinkle in his eye. "And the people. One in particular."

"Okay, you two." Benita laughed, shaking a finger at them.

"It's great to be back in a more rural area, away from the phoniness of people in the big city." Sam glanced out the sliding glass doors at Nell's back yard.

"One thing I would like to keep from this trip though, is my new beauty routine. I can't believe how people treated me in Chicago. Like I was really something," Benita said, her face beaming.

"You are really something, Bean. You always have been and always will be. It doesn't matter how you look."

"Oh I know that, Dad, but I have to admit that it feels nice to have men turn around to look at me. I've never had that before." She laughed and batted her eyes at him.

"Nothing wrong with a few beauty products to keep us ladies looking good, but Benita, you are truly beautiful. And your Dad is right. You've always been a wonderful person. That's the important thing."

"Well, it's time we get back to the bar," Sam said, standing up. "And see how things have gone in our absence. I'll call you tomorrow, Nell."

Sam and Benita soon were on their way home, leaving Nell pondering over Benita's appearance. Sam had said she looked so much like her mother that he couldn't believe the resemblance. If this was how Jess looked when Sam met her, Nell could understand how a young man would have been awestruck. She was gorgeous. What nagged at her was that Sam was thirty-six when he was overcome by her looks. Shouldn't he have been more mature by that time?

Perhaps even more than that, the thought that had a stranglehold on her—could a man who had ever been in a relationship with a woman who looked so perfect—actually want to be in a relationship with her? Slim, smooth, sleek vs. dumpy, bumpy, and lumpy (but a good person).

As these thoughts were hurling through her mind, Nell decided to distract herself by making one of her all-time favorite desserts. It was one that she had made up after reading scores of recipes and watching food shows. She had named it Nell's Layered Lemon Love. One of the best things about it was that it had the ingredients she kept on hand. Another bonus was that she could do it up fancy or fix it the easy way. The taste was almost the same.

She had everything at her fingertips to make it. Nell pulled out a lime and a tub of Cool Whip that she had in the fridge so it was already thawed. She went to her pantry and brought out a prepared shortbread pie crust and two jars of lemon curd.

That's it for ingredients.

Now she'd spoon all of one jar of lemon curd into a bowl. Stir it enough to soften and so it spreads easily. Then she poured the spreadable curd into the shortbread crust. Next, she put the other jar of lemon curd in the same bowl and stirred it to soften. She added half of the Cool Whip and blended it all together.

Nell used care in the stirring so the Cool Whip kept its texture. When everything was well combined, she spooned it over the previous layer. Then she put the last of the Cool Whip over that layer. She zested the lime and sprinkled it over the top and put it in the fridge where it would stay for several hours.

Nell had made this dessert the fancy way only once using a spring form pan and her own homemade crust, lemon curd and whipped cream. The result looked fabulous, but the taste was not too different than the shortcut. Either way the result was tart, fresh, and absolutely delicious! Now to wait...

Chapter 20

Nell pulled up in front of Elena's house and noticed a movement in the flower garden. A rabbit ran out in front of Elena as she set birdseed in the shed and then came over to Nell's car.

"Elena, your flowers look beautiful. You have so many colors of mums, but they blend perfectly."

"Thanks." Elena settled herself in the car, then snapped on her seatbelt. "I know I threaten to plow my beds over every year, but next year I'm going to do it." She flexed her fingers. "Between the pain in my fingers and my back, I've had it. I'm so glad the season is almost done."

"I'll believe you'll stop gardening when it actually happens. You know you give all the people that go by your house a lot of pleasure, and I appreciate it, too."

"I know, I know." Elena's eyes lit up as she turned to Nell. "Right now I'm excited to be back on the hunt. I was so happy when you called yesterday and I could get Julie to work today. I've been thinking about what you mentioned about Annie's boyfriend. Are we going to try to find out more about him?"

"I don't know. We can discuss our options for the afternoon at lunch. Do you have any preferences on where to dine?" Nell looked both ways before she drove away from the house.

"Not really. You usually have an idea because of your blog, so I don't really pay attention to new places sprouting up."

"I know, but not today. There are places I want to review in other towns, but I'd really like to stay in Bayshore. Any thoughts?"

"Is Miner's Fish House open on Mondays? We could scout out the joint and maybe talk to the bartender."

"Elena, you're becoming quite the partner. That's an excellent idea. And yes, it is open today." Nell drove silently for a minute, then added, "Let's go over to the campgrounds first and see what's being done about Ian's camper."

"Are you thinking of peeking in the windows?"

"Possibly. And if it's unlocked…"

"Nell!" Elena yelled.

"If we want to find out anything, we have to be assertive."

But she didn't need to drive all the way to Ian's campsite. As they were driving along the highway next to the Oconto River, they glanced across to the campgrounds and saw an empty space where Ian's camper had previously been parked. No sign of it anywhere.

"I wonder what happened to his camper," Elena said. "Could relatives have come up here to retrieve it?"

"I suppose so, or maybe the police department had it hauled away. I'm sure the campground director wanted it out of there so the space could be rented."

Nell turned her car around in the parking lot of the Bayshore Inn. "At any rate we won't be able to look at it now. I've never noticed his car parked on Main Street since the murder. The police probably hauled it away immediately."

"I'll bet they did. Time to eat?"

"I can't think of anything else we need to do before lunch. Maybe if we get a chance to talk to someone at Miner's Fish House, we'll have more leads."

It was a short trip downtown, but they enjoyed looking at the autumn flowers and decorations as they drove past the old Victorian homes on Main Street. Nell parked the car, and together she and Elena entered the British-style pub.

"Will's tending bar," Nell whispered. "Let's grab a stool and sit there so we can talk to him."

"What's your pleasure today, ladies?" Will leaned over the bar and Nell caught a whiff of that same familiar scent. English Leather aftershave, that's it. She remembered her dad wearing it, but was a little surprised it was still being made. Makes sense for a bartender working in a British pub, though.

"Do you have any of that specialty root beer?" Nell asked as she retrieved her wallet out of her purse.

"We sure do."

"I'll try it, too," Elena added.

"Two root beers coming right up." Will grabbed a couple cold mugs out of the cooler, filled them with the dark elixir, and set the drinks down in front of them.

"Quite a bit of excitement in this bar recently. Were you down here the night of the murder, Will?" Nell remembered he wasn't bartending that night, but wanted to know if he had anything new to add.

"No, that was my night off." Very short and to the point. Nell expected to get more than that out of him.

"We were down here that night," Elena piped up. "Nell was the one who found the body!"

"That must have been horrifying for you." Will's eyes bored into Nell. "Was the murdered man someone you knew?"

"No. I just wanted to take a look at the fireplace after coming out of the rest room and found him."

"I would imagine you've both had to speak with the police. Do they have any suspects?"

"They haven't mentioned anyone to me, but why would they?" Nell had no intention of giving out any information on Keith. *Just who was doing the interrogating here anyway?*

"Well, if you hear anything, please let me know. I consider myself to be kind of an amateur sleuth here at the bar so I'm interested in the details of the murder." Will said, then turned his attention to the waitress who had come to the bar for a drink order.

"Amateur sleuth? Give me a break," Nell snorted.

"Nell?" Elena raised her eyebrows with a chuckle.

"Well, this town isn't big enough for both of us."

"Shall we go sit at a table and order lunch?" Elena laughed as she nodded her head in the direction of the dining room.

"Will isn't being very forthcoming, but I'd like to know how well he knew Ian. We've seen them talking together. Why don't we just eat at one of the tables near the bar?" Nell suggested. "That way, maybe we can ask him some more questions."

"Sure. That's fine with me."

So she and Elena walked over to a table, looked over the menu, and decided to give the pub's American burgers a shot. They signaled to a passing waitress who gladly took their order.

"What do we do next if Will is a dead end, Nell?" Elena asked, her hands around her root beer mug.

"Good question. Let's do a little speculating. If Ian took it upon himself to leave the dolls and the flowers without any directive from Keith, the harassment of Annie and Leigh will end. But the question remains: who killed Ian? And why?"

"Too bad it wasn't a suicide," Elena said. "Then the case would be over."

"There's no way it was a suicide. Ian didn't accidentally fall into a sharp instrument several times, stick darts in the wounds, and then pierce a fireplace poker in his heart as a grand finale."

"Oh, I know that. It would have tied it up nicely, though."

"No one is at the bar right now. I'll go up to ask for a refill and see if I can get any information out of him." Nell gulped the remainder of her drink and left the table with her glass.

"Could I get a refill, please?"

"Sure thing," Will said as he walked over to retrieve Nell's mug.

"So, how well did you know Ian Burke?"

"The murdered guy? Not at all."

"But you talked to him. I've noticed the two of you when I've been in here before." Nell knew she was saying too much, but wanted his answer.

"I've talked to you, too. How well do I know you?" Nell acknowledged he was right, but then he had to top it off. "Hey, why were you watching that guy? Are you sure you didn't know him? Did the two of you have something going?"

The nerve of that pup! Nell grabbed her filled mug of root beer and sat down by Elena. She noticed their meals had been delivered. The burgers had little picks with the British flag stuck in them.

Elena looked at her with big eyes. "I bet he's at the top of a certain list of yours right now."

"Amateur sleuth," Nell sneered, then picked up her cheeseburger and took a huge bite.

"These fries are wonderful," Elena said. "So light and crispy. And they have malt vinegar to sprinkle over them."

"I noticed that when I ordered the fish and chips the other day. But they better have malt vinegar to be calling themselves a British pub," Nell scowled. "They wouldn't be authentic without it."

"Am I detecting a note of irritation in your voice?"

"Well, look who's acting like a detective now? Yes, Will ticked me off. Accusing me of having something going on with Ian. Can you *imagine?*"

"I have to admit, Nell, you did make it sound like you had been watching them. At least Will didn't suggest you've been watching him." Elena glanced over her shoulder.

"Yeah, but who knows what he thinks? I can tell he's a ladies' man. He's always flirting with all the women in here." Nell ate some of her fries—with ketchup.

"He talks to the men, too. Will has the perfect personality for a bartender. He's not afraid to make jokes. People like to laugh." Elena tilted her head and continued. "Sam is that kind of bartender."

"Oh, I know. It's just sour grapes. I'll try to let it go and finish this juicy burger." Nell took another healthy bite.

"The American food here is just as good as their British entrees." Elena put a few more drops of malt vinegar on her remaining fries. "A person could come here for ages, not order the same thing twice, and still get a good meal."

Not surprisingly Nell finished her burger before thinking about taking part of it home. She did leave a few fries on her plate. "We need to talk to the bartender who actually worked the night of the murder. I wonder when he'll be in here again."

"I'll ask Will on our way out. Or did you want to talk to him again?" Elena chuckled.

"Very funny."

The waitress walked over to their table. "Is there anything else I can get you today? Do you need a box?"

"I'm stuffed. I have a few bites left, but I'll just leave it." Elena smiled at her. "Just our checks, please."

"Oh, wait," Nell interjected. "I have a question for you. Who are your other bartenders?"

"I'm sorry. This is my first day here. Will is the only bartender I know."

As the young waitress walked away, Nell grumbled, "I don't want to ask that pompous ass of a bartender for anything."

"I told you, I'll ask him. Relax, Nell."

The checks came out in short order and Elena walked to the bar. "Will, do you know what bartender was working last Thursday night?"

"You mean the night of the murder?" Will lowered his voice eerily and did a Groucho Marx impression with his eyebrows. Elena couldn't stop herself from laughing and looked over at Nell standing by the door, rolling her eyes.

"I'll check the schedule." Will looked at a clipboard at the end of the bar. "Looks like Curt."

At Elena's questioning look, Will explained, "Curt Turner. He started work here a few days after the pub opened."

"Okay, thanks."

"Sure. Come again."

Back at the car, Elena could contain herself no longer. "What's gotten into you, Nell? That bartender hasn't done anything wrong. Where is that famous sense of humor of yours?"

"He has two strikes against him. First calling himself an amateur sleuth and then asking if I had something going on with the dead man. Both statements just rubbed me the wrong way. I know it's not like me, which is only adding to my crabbiness."

"Do you feel up to continuing with our afternoon, or should we just go home?"

Nell paused. "I'll suck it up and continue. The next time Will is working I promise to behave myself. But for now we have a name, Curt Turner. If Curt had been any kind of decent bartender he would have introduced himself to us that night. Then we wouldn't have to go to Will to get his name. Thank you for asking and getting that information, Elena."

Elena winked, "Anything for the cause."

"When I think back to that night, Curt didn't look familiar to me. He's probably not from Bayshore. That would put us at a disadvantage for learning more about him."

"If he's not from here, it will take longer to get info," Elena agreed as she dug in her purse.

"How about going back to my house? I want to find the article that was in the local paper about Miner's Fish House when it first opened. I know I have it in a file. Also I made my Layered Lemon Love dessert."

"That's my favorite. Count me in." Elena put the gum she finally found in her purse and popped a piece in her mouth. "What exactly are you looking for in the article?"

"It gives the names of the owners for one thing. You know, we never see them. There was a picture in the paper, so we can review what they look like. As far as I know neither of them tend bar. I wonder if they take turns cooking."

"Did the article mention if they had kids? Look at how Benita helps Sam." Elena turned to Nell with a little shriek. "Maybe Will is their son!"

"The healthy piece of dessert I was planning on giving you has now shrunk in half." The laugh lines around Nell's face gave her away. She was enjoying the situation, too.

George and Newman were ecstatic to welcome their friend, Elena, into the house. Bellies were offered for rubbing and she was a willing participant. "My goodness, Nell. I forgot how excited these two get," Elena laughed.

"They never tire of getting their bellies rubbed." Nell went to her office to look for her file.

"Here it is," she said walking back into the living room. "The man in the picture looks familiar, but not the woman. Here, what do you think?"

Elena took the article from Nell and looked at the picture. "You know when we saw him? The night of the murder. He was in that group of townspeople that showed up when we heard the sirens."

"I think you're right. He was probably cooking that night and just walked out of the kitchen. Let me reread the article." Nell retrieved it and started to read it over. "It says here that Phil Stewart is originally from Marquette, Michigan and Rita Mitchell Stewart is originally from Mineral Point, Wisconsin. They met at a pasty shop in Marquette while attending college. They are the only cooks at Miner's Fish House, but training others so they can have some time off together." Nell handed the article back to Elena.

"Do you plan to interview them about that night?"

"I think we should. Don't you?" Nell said, making her way to the fridge.

Elena followed, newspaper still in hand. "I do, but what will the owners be able to tell us? If they were working in the kitchen, they wouldn't have seen anything."

"We don't know that. Remember the killer probably came in the back door which is close to the kitchen. Often people don't know what they know. It has to be pulled out of them."

"So you're saying he might have seen something and he doesn't even realize it?"

"Exactly." Nell pulled two dessert plates out of the cupboard and set them on the counter. Then, she reached for and re-read the article, heading back to the living room. "It doesn't say anything about children. The clipping says that the husband and wife are the only cooks, but the waitresses and bartenders *could be* relatives. Come to think of it, I don't recognize any of the workers as former students or townspeople. Did they bring in everyone that works there?"

"We could investigate their whole staff." Newmie jumped up on Elena. "That would keep us busy."

"You've started something now. Look at George looking at me." Nell patted her chair and he came bounding up. "I don't know if it would be worth our time to talk to every single dishwasher at Miner's Fish House. It wouldn't hurt, but I wonder how receptive the owners are going to be toward us talking to the two of them. I guess we could keep going there for meals until we talk to all the waitresses and bartenders. Hmmm…"

"I can see it all now. We'll wait in the alley for the dishwashers and cook's helpers to exit the building and accost them with our questions. We'll POUNCE!"

Newmie jumped off Elena's lap, turned around, and gave her a sharp yip.

"Elena! You scared him."

"I'm sorry, Newmie. Come here, boy."

Newman only scooted farther away.

"That's what you get, Elena." Nell patted George on the head. "My concern is that the Stewarts won't speak to us. Realistically, why should they? We're not the police. They aren't obligated to tell us anything." Jud's words of *small town busybody* echoed in her ears.

"Maybe they like to talk," Elena suggested. "Give some people a little attention and they'll work it for all it's worth."

"Let's hope they are folks of that variety." Nell clapped her hands together and stood up. "Now how about that dessert?"

***

Feeling content after their piece of lemon dessert, Nell and Elena gathered their thoughts and jotted down notes about Ian and the murder:

- Ian knocks on Nell's door looking for Annie
- Ian is watching Annie and Leigh at Miner's Fish House
- Ian visits Leigh at her studio
- Leigh finds a Pippi Longstocking doll lovingly cared for after a knock at her door
- Annie finds a Midwest Annie doll mutilated after a knock at her door
- Ian is seen around town driving his car
- Ian has a camper at Wedgewood Park
- Annie finds a dart with a threatening note
- Leigh finds flowers and a dart with a complimentary note
- Nell finds Ian stabbed with a poker and darts

After discussing each occurrence and trying to make sure they had them in the correct chronological order, Nell and Elena decided another piece of Lemon Love was needed for energy. Then they continued:

- Ed burns his tomato juice stained shirt. Blood?
- Keith is found looking in Annie's house
- Keith had asked Ian to check up on Annie
- Police did not arrest Keith
- Police don't know about Ed

- There's any number of employees at Miner's Fish House that might know something
- Police do not want Nell involved

Therefore Nell and Elena must work stealthily.

By the time they had finished compiling their lists, it was late afternoon.

"I can't think of anything else, can you Elena?"

"No, not a thing more."

Nell gave Elena a ride home and then stopped at the store for a rotisserie chicken and some deli pasta salad. She usually liked to make her own, but it was already late and she didn't want to take the time. She would make a lettuce salad, though.

Her mind was full of possibilities of speaking with the Stewarts as she drove back to the house. Maybe she would ask them some questions about their workers. Any little piece of information could turn into a lead. She pulled in the garage, lifted her bag of groceries, and walked into the house. The boys greeted her as usual.

"Should we go for a walk? How would that be?" George and Newman jumped and ran back and forth to the door. "Just let me put these groceries away and we'll go."

Soon she was ready to hit the road. Nell decided to walk past Annie's house and see if they were outside. She knew the family was living there again. At least until Keith left to go home.

As they walked down Jefferson Street, there seemed to be no action around Annie's house. They had reached the lawn in front of the next house when Annie came running out. "Nell, wait!"

She dashed over to them quickly, somewhat out of breath. "Keith's coming. I wanted you two to meet."

Nell looked back at the door and saw a handsome, dark-haired man stepping down the stairs. He walked over to where they were standing.

"Nell, this is Keith. Keith, Nell." Annie stood smiling at both of them.

Nell offered her hand and Keith shook it. "So nice to meet you, Keith."

"I've heard a lot about you, Nell." Keith gave her an easy grin. "Annie thinks you're some Agatha Christie, or is it Miss Marple? Anyway she's impressed with your detective abilities."

"Thanks, but she's definitely been exaggerating." Nell could feel a little heat spreading over her cheeks. "I sure wish someone would figure out who killed Ian. Annie tells me you knew him. What kind of guy was he?"

"I hadn't really known him that long, but I thought he was a good guy. Honest and trustworthy, and he loved to camp. When he mentioned he was going to Bayshore I asked him to check on Annie." Keith shook his head. "I can see that was the wrong thing to do now, but I didn't mean it in any weird way. I'm so sorry he bothered you at your house. That was never my intention. I can't imagine how his getting killed had anything to do with

Annie."

"Do you know if he could possibly be involved with anything unseemly? Drugs maybe, or gambling?"

"I couldn't swear to it, but he didn't seem like that kind of guy. I wish I could be more help, but I don't know much about him personally."

"That's too bad," Nell said. "The sooner we find the person who killed Ian, the sooner Annie and the kids will be safe."

"I think I have the cure for that." Keith put his arm around Annie. "I'm working on Annie to come back to Cedarburg where we can be a family again."

Nell shot a quick glance to Annie, who shrugged her shoulders.

"Well, the boys are starting to get a little antsy so we better continue our walk. Nice to meet you, Keith. Talk to you later, Annie."

Guiding the dogs along at a pace that was somewhat brisk for her, Nell thought about Annie leaving Bayshore with Keith. He was slick, in her opinion. She wasn't sure about him. Would going to Cedarburg be a cure for Annie, or would she only be taking much harsher medicine? Poison perhaps?

***

After relishing the ease and tastiness of her simple supper, Nell settled in for a relaxing night of watching saved episodes of NCIS. The boys had positioned themselves with Newman on her lap and George on her left side. As soon as Mark Harmon came on the screen, Nell's thoughts went to Sam.

She hadn't heard from him yet today. She had thought of him several times throughout the day, but received no word by either landline or cell. She was sure he was overwhelmed as he and Benita had been gone for a few days. He'd call when he has time, she assured herself.

By the time the sports segment of the 10:00 news came on, Nell didn't think Sam was going to call and hustled the boys outside for the last pee of the night. As she was standing at the sliding glass doors, the phone rang.

"Sam?"

"Hi, Nell. Sorry I didn't call earlier, but a lot of work was waiting to be done here. I received a play by play from the staff about every tiny incident that happened while I was gone."

"I imagine without Benita there, no one else was comfortable enough to make any decisions."

"Maybe not."

"Is everything back in good working order now?" Nell could hear the noise from the bar in the background.

"More or less. I'll have to work here again tomorrow, but Nell, I was wondering if you could come up. I miss you and we need to catch up."

She smiled at the request. "Oh, I think that can be arranged."

"Good. I'll even take a break and buy you lunch. See you tomorrow, Nell."

"Good night, Sam." Now she knew she'd have sweet dreams and wake up tomorrow morning ready for her lunch with Sam.

Chapter 21

As she drove to Marinette, Nell considered how far behind spending the day with Sam would put her in her quest to find the killer. But she needed to see Sam and Sam needed to see her. She had so many questions about Jessica that she wanted to ask him. *Small town busybody.* No, this was different. It was a personal relationship. A personal relationship that her son knew nothing about. Good grief! When was she going to tell Jud about Sam? She promised herself it would be soon as she parked her car in the lot and walked up to the building.

Sam immediately came around the bar and gave her a big hug when she entered the Slam. Some of the tension she had been holding in her body floated away at his embrace. He smelled inviting—like the woods, cedar perhaps and orange blossom. However, looking closer, Nell noticed the weariness around his eyes.

"It's great to see you," Sam said, keeping his arm around her as they walked to the bar. "Do you mind sitting out here for a few minutes while I finish filling the cooler, and then we can go back and grab a bite?" He pulled out a barstool for her.

"Not at all," Nell said as she sat down. "Did you end up closing the bar last night?"

"I did. And I was down here early to open it. I remember telling you when we first met that the owner has to run the whole show. It's true. Diet Sprite?"

"Thanks. I'll bet it felt good to sleep in your own bed."

"I had a little problem with the sleeping part." Sam set Nell's glass of soda down on the spotless counter. "As soon as I got in bed, I had a phone call. Jess. Yelling and screaming like you wouldn't believe. I hung up. She called again. That happened one more time before I turned off the phone. The trouble was, I couldn't get her caustic voice out of my head. She sounds more like her mother every day. Unfortunately, she's not done with us yet."

"Sam, no. Doesn't she realize her behavior will turn you and Benita even more against her?"

"Jess isn't accustomed to being told no. She likes to call all the shots and have everyone else dance to her tune. I have a sneaking suspicion that turning off my phone last night will cause her to come back up here." He shook his head and went back to his work.

"I know how much you would hate that, Sam. At least now you know that she can't turn Benita against you."

"Yes, that's true. The Bean saw the true picture of her mother in Chicago I'm sorry to say. How the most wonderful young woman in the world was given the miracle of birth by a viper is beyond me." Sam put the last of the bottled beer in the cooler. "Enough about that. Let's go in and eat. You can fill me in on the murder in Bayshore. I'm sure you know all the details."

They walked toward the dining area and Sam stopped in the kitchen. "Bean, Nell's here, so can you watch the bar?"

Benita came out of the kitchen with a different bearing than before. Even though she wore jeans and an apron and had her hair pulled back, she exuded a glow. Nell couldn't put her finger on it immediately. Maybe it was an air of confidence. Whatever it was, at least that was something good that came out of the whole mess with her mother.

"Hi, Nell." Benita took off her apron and shook her hair loose. "Nobody that orders a drink wants to see a cook's apron. You two take as long as you want. I have it under control."

"Thanks, Benita," Nell said.

Several tables were full as Sam and Nell went in the dining area. They found a quiet spot in the corner and sat down. The waitress came with menus.

"You might be able to guess that I haven't told the Bean yet about her mother's calls last night."

"She did seem pretty happy. Why haven't you told her?" she asked, looking him in the eyes.

"As soon as the Bean found out what Jess was up to, she was uncomfortable." Sam shook his head. "I know my daughter very well and she just wasn't herself. As soon as we were in the car heading home we each breathed a sigh of relief. I don't have the heart to tell her that we haven't heard the last of Jess."

"You might have the right idea, Sam. Let Benita relax until you actually hear something from Jessica. The light of day may have brought clarity to her and maybe she'll leave you alone. Who knows?"

"I'm pretty sure that I know. Jess must already have the mark in mind. She won't want to let a big fish get away."

"Why can't she snare him herself then, and not involve her daughter?" Nell snapped, nostrils flared as she opened the menu.

"I feel a little uncomfortable talking about this, but you know...some guys have fantasies." Sam rubbed the back of his neck. "Being with two women—two beautiful women, twins maybe, would be a highlight for a certain kind of man."

"And Jessica would subject her daughter to that? What kind of *monster* is she?" Nell was angry now, and did her best to keep her cool. It wasn't easy, but this wasn't Sam's fault.

"That's a good word for her—monster."

"Why haven't the police stopped her?"

"My guess is that no one has admitted it to the police. I was too embarrassed myself, and I'd bet the other men she suckered out of cash were wealthy enough to chalk it up as a bad experience, rather than have their shame paraded out in front of their friends."

The waitress came to the table. "Are you ready to order?"

"Nell?" he asked.

"Yes, I'm ready. I'll have the fish sandwich."

"Would you like to make it a basket with fries and coleslaw?" the young waitress asked.

"Sure." Nell nodded.

"Sam?"

"Beth, will you ask Polly if she'll make me a fried egg sandwich with some American fries?"

"You know she will," Beth laughed.

"One of the perks of being the boss."

As Beth went back to the kitchen, Nell looked over at Sam thinking how much her late husband loved those sandwiches. "Fried egg sandwich, huh? I didn't see that on the menu or I may have ordered one for myself." She winked at him.

"Actually customers can ask for items that aren't on the menu, too. As long as the cook knows how to make it and we have the ingredients, there's no problem. All someone has to do is ask."

"Good to know." She took a sip of her soda.

"Now, what's the latest on the murder? I'm still worried about you. I'm so sorry you had to find that dead man's body by yourself."

"I have to admit the vision of his bloody body lying there with that fireplace poker sticking in it haunts me daily. And the darts! I think once the killer is brought to justice, I'll be able to come to terms with it. That's why I want to get this case wrapped up soon."

He slid his hand across the table, and took hers. "You know you don't have to be the one to solve this case. That job belongs to the police."

She squeezed his hand in return. "I know, but I'm right in the middle of it. I'm sure I'll come up with information the police will never find."

"And what do the police think of your help? Have they mentioned anything to you?"

Nell paused. She had hoped she'd be able to avoid telling Sam what Chief Vance said to her, but he had asked her directly. "Chief Vance told me to stay out of their way. But I'm sure he has no idea how much I can help."

"Okay, but if your involvement goes poorly I think there's something they could charge you with, like hindering an investigation or something. Are you prepared for that to happen? How do you look in stripes?" He winked at her.

"Not too bad if the stripes are vertical, but horizontal lines get ugly." Nell looked at Sam with a chuckle.

Beth came out with the tray of food and both of them were more than satisfied with their choices. More than anything, they needed this time together. That was all part of being a couple—working through disappointments as well as joys.

As Sam walked Nell to the door through the now empty bar, he whispered in her ear, "Remember a couple months ago I was able to help you through a hard time. I'm less than zero help now."

"Don't think that way. Your plate is too full as it is. You have this place to run and a vindictive ex-wife. I can take care of myself."

"I know you can. You're a strong woman, and that's part of your charm. But I'd like to think that maybe you need me a little, too."

"Oh, Sam." Nell leaned into him, gave him a quick kiss on the lips and murmured, "I need you a little."

Then she turned and was out the door before she told him she needed him a lot more than that.

***

Nell did her particular version of running to her car. She settled herself in the driver's seat and took a moment to catch her breath. Were Sam's feelings growing deeper towards her because Jessica showed up again and was behaving so poorly? At least she truly believed that Sam had no interest in his ex-wife. Unlike Sam, Nell wasn't sure Jessica would come back here. Sam and Benita left Chicago because they were upset with Jessica. What would make that woman think she could change their minds if she came thundering back to Wisconsin? It didn't make sense to Nell, but nothing that woman did made any sense.

Since she was in Marinette, Nell thought of some other errands she could run. There were a couple cute home décor shops that she hadn't been to in ages. Although her house was fully furnished, it was always fun to check them out.

Nell spent several hours browsing through the shops. She found some burnt orange cloth napkins that would look nice with her brown tablecloth. An autumn colored centerpiece was too beautiful and reasonably priced to pass up. She had a smidgen of guilt for buying dining room accessories at a spot other than Elena's, but she had certainly spent enough cash there through the years. She purchased some other odds and ends and had just one shop left. Clyde's Antiques was a must stop even though she rarely found anything there to buy. His merchandise was top of the line, but Nell didn't have a need for most of it. She loved to walk through the shop anyway.

Today Clyde was bent over waiting on someone when Nell came in the door. She waved a greeting at him and then waded through crocks and glassware, old books and vinyl records. She came upon a small section of the store dedicated to sports memorabilia. She was drawn to several pictures of Vince Lombardi. They were obviously reproductions from the price. She found a framed shot of the coach that she had never seen before. Sam had his dining area at Sam's Slam decorated with Packers' stuff. Should she buy it for him? How would he feel about the gift?

***

Nell parked the car in front of Sam's Slam with a smile on her face, anxious to see Sam's reaction to the picture. She'd made a brief stop at a dollar store for a gift bag and tissue paper, making the present appear festive. Her plan was to stay long enough to surprise him with the picture and then go home.

Nell opened the door to the Slam and noticed Sam with his back to her at the other end of the bar talking to a customer. Benita was also looking away from her as she was seated at the bar instead of working in the kitchen.

"Benita, I'm so excited. I have a surprise for your dad." Nell walked over and lightly touched the woman's shoulder.

"Take your hands off me, you bitch! Who the hell are you and what are you planning to give to my husband? A disease?"

Nell's excitement turned to horror as she realized the woman was not Benita, but Jessica. She was taken completely off guard and momentarily speechless.

Sam came to her rescue. "Jess, get out of here. No one wants to talk to you. Not me, not the Bean, and definitely not Nell."

"Is *this* your Nell?" Jessica asked Sam with a vicious laugh. "She looks old enough to be my mother, no make that grandmother." Then turning to Nell she cooed, "What's the matter, Chubs, cat got your tongue?"

"This is the last straw, Mother. Nell is a dear friend and you have no reason to treat her in such a degrading manner." Benita was suddenly at Nell's side and locked their arms together. "Nell, come back to Dad's office with me. Mother, I will never work with you so get that stupid idea right out of your head. As of this moment, I never want to see you again." Benita hustled Nell away in a whirl.

Once back in the office, Benita apologized profusely for her mother's boorish behavior. "I was so happy driving away from Chicago. Why did she have to come back here? She's a horrible, horrible person. I would have rather never known my mom than have her be this callous shrew. I'm ashamed to have her genes."

"You are nothing like her, Benita. You're kind-hearted and caring. The only genes that came to you from her was your beauty." Nell shook herself off and regained some of her lost composure. "I'm a little ticked that I couldn't come up with some snappy retort, and just stood there gaping. How embarrassing!"

"You did just fine. If you had said something, anything, Mom would have engineered it into an argument and made a gigantic scene. By staying quiet you did the best thing possible. It showed you have class and can't be goaded into playing her game."

Sam appeared in the doorway of the office. "She's gone. I walked her out the door. I doubt she's gone for good, though. My guess is you're going to be her new target, Nell."

"I made a big mistake stopping back here. I should have just gone home."

"When Jess showed up an hour ago I was so relieved that you had already left. Why'd you come back anyway?"

"Oh, I almost forgot." Nell pulled her gift bag up and handed it to Sam. "A present for you."

"You're kidding." Sam pulled out the picture and tore off the tissue paper. "This is a shot of Lombardi I've never seen. We'll find a good spot for it in the dining room. Thanks, Nell, for being so thoughtful." He leaned over and enveloped her in a bear hug.

After breaking apart, Nell voiced her concern. "Any ideas how I can protect myself from Jessica? Do you think she's waiting outside for me?"

"Rest assured she won't physically attack you. She might scratch one of her soft hands. Besides, she's too vain about her face and wouldn't want to risk even a blemish on it." Sam paused. "She may be watching from somewhere to see which one is your car, though."

"Oh, great," Nell sighed.

"Why don't I give you a ride home? You can leave your car here and I'll bring it back after I close up the bar. Benita can follow me to your house."

"Don't you think she'll follow us?"

"No. If she's watching for you to go to your car, she's looking at the parking lot. I parked my car behind the kitchen today to bring in some supplies. She wouldn't see us going out the back door and we can use the back driveway, too."

"That sounds good. How soon can you go?"

"Right away. I'm sure George and Newman are missing you."

"You know me too well."

"Believe me, it's my pleasure."

***

Even though Jessica had caused stress in Nell's life, she still enjoyed the short ride from Marinette to Bayshore with Sam. He was able to soothe some of her concerns, too. Sam assured Nell again that she needn't be afraid of Jess killing or physically harming her. Her game was more of the nasty phone call, smashing a car window variety. Still very annoying, but could be lived through.

"Also, I plan to contact an attorney acquaintance of mine about the possibility of a restraining order against Jess. I don't know enough about the law to know if we could get one, but the threat of one might be enough to make her clear out of town."

"That would be wonderful, Sam."

"The Bean has made it very clear that she is not going to participate in her mother's scam, so if Jess was smart, she'd hightail it home and start working her con solo."

Sam walked Nell to her door and she asked him in.

"Not tonight. I'm needed back at the Slam. Benita and I will bring your car back in a few hours after we close the bar. Is it okay to leave the keys under the mat?"

"Yes, but I wish you didn't have to bring it back in the middle of the night."

"Not a problem. It's more important for me to know that you're safe." He pulled her in for a kiss, a deep one that made Nell light-headed. "But I have every intention of coming back here soon. Finally get that fire going in the backyard."

The sound of the boys almost flipping out on the other side of the door may have killed the mood a bit, but she still murmured, "Can't be soon enough for me."

Nell unlocked her door, then handed Sam the keys as he made his escape before George and Newmie caught sight of him. She bent over making a big deal of greeting the boys. "Are you hungry? Is it time for supper?" She filled their bowls with fresh water and food.

While they were eating, Nell took a moment to think about Sam. It'd been just a couple of months yet she felt like she'd known him much longer. Is this what she wanted?

She had loved being married, and maybe being half of a couple was just what she needed. Neither one of them were getting any younger.

She went to the fridge and pulled out the leftover chicken and pasta salad. Another simple meal would fill the bill tonight. As she ate, at the bistro table not in front of the TV, Nell thought about Jessica. What a cold-hearted, selfish woman! Benita is nothing like her, but Nell could understand if that was her fear. Sam had done a wonderful job of raising Benita on his own. Now if Jessica would just leave them all alone.

Nell thought about Jessica's youthful appearance. She was beautiful naturally, but must have had some work done because she really did look to be in her late twenties. She and Benita could be twins. Nell imagined Benita was uncomfortable with that fact. But truthfully, Nell would rather have her own looks and personality than to be flawless and evil. Yes, she was a bit of a chub and her light brown hair was streaked with gray, but she was happy. She had recently chosen to stop coloring her hair because she'd earned the gray. Her life had been spent trying to help people, not swindle them for her own financial gain.

After eating, Nell didn't go to the TV for an episode of Seinfeld or a food or crime show. She didn't even turn it on for white noise. With two sleeping dogs beside her, she leafed through a decorating magazine, but she didn't like those fancy rooms any more than her own pleasant space. She was comfortable in her own skin. Maybe the dust up with Jessica had made her realize her own worth. Sam seemed to be quite taken with her. And Benita stepped right in to help her today. Sometimes nice gals do finish first.

Still she couldn't help but wonder what Jessica would do next?

Chapter 22

The old Sable was in her driveway—evidence that Sam had been there. Nell pulled it in the garage and hurried in the house when she heard the phone ringing. "Hello."

"Hi, Nell. I worked at the shop yesterday. Did you do anything on our case without me?" Elena's anxious tone let Nell know she would be happy with her answer.

"No. Yesterday I went to Marinette to see Sam and had quite an interesting experience." She then filled Elena in on all that happened.

"Sam's ex-wife sounds awful! She attacked you, not physically, but certainly verbally," Elena proclaimed.

"I agree, awful is putting it lightly. But as long as she goes back to Chicago I'm going to put her out of my mind."

"*Will* she go back?"

"That's kind of a wait-and-see game. But Sam mentioned the possibility of a restraining order, so maybe she'll clear out."

"I hope so. You sure don't need some woman out to get you."

"No truer words were ever spoken." Nell breathed a sigh of relief.

"I'm going to clean up the beds of the summer flowers this morning. Would you have any interest in getting together this afternoon to discuss what we should do next for our case?"

Nell smiled to herself. It was the second time Elena referred to it as "our case."

"I have an idea of what should be done next. We need to call down to Miner's Fish House and see if we can talk to either Phil or Rita Stewart, whichever one is cooking today. I'll attempt to speak with Will again, or there's the possibility Curt Turner might be bartending and we could talk to him instead."

"Great plan, Nell!"

"I'm glad you think so. Do you want to make the call?"

Silence.

"Hello?" Nell asked. "Did I get disconnected?" she said into the phone.

"No, I'm here," came Elena's soft voice on the line.

"I was just joking, Elena," Nell laughed. "Of course, I'll make the call."

"I…I didn't mind asking Will a question, but arranging a meeting with Phil Stewart isn't to my liking. You know, Nell, that's why you're…Batman and I'm only Robin."

Nell hung up the phone, but she couldn't stop laughing.

***

Taking her own car downtown, Nell was occupied thinking about her phone conversation with Phil Stewart. He had been friendly and inviting. She parked her car, and as soon as she stepped up on the sidewalk, she heard a voice behind her.

"Mrs. Bailey, wait up." Nell turned and saw Zane Colsen, a former student running down the sidewalk to catch up with her.

"Hi, Zane. How are you?"

"I'm fine, but you, Mrs. B., how are you?" Zane pushed his pink tipped blond hair out of his eyes and shuffled his backpack to his other arm. "I heard about you being involved in another murder."

"I wasn't involved in it, Zane. I just found the body."

"That's involved. I heard you were questioned by the police and everything. How could this happen to you again?"

"Just a coincidence, I guess." Nell glanced at her watch. "Why aren't you in school?" *Old habits die hard.*

"The teachers had a meeting or something. It's an early release day." Zane took a deep breath. "Anyway Mrs. B., remember after your first murder case I interviewed you for the school paper?"

"Yes, I remember. That interview was only a month ago."

"Everybody liked that article, so I'm wondering if I can interview you again. Please, please, please, say yes." Zane looked at her pleadingly with crossed fingers. Nell still envisioned him as the middle school boy who had difficulties getting along with his classmates. She had had to speak to more than one of them who called him Zane the Pain. Even though he had grown half a foot since she had him in class, it was hard to believe he was a sophomore and would soon have a driver's license.

"I'll tell you what, Zane. We'll wait until the case is closed and then if I have any details other than being in the wrong place at the wrong time and finding the body, I'll do the interview."

"Thank you so much. I've been reading detective books from the school library and now I'm going to the public one, too. I've become quite interested in solving crimes, Mrs. B."

"I'm delighted to hear that you're reading. Keep it up!"

"Bye, Mrs. Bailey," Zane called as he walked in the other direction. "I'll contact you soon to find out how the case is going."

"Okay, Zane," Nell answered, smiling. *Another amateur sleuth.*

As Nell neared the pub, she noticed Elena getting out of her car. She waited outside the door so they could enter together.

"I'm anxious to hear what the owner has to say," Elena chirped. "How cooperative was he when you called?"

"He's willing to talk, but I didn't speak with him long. I didn't want to

123

give him a chance to change his mind." Nell pulled the door open and they entered.

Will wasn't tending bar. It was the fellow who was the bartender the night of the murder. Curt. What good fortune! After they were finished with Phil Stewart, she and Elena could stop for a chat with him.

"Phil is expecting us. Should we go back to the kitchen?" Nell said.

"Oh, no," Curt replied. "He'll need to come out to speak with you. I'll let him know you're here. What are your names again?"

Nell told Curt their names.

A few minutes later, a large man came out to the bar who Nell recognized from the newspaper article. She silently agreed with Elena that he was in the crowd of onlookers after the murder. Nell and Elena introduced themselves and commented on the good food they'd eaten at the establishment.

"I'm glad you've enjoyed our menu. Why don't we head into the dining room? There's a private table there where we won't be disturbed." Phil led them to a table and they were seated. "Now, Officers, what is it you'd like to know?"

"Actually we're not with the police," Nell began.

"*What?* You said you were investigating the murder?"

"We are, but on our own." Phil started to rise from his chair as Nell blurted, "I was the one who found the body that night here, and Elena was with me. Please don't leave. We have special insight to the crime."

"Being first at the scene of the crime doesn't give you any added insight," Phil sneered with a curled lip. "I have a lot of work to do in the kitchen. Have a good day."

"Please wait!" Elena reached over and touched his arm. "Nell and I are very good customers here. Nell writes a restaurant review blog that hundreds of people in Northeast Wisconsin read for dining suggestions. She's just getting ready to give you a good review. You wouldn't really walk away from us, would you?"

The wheels could almost be seen turning in his head as Phil thought about potential profits. He sat back down.

Nell didn't care for the appearance of blackmail, but she knew she'd already given Miner's Fish House a good review. He didn't know that, though. Phil probably didn't know anything about Noshes Up North. Good thinking on Elena's part.

"I suppose I could spare a few minutes," Phil relented. "What do you need to know?"

"How well did you know Ian Burke, the murdered man?"

"I didn't know him. Not at all. I don't get out of the kitchen much. You two say you've been in here often, but we've never spoken before now." Phil paused. "I do know he was in my place a lot in the last few weeks because I look over the checks that are cashed here before I take them to the bank. He sometimes wrote more than one check a day. It seemed odd, too, that he didn't use a credit card. Always a paper check. That's getting more and more unusual these days."

"Two checks a day is odd. Did it raise any red flags that something was amiss?" Nell made a few notes in her iPad.

"I took a pack of checks to the bank on Friday, the day after the murder. That's when I noticed he had written so many. To my relief, his checks were good."

"You don't have a restrictive check writing policy," Elena piped up. "Are you planning to initiate stricter rules on that? I own my own business, The Dining Room, and most of the locals are good for it."

"I haven't been in business long enough here to get burned. If a bunch of rubber checks come through I may need to change my trusting ways," Phil said, smiling at her.

"Have any of your staff mentioned Ian?" Nell inquired, putting the focus back on the case. "Who cashed most of his checks?"

"The time it's cashed isn't imprinted on the check, so I don't know who was tending to the bar. None of my staff had spoken or complained about him to me." Phil got up from his seat. "Now I really do need to get back to my duties."

"Thanks for taking the time to speak with us. We appreciate it." Nell leaned over to shake his hand.

"We'll be back for many more meals." Elena gave him a little wave.

Phil nodded at them and rushed back to the kitchen.

"I didn't think he was going to talk to us," Elena said.

"You saved the day, my friend. He was ready to leave right then and there until you mentioned my blog," Nell grinned. "You're a quick thinker."

"That's a compliment coming from you." Elena nodded her head toward Nell.

"I want you to think back to the night of the murder. As I was looking at Phil, it came to me that Will was standing by him with the other onlookers that night. Do you remember him?"

"Yeah, now that you mention it, I do." Elena's eyebrows knit together. "Is that a big deal?"

"When we talked to Will, he said he wasn't here the night of the murder. But he was. Why would he lie about that?"

"I'm not sure," Elena said. "That's interesting, though. I bet we'll be getting to the bottom of that soon, won't we?"

"Hope so. Let's walk back to the bar and see what Curt can tell us." Nell slipped her iPad back into her purse.

They positioned themselves at one end of the bar and ordered a couple of sodas. Curt wasn't too busy, so Nell asked her first question. "Curt, how well did you know the murdered man, Ian Burke?"

"How do you know my name?" he asked, surprise written clearly on his face.

"Will mentioned you were the one working the night Ian was killed," she answered. "Did you know him?"

"Me? No. I didn't know him."

"Not at all?" Elena prodded.

"Didn't you cash some checks for him? Quite a few checks?" Nell asked, pulling her soda closer.

Curt glared at her. "I waited on him a few times, so I may have taken one or two checks. I don't know."

"Last Thursday night *you* took his drink back to the game room instead of the waitress. Why was that?" Nell asked, doing her best to keep calm.

"Who are you? Why are you asking me all these questions? You're talking to me like you're accusing me of something."

"Don't you recognize me? I was the woman who found his body the night Ian was murdered." Nell shivered. It was still a hard image for her to get out of her head.

"Yeah, I recognize you, but I don't understand why you're grilling me. You know, I could ask you some pretty pointed questions, too." He picked up a glass and cleaned it with a rag the same way she had seen Sam do so many times.

"Relax, Curt." Nell glanced at Elena. "Don't be upset. We just want to find out a few things about the victim."

"I guess that's okay." Curt put the glass down and wiped his hands on his apron. "I had been back in the game room to attend to the fireplace. While I was there, Ian asked for another beer, so I grabbed a bottle and brought it back for him. The waitresses were busy, and I had the time. That was the last I saw of him. Alive, that is."

"Did you use the fireplace poker?" Nell asked, pulling out her iPad again.

He heaved a heavy sigh. "Yeah, but I put it back in its holder."

"Was Will around here that night?" Elena asked. "We didn't see him, and he's usually here."

"No. You saw me tending bar."

Nell prodded him this time. "Are you sure he wasn't in the building? I thought I saw him after the body was found."

"Could be," Curt shrugged. "I didn't see him, but he could have been down here. He just lives upstairs, ya know."

Nell was surprised by this clue. "He lives upstairs? I thought the Stewarts lived up there."

"They own the building and live in the main apartment, but there are lots of rooms they rent out. I live up there, too."

"Who else lives there?" Nell was curious now.

"All the bartenders, waitstaff, and kitchen helpers. But it's just to start out," Curt said, grabbing another glass to clean. "We're all looking for apartments away from the pub. A few workers are married with kids and needed the work down here. They're checking it out to see if they're going to stay. If so, they'll bring their families here."

A group of women, shopping bags from the stores on Main Street in each of their hands, came through the door. They arranged themselves at a table and set their packages on the floor.

"Where are most of you from? I don't recognize any of you from around town."

"Mostly in the U.P. I'm from Escanaba, Michigan myself. Excuse me, I've got to go check on the new customers." He walked over to attend to the shoppers.

"I'll leave enough to cover our sodas, plus a tip. Let's go over to the Mocha Chip and digest what we've learned today," Nell suggested.

"And maybe digest a late afternoon treat?" Elena teased.

Nell winked. "You know me well."

***

Nell took a big bite out of her white chocolate raspberry swirl cheesecake. "Mmm...this is so good, but back to the case. If Will lives upstairs, it's no wonder he came down when the police arrived. I bet all of the workers did."

"It would probably be suspicious if someone *didn't* come down, unless they were in the shower or something." Elena nibbled on her mini cream puff.

"Goodness, Elena!" Nell exclaimed. "How can you eat just one of those tiny things? There's not enough food there to fill a tooth."

"I just needed a *taste* of something sweet."

"And you didn't get any more than that." Nell stirred her decaf thoughtfully. "Before we thought the killer needed to go out the back door to get away with bloody clothes. Now we know he could have just as easily gone up to the second floor to change."

"You know, that takes Ed and Keith off the suspect list."

Nell tapped her fingers on the table. "I've done no such thing, Elena. I'm exploring all the possibilities. I just wish we had some kind of motive." Another forkful of cheesecake found its way into Nell's mouth.

"What about the possibility of someone getting upset if Ian was the man doing all the mischief with the dolls and notes?" Elena offered.

"That motive would lead back to Ed or Keith. They're not off my list, but I don't want it to be either of them. What would be another motive?"

"Maybe this Ian guy slept with someone else's wife, cheated in business, or cut someone off in traffic. He may have been followed here from where he lived in the Milwaukee area. Oh, Nell, how are we ever going to know?"

Nell was looking out the window at Miner's Fish House when she made eye contact with Chief Vance in his squad car as he was slowly driving down the street. His eyes opened wide and his face turned maniacal as he pulled his car over to the side of the road and parked. Soon he was out of his vehicle and heading toward the shop.

"I don't think this is good," Nell whispered to Elena, keeping calm.

"I'll be back in a jiffy." Elena started to rise from her chair. "I'm going to the restroom."

"You'll do no such thing." Nell pulled at Elena's hand. "Stay here. Please."

Elena looked in her purse for gum as Chief Vance came in the coffee shop and headed straight their way.

"Hello, Chief," Nell squeaked as he stood before their table.

"I'm going to dispense with the small talk," he bellowed in no attempt to be quiet. "I've just received a call from a citizen complaining about you harassing him. What are you doing, Nell? I told you to stay out of it."

"Asking a few questions isn't harassment. What about my rights? I'm a citizen, too."

The chief lifted his hands in frustration. "What rights of yours are in jeopardy?"

"How about free speech?" Nell argued.

"No one is trampling on your right to free speech." The chief shook his head. "But, Nell, these people were working. And even if they weren't, they don't have to talk to you."

Nell sat up straighter in her chair. "I'm not forcing anyone, Chief. If they don't want to talk to me, they don't have to answer my questions. Besides, whether you think so or not, I know I can help solve this case."

"It's not that simple. I already told you to stay out of it and you're right in the thick of things. You have no business asking anyone, anything. There's a murderer out there, Nell. I don't want you to get hurt. Do you understand?" Chief Vance looked down on Nell with cold hazel eyes. "This is your official warning. Don't make me talk to you again. You won't like the result."

With that, he turned on his heel and left.

"Well, Nell. We had a nice little run with our detective charade, but I guess it's over now." Elena finally put the piece of gum in her mouth.

"What are you talking about? Why should it be over?"

"Nell!" Elena stared at Nell.

"We need to be more secretive is all." Nell ate the last bite of the tasty cheesecake. Looking at Elena's shocked face, she said, "He's not going to put us in jail, Elena."

"Hope not." Elena glanced at her watch. "I'm going to take off now. I need to talk to Julie at the shop. She was expecting me forty minutes ago. I hadn't realized how late it was."

"I'll walk out with you."

They walked over to the door. "Elena, you don't need to do anything else with me. You've done more already than any friend should have to do."

"I just don't want any trouble with the police, that's all."

"I don't either. Tonight I'll think everything over. There may not be anything more for us to investigate anyway." She hugged Elena and they went their separate ways.

***

Nell returned to the love and affection of her boys, and a very interesting phone message from Sam.

"Jess went back to Chicago today, Nell. She wanted me to apologize to you for her rude behavior. She actually seemed sincere. Call me when you can and I'll give you all the details."

At least something good happened today.

After taking the boys outside to play for a bit, Nell gave Sam a call.

"Yes, she's gone. We're breathing a big sigh of relief here, and I think you can, too." Sam's voice was more relaxed than Nell had heard it in days.

"Why did she decide to leave?" Nell asked. "And why do you think you can trust her now?"

"I'm not saying she can be trusted, just that she's gone." Sam's voice turned serious again. "I think she left because she couldn't change the Bean's mind. Jess apologized to her and left on decent terms. I'm sure she wanted the door to be left open for her to come back." He laughed. "She probably wanted to return to Chicago before her big fish got away."

"I'm so glad she's gone."

"I know, my honey. I know." Sam's sexy, deep voice sent a little thrill up Nell's spine.

I'm *his honey.* She gave herself a little shake and asked, "How is Benita? I'm concerned with how disappointed she must be with her mother. She was without her a long time and then to have her turn out to be so selfish and cold. Poor girl."

"I'm concerned about her, too. She's acting strong as if she doesn't care, but I know she's hurt by the way Jess wanted to use her," Sam sighed. "I've tried to talk to her, but she brushed me off."

"Give her time, Sam."

"I'm still getting caught up here at the Slam, but I want to find a night where we can go to a different place and enjoy a nice evening. How does that sound, Nell?"

"A little bit like heaven! Just let me know the night."

"I'll call you soon with a tentative date. You are in my thoughts so often, Nell. Thank you for…being there these last few days."

Nell tingled as they said their goodbyes. It was so nice to know Sam was firmly hers again.

Chapter 23

Nell was up early and out with the boys. She had a lot to accomplish today.

One of her top priorities was contacting Leigh, either by phone or going down to the shop. They hadn't spoken in several days. Nell was curious about Ed destroying his shirt. And she was so irritated with Chief Vance she *almost* didn't care if he knew anything about it. Let the police department hunt up every clue on their own like she and Elena had. They sure didn't give her any help. *Did she dare walk into the establishment of one of her best friends, or would the chief accuse her of meddling?*

She had a bunch of phone calls to make today—to Annie, Benita, and Jud. Nell thought she would give Annie a call and see how things were going with Keith. Something about him seemed off to her. She couldn't put her finger on it, though.

She wanted to call Benita and give her encouragement, too. She didn't want to overstep her bounds, but if there was any way she could help Benita, she certainly would. Of course, she wanted to talk to Sam today, too. That was a given.

As much as she had been putting it off, Nell knew she needed to call Jud and tell him about Sam. Their relationship was deepening and her son needed to know. And he deserved to hear it from her.

She was a bit concerned that one of Jud's high school chums who still lived in town might hear about Sam and contact Jud. Her whole problem with sharing the news was that they had such a strained relationship already and it was finally starting to get back to normal. She had to come up with the right words to make him understand that Sam wasn't a replacement for his father.

And last, but not least—after her phone calls, she needed to attend to her blog. It had seemed it had been last a lot lately. She hadn't kept up with her usual entries. There was more work to be done on the computer than she could accomplish at one sitting, but she'd get as much done as she could today.

Starting at the top of her list, she reached for the phone and called Leigh.

"Nell, it's so good to hear from you. I'm just about ready to go down to the shop. How are you?" Leigh voice was pleasant as if totally unaffected by the recent murder.

"I'm okay. I meant to talk to you earlier about this, but I was thinking about Ed's shirt and wondering if he'd mentioned it to the police?"

"No. He's not going to talk to them either," Leigh retorted. "He hasn't done anything wrong and he's chosen to stay silent. Why should he draw the spotlight to himself when he and I know he's innocent?"

Nell paused. Maybe the police wouldn't care about the shirt anyway.

"And don't you even *think* about talking to the police yourself and directing them toward Ed." Leigh was firm.

"You don't have to worry about me talking to the police, Leigh." Nell then related her recent conversation with Chief Vance.

"It would be horrible to be charged for interfering," Leigh commented. "Maybe it might be better if you let the police handle it."

"I guess that's what I'm going to do, but I sure hope nothing else happens."

Nell sat in her chair petting the dogs as she thought about their conversation. She understood why Ed didn't want to draw attention to himself. She truly believed he was innocent, too. How she longed for the time when she and Leigh could have a conversation without this murder hanging over their heads. Soon, she hoped.

Next on her agenda—Annie. She wasn't sure if this was her day off or what hours she was working at the hospital this week. There was one way to find out.

"Hello."

"Hi, Annie. This is Nell. Is this a good time to talk?"

"I'm at work, but I have a couple free minutes. Has anything happened?"

"No, I was just wondering how you were and if the police have left Keith alone."

"I'm great. Keith left this morning to go back to Cedarburg, but I wish he was still here. It was so good having him at the house. I didn't realize how much I missed him," Annie admitted. "The police no longer consider him a person of interest."

"That's good. Did an officer come to your house with that information?"

"No, someone called Keith on his cell and told him. Why?"

"No reason, Annie. I was just curious. Well, I know you're busy. I'll let you go."

Nell realized she hadn't handled that very smoothly. She hoped she hadn't irritated Annie. But just because Keith said he was contacted by the police didn't necessarily make it true.

She had made two phone calls and couldn't say that either of them had ended in a satisfactory way. She hoped the next one would go better.

"Sam's Slam."

"Hi, Sam."

"What a wonderful surprise! I hope everything is going great for my favorite person in Bayshore."

How sweet! Sam could always brighten her day. "It is, but I wanted to hear your voice. Is Benita around? I thought I'd check on her."

"You can rest assured you can hear my voice anytime day or night. I'm

131

just waiting for the invitation to start a fire in the fire pit in your yard," Sam drawled. Nell could almost see the smile on his face and knew he was probably thinking of starting a fire somewhere else, too. She certainly was! "Here, I'll hand the phone over to the Bean."

"Nell?"

"Benita. I was thinking of you today and want to make sure you're alright after everything…"

"Thanks, but I'm fine. Really. Dad is worried, too. But honestly, I didn't have high expectations for a woman that hadn't taken the time to visit me in twenty years. And even though I wasn't looking for some fictional TV mom, I didn't expect she'd try to involve me in some sort of illegal sexual con game either."

"I just know how disappointed you must be. I don't like to see you hurt."

"I appreciate your concern, Nell. More than you know. I've had many good women in my life and you are quickly becoming one of my favorites. You have changed Dad's life for the better." Benita paused and Nell could hear a soft sigh. "I know you sincerely care about me, too. Thank you."

"Here I call to help you feel better and you end up giving me a gigantic boost. Thank you, Benita."

"Let's go to lunch sometime. Maybe shopping afterward—make a day of it. Without Dad."

"That sounds fantastic! Yes, we'll do it soon."

When the call was over, Nell couldn't stop smiling. She hadn't realized she meant so much to Benita, and she'd like to spend a whole day with her? Lunch and shopping? A dream come true. She'd always wanted a daughter. Best not to get ahead of herself, though.

With happy thoughts dancing in her head, Nell once again put off the call to Judson. She didn't want to spoil the mood. She promised herself she would call him soon and explain everything. Jud's understanding about Sam was becoming more and more important to her. Especially now that she knew Benita had fully accepted her relationship with Sam.

She went to her laptop to do some serious work on her blog. But first, she needed to read over some of her followers' messages.

Red Stiletto

Thank you, Nell, for the wonderful review of The Whole Enchilada in Cecil. My friends and I enjoyed a day of shopping in Shawano and I suggested we try it for lunch. We were all delighted with our food. Everything looked and tasted more authentic than some of the other Mexican restaurants we had visited. I plan to return often, and so do the other women in my party. Keep up the good reviews!

Professor and Mary Ann

Did an internet search and came upon your blog. My wife and I are coming up from Madison to just north of Green Bay for a "Vacation in the Woods." I love a good broasted chicken dinner on Sunday. Could you give us a few suggestions?

Chuck's Angel

I just went to a new bakery in Suamico called The Bee's Knees. Most of their baked goods are made with honey rather than sugar. I've been there three times and everything I tried was delicious. I'd be interested in reading your opinion of their offerings.

A few months ago opening her blog filled Nell with trepidation, dreading the possibility of finding another nasty post from Northwoodsman. Now, just in the first three messages from her followers, she received a compliment, was asked for advice, and was alerted to a new eating establishment. This was her dream come true, and it had become real.

The hysterical barking of her dogs interrupted her peaceful moment. It sounded like they were at the front door in the living room. *What on earth?*

Nell walked over to the door and saw her former student, Zane, standing there looking frightened. "George. Newman. Settle down."

She opened the door. "Zane, what is it? What are you doing here?"

"I don't want to get close to your dogs, Mrs. B. I was bitten by a beagle once and now I don't take any chances," Zane said.

"Boys, stay." Nell quickly walked outside, but stood where the boys could still see her. She hoped it would be enough to keep them there and they wouldn't come out the doggie door and scare Zane even more.

"I understand your concern, although my little guys are just protecting their territory and are harmless. Their barks are way worse than their bites," Nell assured. "What's up?"

"I've been keeping an eye on Miner's Fish House since the murder," he whispered looking over his shoulder. "I think there is something going on with some of the workers there."

"What makes you say that?"

"Two guys always come out the back together and talk low, like they're hatching some evil plan or something." He glanced behind him again.

"How long do the men stay outside?"

"About twenty minutes, but I can't get close enough to hear what they're talking about without them seeing me."

"Hmm… Could you see if they were smoking?" Nell mused.

"Yeah, they were," Zane admitted. "Do you have proof the murderer is a smoker?"

"No. It would be my guess it's their break time. They could be talking about the boss or another worker and don't want anyone to hear them."

"Or, they could be talking about who to kill next, Mrs. B. I'm going to help you get to the bottom of this murder."

"No, Zane. You can't. I want you to stop your surveillance of Miner's Fish House right now." At Zane's slumped shoulders and disappointed expression, Nell softened her tone. "I know you want to help and I appreciate your thoughtfulness. Think how devastated I would be if something happened to you? This is not a fiction book or made-up movie. A real murder took place here in Bayshore. A killer is out there somewhere and I don't want you anywhere near him."

"I've got this, Mrs. B." Zane pulled his shoulders back and inflated his chest. "I know I could find clues that will blow this case wide open."

"No! Please, for my peace of mind, stop this right now. Zane, please…"

Zane backed away from her, then got on the bike leaning next to the garage and took off. He was soon out of sight without agreeing to stop investigating.

Why wasn't he in school today?

Once Zane was gone, Nell's motivation to work on her blog rapidly dissipated. She couldn't help but dwell on her conversation with him. It was too close to Chief Vance's speech for comfort. The chief didn't want her to get hurt, either. Maybe she should give it a rest for a bit. *Unless a clue fell into her lap.*

Chapter 23.5

I may need to accelerate my plan to leave town. Nosy townspeople. Some think they can solve a murder. One had thoughts about what he could do and look what happened to him. I won't let some old woman stand in my way, either. Some stupid old woman.

Chapter 24

Thunk! The sound of a clue falling into her lap.

The shrill ring of her landline phone woke Nell up from a sound sleep. Her first thought was about the safety of her son. She looked at the clock. Almost midnight.

"Hello?"

"In est th woman huh askin bot murther?" A garbled question from a woman's voice.

"I'm sorry," Nell said, "but I can't hear you." She sat up in bed and shook her head to wake herself up.

"Is this the woman who was asking about the murder?"

"To whom am I speaking?"

"Oh, sorry. This is Lynn. I've waited on you a couple times at Miner's Fish House."

"Yes, Lynn. I remember you."

"I don't want to talk loud enough to be heard by others, but I want to speak with you about the murder." Lynn's voice lowered again. "Could we meet somewhere?"

"I'm having trouble hearing. Did you just ask to meet somewhere?" Nell asked. "Please tell me you don't mean right now."

"Tomorrow. Could you meet me tomorrow?" A short pause and then, "But not here. It has to be somewhere else."

"That's fine. Where and when?"

"Could we *accidentally* run into each other at the pharmacy on Main Street? Say at 10:30 in the morning?"

"See you then, Lynn."

Nell was relieved the late call wasn't about Judson. She went out to the kitchen for a glass of water and thought about Lynn. What kind of information about the murder does this young waitress have? Had she been working the night of the murder? Nell couldn't remember seeing her. Perhaps Lynn saw something she didn't want to mention to the police. Nell could feel her heart pounding faster as her excitement rose. She wondered if Lynn, like the other workers, lived upstairs from Miner's Fish House. Could that be why she spoke so softly on the phone? She didn't want to be overheard.

Nell sighed. She was in for a restless night as her mind was bound to consider every possibility before she'd be able to fall asleep.

The boys and Nell were up early and out the door for a walk. Nell's busy mind hadn't let her get a good night's sleep. Her thoughts ranged from Lynn's info being enough to solve the case to it being very minor. And she thought about Zane's clue about the two men smoking outside. She tried not to get her hopes up.

All her chores were finished in short order and Nell almost counted the minutes until she could leave to go downtown. She wanted to get there early, so Lynn didn't have to wait for her. Luckily, there was a large assortment of goods to browse through at the Bayshore Pharmacy. It was a delightful place to shop for home décor and various other items. Being in a small town, they catered to the various needs of the community.

Nell had just finished walking down the first aisle of the store when she turned the corner and saw Lynn. They wandered over to the display of candles where they could stand together for a time without drawing attention to themselves.

"Hello, Lynn." Nell gave her an encouraging smile.

Lynn nodded her head. "Thanks for meeting me."

Nell waited for more, but was met with silence. "Do you have something you want to tell me?"

"I do, but this is harder than I thought. I feel like a snitch."

"Lynn, someone was murdered. If you know even the smallest bit of information you need to let someone know. You can talk to me or the police. The guilty party has to be caught."

"I think Phil killed him," Lynn blurted, pushing her bangs out of her face.

"Phil?" Nell was taken completely off guard. "What makes you suspect him?"

"His wife, Rita, has hardly stopped crying since that night. She as much as told me she thinks Phil killed the guy." Lynn's face turned red and she looked like she would either start crying herself or screaming any minute.

"Think. What were the exact words Rita used?" Nell mentally crossed her fingers for Lynn to remember.

"I don't know the exact words, but something to the effect of 'what has my Phil done and what's going to happen now?' Then Rita burst into a flood of tears."

"Are you sure this happened after the murder?" Nell prodded.

"Of course it happened after the murder." She looked at Nell with a question in her eyes. "What did she have to cry about before?"

"Well…we never know what's going on in other people's lives. There are a variety of reasons she could have been upset. Did she mention why she thought Phil had done something? She must have a reason to suspect him."

"Nope. That's all she said to me. But she's been moping around, driving everyone crazy." Lynn straightened her shoulders and walked over to the half price autumn decorations.

Nell sauntered over to stand next to her again. "This is something the police should know. You should go down to the station and make out a report."

"*Are you crazy?* I'm not getting involved with the police," Lynn snapped. "I probably shouldn't have even contacted you."

Seeing that Lynn was getting upset, Nell moved on to another question. "Has anyone else acted in an odd manner since the murder? What about Phil? How's he been?"

"He's been cool as a cucumber." Lynn shook her head. "Hasn't seemed to bother him at all. He's concerned some customers may not want to come in because a murder happened there. He's all about the money."

"Knowing human nature as I do, some customers would go *because* a murder took place there."

"Sickos! Some people are so warped," Lynn snarled.

Nell thought back to when she and Drew had visited London and went on the Jack the Ripper Walking Tour. They had stopped at the Ten Bells Pub where the prostitutes hung out, who were later killed by the Ripper. The door where one was stabbed was pointed out to them. Drew passed right by it, but she went over and touched it. Sicko? Perhaps. At least she would be according to Lynn's standards.

"How about any of the other workers? Any difference in their behavior?"

"It's hard to say. We've only been open a few weeks, and I haven't worked with any of them before, so I can't tell."

"Lynn, do you think Rita would be receptive to talking to me?" Nell asked.

"No!" Lynn shrieked, causing other customers to look in their direction. She lowered her voice. "You can't mention me. I don't want to get involved. I need this job."

"I won't mention your name," Nell whispered. "I just mean, Rita must tell someone what she knows. We don't want a murderer to roam free. None of us would feel safe again."

"But it's her husband. She doesn't have to testify against her husband."

"It's up to her. She could speak to the police." Nell reached for Lynn's arm. "Help me out here. When would be a good time for me to contact Rita…alone? If Phil is a murderer we don't want him knowing about it."

"There are two shifts for cooking—10:00-4:00 and 4:00-10:00. Sometimes Phil works early and Rita late, or the other way around." Lynn shook her head. "It doesn't matter either way. You can't talk to her when she's working, or other workers will know. Someone would surely let it slip to Phil. They're all loyal to him. And you can't talk to her upstairs either. You'd have to come into the bar. It won't work."

"There must be some time during the day that she leaves. Doesn't she go anywhere?" Nell could see the uncertainty on Lynn's face. "Please tell me, Lynn."

"They do have a little dog, Ringo. They take him for a walk during the day," Lynn admitted. "Early in the morning either one could take him. When

Phil works, Rita takes him around lunch, so you could *accidentally* run into her."

"Which one is working right now?"

"I'm not working until this afternoon, but I think Phil is cooking the lunch shift."

"Where do they walk?" Nell knew she was pushing her luck, but needed to find out.

Lynn rolled her eyes. "I don't know. I've never followed them. I just know that each day someone goes out the back door with the dog about 11:30. They aren't gone long, so you'd need to watch for them coming out the back."

Nell took out the small notebook she kept in her purse. "Thanks so much for your help. Could I get your phone number in case we need to talk again?"

"I can't have my phone going off while I'm working," Lynn hesitated. "I guess this would be okay. My number is 555-4250, but please send me a text and I'll get back to you so no one can hear me. You do know how to text, don't you?"

"Yes," Nell bristled.

"If you talk to Rita, remember to keep my name out of it," Lynn reminded as she turned to leave.

Nell sighed. It seemed no one wanted to be involved in this murder investigation...

                                    ***

Nell hustled over to the alleyway behind Miner's Fish House. It was already after 11:00. She needed a place to hide so she'd see Rita when she came out with the dog. A large dumpster was behind the building, so she scurried over there. Just in time.

The back door opened and Nell could hear heavy feet coming in her direction. Could someone be emptying garbage? That's all she needed— smelly garbage. Nell maneuvered herself so she was on the opposite side of where the dumpster lid opened. She heard it being lifted, a bag thrown in, and the lid slamming down. Despite expecting it, the loud bang still startled her. Then the sound of footsteps walking away. *Whew!* Close call.

As Nell waited, she thought about Zane. Where had he hidden when he was doing his surveillance? The dumpster was the logical place. She stretched her neck, scanning all around the alley, praying she wouldn't find him somewhere nearby. How had her life gotten to this point? Almost sixty years old and here she was hiding behind a dirty dumpster waiting for a dog to relieve itself? Good grief!

Her patience was rewarded. The door opened and Nell could hear soft cooing sounds. She dared to take a peek around the dumpster and saw Rita carrying a Yorkshire Terrier out the door. She set him down and picked up a pooper scooper in a crate nearby. Rita then spoke in a louder tone.

"Go for a walk? Ringo gonna go for a walk? What are we gonna see today? How about a fat squirrel like yesterday? Oh, Ringo, he was almost bigger than you!" Rita chuckled. "Let's see what we can find."

Did she sound like that when she talked to George and Newman? Nell waited a few minutes and then stood up straight. Her back hurt from crouching as she stretched it out. She took off in the same direction that Rita and Ringo were headed. Manufacturing a reason to talk to them would have been much easier if she could meet them face to face. They turned out from the alley and on past the beautiful Victorian homes on Main Street. Nell kept her distance so she didn't look suspicious.

Ringo stopped and moved into a familiar pose. The jaws of the scooper were put to use. Woman and dog turned and headed back the same route on which they came. Nell would have the opportunity to meet them face to face.

As the distance between them lessened, panic overwhelmed her. How could she casually bring up the subject to Rita of her husband committing a murder? She had never even met this woman. Who would question her about such a thing?

She would.

And she would find a way. Just a few yards more.

"You have the cutest dog. Is it a Yorkie?" Nell smiled at Rita knowing most animal lovers liked to talk about their pets.

"Yes, this is Ringo. He's my little cutie." Rita beamed, and Nell knew she had hit on the right topic.

"Ringo?" Nell laughed. "A British male with lots of hair in his face—that works."

"You get it. It goes right over the heads of the younger crowd I work with every day." A slight frown appeared on Rita's face and she started to chew on her fingernail.

"You're the owner of Miner's Fish House, aren't you?" Nell asked. "I remember seeing your picture in the paper."

"Yes, my husband and I own it." Nothing more was offered.

"It's a great place." Nell smiled. "I've eaten there several times with friends and love the food and atmosphere." Nell was hoping to get Rita warmed up a little. "You're a wonderful addition to Main Street."

"Thank you." Silence.

"Actually I'm the one who found the body last week and…"

"I have to get going." Rita started to walk away. "I'm expected back."

"Wait, please," Nell pleaded. "I was wondering…"

Without another word, Rita held tight to the scooper, picked up Ringo, and took off at a pretty good clip.

Nell knew it would be useless to follow her. She was certain Rita wouldn't talk to her today. Another way would need to be found to get the information from her.

Rita had spoken to Lynn before and maybe she would again. She'd give Lynn a call later and see if she would do a little undercover work for Nell.

No...she'd send her a text.

***

Back at home Nell made a tuna sandwich on whole wheat toast for lunch. She topped the tuna with a couple thick slices of tomato and several leaves of crispy lettuce. Nell was well pleased she made a healthy choice for lunch. How she would have loved some potato chips and dip to go with it. Or ice cream with caramel sauce for dessert! *Yikes!* She needed to banish those kinds of thoughts.

She looked down and saw George and Newmie staring up at her. "Don't worry, I'm saving some of my sandwich for you." She bent down to give them each a crust with a little tuna on it. Each morsel was swallowed whole, barely being tasted.

Nell quickly tidied up the kitchen and walked outside with the boys. She sat down on a patio chair while George spied a squirrel way in the back of the yard and took off. Newmie followed George, and soon the two were busy protecting the yard and smelling the path of the intruder.

She smiled while watching them, but Nell's thoughts had turned once again to the murder. She wasn't sure she could talk Lynn into approaching Rita for more information. Both women were hesitant to share what they knew. Lynn, in order to keep her job and Rita, not wanting to get her husband in trouble. At least Nell thought that was the reason.

The autumn days were starting to turn colder and Nell appreciated her thick-sleeved shirt. It wouldn't be long until her jacket would be needed, and then a full-fledged winter coat. Warm weather didn't last long enough in the northern part of the state.

The boys had found a sunny spot and were sprawled out near each other in the middle of the yard. Nell caught a movement out of the corner of her eye and glanced over to the next yard. A deer had walked out of the woods, but must have noticed the dogs. It stood like a statue for a moment, then stepped back into the woods. George and Newmie were totally oblivious as they snoozed while basking in the sun. Oh, to have a dog's life!

Nell would've liked to have gone out with Sam tonight, but it was Friday. That's when half the population in Wisconsin's small towns went out for fish. She knew he'd be busy, especially since he was still catching up on things from being away. The Packers had a home game on Sunday which meant the bar would be full, too. Unless Sam could get away tomorrow, which she doubted, she wouldn't see him for several days. She'd like to run some of her thoughts about the murder by him, but that didn't appear to be in the cards.

Elena hadn't called her, either, so Nell figured she was lying low hoping Nell was done sleuthing. She had intended to let it go for a while, but that clue had fallen right in her lap. She couldn't possibly be expected to ignore a suspect's name! She'd give Elena a little time before sharing that bit of news. She didn't want to drag her back into the investigation quite yet. That is, if there was going to be a continued investigation. She considered what to do next.

The thought of contacting the police went back and forth in her mind. She could tell them what she knew and not get involved any further. Except she'd need to give them Lynn's name. She didn't want to hand over that information. She'd not only lose her trust, but also lose Lynn as a source.

Of course, *if* she was going to stay out of it she wouldn't need a source. But she had a sneaking suspicion that if she went to the police with Phil's name, the chief would still be irritated with her. Probably even accuse her of meddling after their talk at The Mocha Chip.

Realizing there was no way she could win—at least none that she could think of right then and there—Nell relaxed and enjoyed the beautiful fall day.

Chapter 25

"What's this about you finding a dead body?" The voice on the phone bellowed early the next morning and Nell quickly realized it was Stacy Craig. "Once again I'm the last to know."

"First, good morning. Second, I'm not in danger this time, so you don't need to worry about a thing," Nell replied.

"That's the reason you should have said something. A couple months ago you didn't let people know because you didn't want anyone to worry. What's your excuse with this murder? I had to read about it on Facebook."

Stacy had been Nell's student early in her teaching days and now was a good friend. For the last several months she had been living in Minnesota helping her sister, Betsy, take care of their mother. She hadn't immediately told Stacy about being a target a couple months back and had not heard the end of it.

"No excuse. I just haven't told anyone who I'd have to call." Nell remembered Jud called her when she told him the story. She thought about her sister Renae, her brother Gary, and her good friend, Kris. She hadn't let any of them know because if she called one, she knew she'd need to call them all. She would end up being on the phone a long time. Somehow she just didn't feel up to it.

"Why are you getting into all these adventures without me?" Stacy scolded, then laughed. "The most exciting thing that happened when I was there was when you fell in the Oconto River."

"Fell in?" Nell countered. "I still think you pushed me."

"I would never be so disrespectful to one of my elders."

"All right for you. Now you'll never find out what's going on."

As the two bantered back and forth, the whole story eventually came out.

"I'm adding my two cents worth whether you want to hear it or not," Stacy said. "Stay out of it. No more investigating. I'm serious." Then she added with a little sass in her voice, "You don't have me over there to protect you, so who knows what kind of trouble you'll find."

After ending the call with Stacy, Nell gave in and talked to Renae, Gary, and Kris. They were all thankful that she let them know what had been going on with her, which only made her feel guilty she hadn't told them sooner.

Just as she knew it would, making those calls had eaten up almost three hours. Nell rubbed her ear and told herself she really should get used to using the speaker phone feature.

She wrote a short text to Lynn asking for some undercover assistance and was immediately rewarded with a one word answer. *No.* It was what she expected.

She walked outside with the boys. A ball was right between the edge of the patio and the grass. George went over, put it in his mouth, came back, and dropped it in front of Nell. He then looked up at her with his soft, brown eyes. Who could resist? It was relaxing for her to let her mind be free of all concerns and throw a ball to her two spirited canines.

Once back in the house, Nell fixed a quick tuna sandwich for lunch and made a plan. She picked up the phone and punched in Leigh's cell number.

"Nell, how are you?"

"Great. I was just wondering if you could spare an hour sometime this afternoon."

"I think that could be arranged. What do you have in mind?"

"Let's meet at Miner's Fish House at 2:00. I'll tell you then."

"Okey Dokey. See you in a bit!"

***

Nell met Leigh at the appointed hour and they seated themselves at the bar. Will was working and Nell wanted to make another stab at eliciting information from him. He brought them their sodas, but then left.

"While Will is occupied elsewhere I'll try to clue you in on what I've found out since the last time we spoke." Nell kept her voice low as she told Leigh about the call from Lynn, and their meeting at the pharmacy.

"No!" Leigh whispered. "The owner is a murderer?" She looked over her shoulder.

"Can you believe it? I never suspected him."

"Have you told the police?"

"No, I thought I'd do a little more investigating first. I hid behind the dumpster and followed his wife, Rita, yesterday."

"What has gotten into you? This is insane." Then in Leigh's next breath she added, "What happened?"

"She ran off and wouldn't speak to me after I told her I was the woman who found the body."

"This could be dangerous being here. If she's covering up for her husband who is a murderer, who knows what she'll do. She may come after you if she thinks you're going to find out he did it. Or she could tell him and who knows what would happen then."

Will still hadn't returned to the bar, so Nell pulled an envelope out of her purse. "Take a look at this picture." Nell unfolded a newspaper clipping from the envelope. "It's the article about Phil and Rita when they opened the restaurant. The Bayshore Reporter did a feature story on their new place and how their love of pasty brought them together."

"This is the owner? I recognize him," Leigh began. "But not from the pub.

144

He's been in Metallic Dreams several times. He came in a few weeks ago and bought a decorative plate I made."

"Did you wait on him?" Nell was curious now, and inched closer to Leigh.

"Yes. I remember him well. He seemed to be a thoughtful, intelligent man. He inquired as to how I twisted the metal for the plate. I went through a few of the steps and he was appreciative that I took the time." Leigh shook her head. "I can't see him murdering someone."

"It looks to me like he made a connection with you." Nell stuffed the news clipping back in her purse when she saw Will coming from the dining area.

"I hope I didn't keep you waiting too long. Are you ready for another round of sodas?"

"We're still working on the first glass," Nell answered. "Will, have you always been a bartender?"

"Heck, no." Will stood in front of them as he warmed to the topic. "I've done lots of different jobs. I was a stock boy at a grocery store while I was in school. Before that I had a paper route. I hired on as extra help on a dairy farm. That wasn't for me. Did a little factory work, too. Then I did roofing work for seven years. I was good at it and made decent money, but I had to give it up."

"Why's that?" Nell asked.

"I lost my footing and fell. Hurt my back. I feel pretty good now, though. Every now and then I'll get a twinge. I guess I didn't want to take the chance of seriously getting hurt. I've bartended the last few years. It's worked out for me." He grinned.

"Is this the first place where you've worked for Phil and Rita?" Nell hoped for a little kernel of a clue.

"No, I worked for them in Escanaba first," Will explained. "At the P and R Club. Miner's Fish House is a little more upscale, but the old P and R had good food, too."

"Are all the workers here from Escanaba?" Nell prodded.

"Most are, but a couple just came down a few days ago from Rapid River." Will raised his eyebrows at Nell. "Is there a reason for the questions about the staff?"

"Not really. I guess I was just wondering if any Bayshore locals would ever be able to get a job here," Nell covered her tracks. "It looks like Phil only hires workers from Michigan."

"Oh no, Phil's a great guy. He just wanted to come down to Bayshore with a team ready to go. He knows most of them will eventually go back. He'll hire from here then, as he gets to know the community."

"Is Phil easy to work for—a good boss?" Leigh asked.

"Absolutely. He and Rita are great." Will bent over and whispered, "They both take such pride in providing delicious food that they never get out of the kitchen. I keep telling them to come out in the pub. They need to meet their customers. People loved them at the P and R Club."

"That's good advice," Leigh agreed. "Customers like to chat with the owners."

"Right now Rita isn't talking to anyone. She's a little freaked out because of the murder." Will looked from Nell to Leigh. "I guess I don't need to remind you. Both of you were here."

"You told me you weren't here, Will. I know you weren't bartending, but I thought I saw you in the crowd after the body had been discovered," Nell pressed.

"I came down from my room upstairs. A murder is big news."

"During the course of the evening—your night off, did you hear anyone come back up to their room?" Nell tried to keep the excitement out of her voice, to stay calm.

"Sure."

"Who? Who came back to their room?" Nell was ready to leap over the bar to get the answer.

"I don't know exactly. I was talking on my cell to my wife."

"Your wife?" Nell sputtered. "You're married? I mean, you don't wear a wedding ring."

"Yeah, hazard of the trade. Better tips." He winked. "I've been looking for an apartment so she can move to Bayshore, but now my circumstances have changed so I'm not so sure I'll stay here."

"Hmmmmm." Nell paused. "Any idea into which room the person coming back went?"

"I'm not sure. There were lots of people going up and down the stairs and in and out of their rooms all night long. There are two shifts for work here so the stairs get plenty of traffic. Most of us prefer to use the back door to the pub when we come and go so we don't have to trudge through the bar." Will turned to greet a couple who sat down at a table.

"Every time I think I'm going to make some headway on this case, there's a roadblock put up in front of me," Nell grumbled. "There's no way of knowing if Phil left the kitchen, killed Ian Burke, and then went upstairs to change his clothes."

"Since Phil was cooking, then Rita was not. Wouldn't she have noticed him coming in the apartment with bloody clothes?" Leigh pulled her stool closer to Nell's.

"That's probably why Rita knows Phil is the killer. And he wouldn't have been too busy in the kitchen. Remember how dead it was there that night? Hardly anyone was here except us."

"Let's go down to the police station right now." Leigh stood up.

"What's the matter with you, Leigh? We can't take our information to the police. I'm not supposed to be trying to find the killer. Remember Chief Vance threatened to charge me with interfering with an investigation or something."

"What's the matter with *you*, Nell? If you're not supposed to be investigating, why are you? And if you don't tell the police what you know and someone else is killed, how will you live with yourself?"

"I know, I know."

"Truthfully, I have a hard time believing Phil is any kind of killer," Leigh admitted, "and I barely know him. He came into our shop again a couple days ago. I hadn't connected that he owned this restaurant. I had put out a display of some of my jewelry pieces. He told me how impressed with my work he was and bought a pair of earrings for his wife. He was dressed real nice and didn't act at all like a murderer."

"A smart murderer wouldn't act like one. But I have an idea. Are you with me?" Nell questioned.

"I think so. What are we doing?"

"Follow me."

Nell left a tip at the bar and walked toward the back. Leigh was close behind and then Nell made a sharp right turn.

"Are we going out the back door?" Leigh whispered trying not to draw attention.

"You'll see." Nell made a sharp turn to the left and started ascending the staircase.

"What are you doing?" Leigh grabbed her arm. "You can't go up there."

"Just watch me—while you're following me."

At the top of the stairs was a door on the right, and on the left a long hallway with doors on each side. "My guess is this is the apartment." Nell nodded to her right.

"Let's leave before we get caught," Leigh pleaded.

They could hear music coming from behind the door. Nell knocked. The music stopped. Nell knocked again. Ringo made a little bark. Slowly the door opened and Rita stood before them.

"I suppose you intend to hound me and I'll have no peace until I talk to you." Rita opened the door wider to let them in the apartment. She held the Yorkie in her arms.

"I'm so sorry," Nell began. "Really I am. My name is Nell and this is my friend, Leigh. May I call you Rita?" At her nod, Nell tried to find the right words. "Thank you for letting us in to speak with you. I take no joy in what I need to do today."

"What is it that you must know?" Rita demanded. "I understand you were the one who found the body of that poor man, but what do you want from me?"

"I want to know your husband's relationship with the deceased. What was the bad blood between them?"

"Why would you say such a thing? Phil didn't even know that man. There was no bad blood." Rita glared at Nell.

"But why then were you concerned about what Phil had done, and what would happen now?" Nell was scrambling, hoping another lead wasn't about to be destroyed.

"What do you know of my concern about what Phil had done?" Rita stared at Nell with eyes like ice.

"Someone overheard you say it," Nell offered, not wanting to get Lynn into trouble.

"If you must know, it was Phil's idea to come here. He said Bayshore was a growing community with a lot of potential. I wanted to stay in Escanaba where our place was paid off and not start all over with a huge mortgage," Rita admitted. "I've been so upset after the murder happened that I blamed Phil for talking me into coming here. I'm worried that customers won't want to relax in a pub where someone was so viciously killed."

As much as Nell hated to admit it, Rita's story worked. It was quite possible Phil was not the murderer. Darn. Back to the drawing board.

Nell and Leigh turned to leave and Rita walked with them to the door. "I hope you change your mind about Bayshore," Nell said. "Your husband is right. It is a wonderful community. Rita, would you like to meet us sometime for coffee over at The Mocha Chip?"

"I'd love to meet you." Rita smiled, her icy eyes now twinkling. She looked like a different person. "I really miss not having friends here my own age like I did back home."

"How about tomorrow?"

Rita beamed and said, "I don't work until four, so you pick the time."

Nell looked at Leigh. "Ten?"

At her nod, Nell clapped her hands.

Standing outside of Miner's Fish House before they departed, Nell and Leigh recapped their experience. They each were pleased that Rita could explain her comments about her husband. Leigh, because he seemed like such a pleasant, thoughtful, and nicely dressed man. Nell, because she didn't want Miner's Fish House to go out of business. And they had helped Rita come out of her shell.

George and Newmie yipped their approval when Nell walked in the door later that day. She found the leashes and took them on a long walk. As they moved along (at a snail's pace so the boys could check their pee-mail), Nell felt a sense of relief for the first time in days. Thankfully she hadn't taken Leigh's suggestion and gone down to the police station to report Phil as the murderer. However, she also felt a sense of defeat. She wanted to find the killer. Actually, she didn't need to physically be the one to do the finding, but the culprit needed to be found. And soon. She wouldn't rest easy while a murderer walked the streets of Bayshore.

She suspected that the police were doing everything possible to investigate the crime. There were no complaints from her about the department. Chief Vance ran a tight ship with wonderful officers. Her favorite, of course, was Paul Carson as he had been her student years before. Nell was so proud of him and all he'd accomplished.

When he was in school, she hadn't thought of Paul as becoming an officer of the law. She had other students who went on to become doctors, lawyers, teachers, and many other occupations. A lot of them surprised her, too. But that was alright. Her own teachers probably wouldn't have thought Nell had been capable of being serious long enough to get through college. Then to think she chose a profession where she was responsible for the learning and behavior of children. What would her students have thought had they known how much time she had spent in the hallway of her school for not being able to stop laughing?

Maybe some of them wouldn't have been too surprised.

She thought of other former students she had taught through the years. She'd taught many children of her former students, too. It was rewarding to read about their achievements in the local paper once they went to high school and then on to college. Academics, sports, drama, and music were areas that talents were duly recorded. But there were plenty of other good kids whose accomplishments never made the paper. And Nell remembered those students, too.

She thought of her years of teaching and everything she had learned about herself as a person as she pulled out the leftover wild rice soup from the fridge. She had learned to restrain herself from laughing uncontrollably in front of her students, that's for sure.

Most of the time.

Smiling, Nell put the soup on the stove. She pulled out crusty bread and butter—the real stuff. After all, she was a farmer's daughter from Wisconsin and still appreciated the taste and feel of real butter.

The phone rang and she was lifted out of her reverie. She could see it was Sam.

She turned down the pot of soup and answered the phone. "Hi, Sam."

"Nell." Just that one word spoken in his soft, deep voice sent a little tingle up her spine.

"I figured you're still busy catching up at the bar from being gone."

"You're right. I had hoped that I would have been able to get away today so we could get together, but it didn't happen. I'm sorry."

"No, it's okay. Really I understand, Sam."

"I know you do, but this has been a hard two weeks for both of us," Sam sighed. "I was all caught up in Jess coming back and you've been busy after finding that body. How are you holding up?"

"I'm okay, just a little discouraged. I thought the killer was Phil, the owner of Miner's Fish House, but Leigh and I talked to his wife today. I don't think he did it. I need another suspect."

"Whoa, Nellie! I can tell we need to talk. I'm way behind on your investigation. We need to catch up."

Nell thought back to a few months earlier when she hated it when Sam said "whoa, Nellie." Now she considered it a term of endearment. "We definitely need to catch up," she laughed.

"Why don't you come up to the Slam for the game tomorrow?" Sam suggested. "I need to be here, but you could be, too."

"It's a noon game, so I might be able to come up for part of it. Leigh and I are meeting Rita at 10:00."

"Who's Rita?"

"She owns Miner's Fish House with her husband, Phil."

"Ah... The guy you previously thought was the murderer?"

"Right."

"I hope you can come up, even if it is late. Ask Little Irish and Ed, too. I want to see her wear that cheesehead with the antlers like she did three weeks ago," Sam laughed. "I better get back to work. Hope to see you tomorrow."

"I'll try."

"I miss you, Nell." That deep voice got to her every time.

"I know. I miss you, too." But Sam had already hung up.

Chapter 26

The early church service was busier than usual as some people were going to the game in Green Bay, and others wanted to have time to relax at home before the game started. Either way, Nell always preferred the first service as she was up early anyway. Her meeting today at The Mocha Chip made the earlier time a necessity.

Without changing from her black dress pants and teal blazer, Nell drove downtown. She found Leigh, sporting tight black jeans and turtleneck with a large dangling piece of art hanging from her neck. She sat at a table at the coffee shop, but without Rita. Nell ordered her coffee at the counter and walked back to the table.

"Do you think Rita changed her mind?" Leigh asked.

"I hope not. She needs to get out," Nell answered. "Yesterday she was excited about the idea."

The waitress walked toward them carrying a steaming cup piled high with whipped cream and a piece of dessert on a fancy plate. She set them down in front of Nell.

"What did you order?"

"I went with the Pumpkin Spice Latte, foregoing my usual Caramel Addiction in honor of the autumn season and a double fudge brownie." Nell looked at Leigh's small cup. "What do you have?"

"Black coffee."

"That's why you're thin and I'm…" Nell looked down at her body. "… not. It's all about choices. Speaking of choices, Sam asked if you and Ed could go up to the Slam for the game today. He was really impressed with your cheesehead with antlers a few weeks ago."

"That was a lot of fun. It gave me a chance to get to know Big Irish better. He's a good guy, Nell."

"I think so, too." Nell glanced out the window. "Here she comes."

Rita waved when she came in and proceeded to the counter to order. Soon she took her seat at the table like an old friend.

As a way of getting acquainted with each other, they shared their job histories.

"My stars!" Rita exclaimed to Leigh. "I should have known it from your beautiful red hair. Phil has been to your shop and raved about the work that you and your husband do. The earrings that he bought for me are so gorgeous and unique. I haven't gone any place to wear them, but I know they'll be conversation starters."

Leigh set her cup on the table. "I'm glad you like them. I've appreciated your husband's encouragement and his business. I hope he buys you many more pieces of jewelry."

"I know he will, but rest assured that Phil will visit Metallic Dreams a lot—even when he isn't planning to buy." At Nell and Leigh's quizzical looks, Rita continued, "Phil has a thing about red hair. It used to bother me a lot. When we first married I colored my mousey brown tresses auburn thinking he'd like it. But he only liked natural redheads and I've never colored my hair since."

"What's the deal with red hair?" Nell almost squeaked with a pointed look at Leigh.

"That's what I wondered, too. Phil's mom took me aside after my fiasco with the hair dye. She said that while in high school his cousin, who had lovely red hair, died of cancer. Trudy was her name and I guess she was quite tiny. Apparently Phil always thought she needed protecting so he watched out for her. His mom said it broke his heart when he couldn't stop the cancer from taking her."

"I'm so sorry," Leigh said. "It must have been awful for him."

"I bet you remind him of Trudy. You're tiny with red hair. Excuse me a minute." Rita left the table to grab more napkins.

"Good grief! Phil could still be the killer," Nell whispered. "He has a fixation with red hair and two redheaded dolls were used as warnings. That's too coincidental for me."

"Should we say something to Rita about it?"

"I don't know. Shhh. She's coming back."

"I brought an extra napkin for each of you, too. I can't tell you how wonderful this is for me to have a chance to get away. I'm usually either in the kitchen, upstairs, or taking Ringo for a walk. You ladies have made my day."

"We're happy you could come out with us. Yesterday you mentioned you weren't keen on the idea of coming to Bayshore, but give us a chance. It's a great place to live."

"Please don't get me wrong." Rita glanced around the room. "I have nothing against Bayshore. It was the idea of starting over with a big mortgage that bothered me," Rita assured.

"Good." Nell decided to go for it. "Leigh had a strange incident happen to her a couple weeks ago. A doll was left on her doorstep."

Leigh's eyes widened in surprise, but she helped Nell continue the story. "Yes. Its long hair had been cut off and the doll was in a box."

"That *is* strange," Rita acknowledged. "First you tell me what a wonderful place Bayshore is and then as proof you reveal this weird story."

"The doll was Pippi Longstocking." Nell and Leigh waited for Rita's reaction.

"Am I missing something here? So the doll was Pippi Longstocking—is that supposed to mean something to me?"

"Pippi Longstocking has red hair!" Nell threw her hands in the air.

"I know Pippi has red hair. I have a vast collection of dolls, although many are in storage since the move." Rita shook her head. "I had a room in Escanaba just for my dolls. Once some of the workers move out, I'll use one of their rooms and set out my collection again."

"Do you have a Pippi Longstocking?" Nell prodded.

Rita smiled. "Yes, I do."

"How about a Midwest Annie?" Nell rubbed her left eyebrow waiting for the answer.

"Yes, and I have both of them right here in Bayshore at our apartment. They were my latest purchases," Rita snapped. "What difference does it make?"

Leigh leaned over to Rita and took her hand. "Another one of our friends had a mutilated Midwest Annie doll left in front of her door."

"I hate to say this, Rita, but we see a connection." Nell drained the last of her coffee.

"I thought you two were being friendly. Now I see you just wanted to use me to get more information," Rita hissed as she pulled her jacket back over her sweater and jeans and started to leave the table.

"Please don't go, Rita. We *were* being friendly. It wasn't until you mentioned Phil's fondness for red hair I thought of these questions." Nell motioned for her to sit back down.

"I don't like your implications." Rita gave Nell the stink eye. "Stay right here. I'm going home to find the boxes containing my dolls and I'll be right back to show you I still have them. Then you'll know the truth."

After Rita stomped out of The Mocha Chip, Nell and Leigh both ordered another coffee. Leigh picked out a buttercream filled Long John with caramel drizzled on top.

"I hope she finds those dolls," Leigh murmured. "I think Rita and Phil are good people."

"In that respect, I agree with you. But it sure would be nice to have this murder wrapped up."

They each made a trip to the rest room. When Leigh came out, she motioned out the window. "Here she comes."

Nell turned to look and saw Rita with a terrified look on her face. She was empty-handed.

Chapter 27

R ita stormed into the dessert shop with bleary eyes and wet cheeks. She found her seat and sniffled, "They're both gone! I don't understand it. I can't imagine what happened to them."

Nell started to speak, but Rita cut her off. "Oh, I'm sure you can imagine. You already have a scenario playing in your head. But my husband is not a killer! And he wouldn't stalk someone with dolls, either. When we get a chance to be alone I'll ask Phil about them. He may have just put the boxes in storage somewhere else. I bet that's what he did."

Rita was coaxed into sitting back down and having another cup of coffee. She listened as Nell and Leigh took turns telling the details concerning the dolls, notes, and flowers. The story sounded bizarre even to Nell as she told it, but she tried to make Rita understand their concern.

"Truthfully, after hearing all you had to say, it does seem like Phil could be the killer. In theory, that is," Rita said. "I know he didn't do any of those things and I'm anxious for tomorrow to be able to show you the dolls. I just know Phil put them in the basement or somewhere else." Rita stood up to leave.

"I hope you're right," Leigh said softly.

"That's the outcome that will be in my prayers tonight." Nell pushed in her chair and headed for the door.

Leigh and Nell stood outside the Mocha Chip as Rita crossed the street. "I bet she's going to have a long night. She's anxious to speak with Phil about the dolls, but has to work in the kitchen." Leigh walked toward her shop.

"Phil must be cooking right now. His afternoon will be slow because he won't have much business." At Leigh's raised eyebrows, Nell explained. "Remember there's no TV. No way to watch the Pack. In this area, that means no business."

"I was so wrapped up in this murder discussion, I completely forgot about the game. Are you still planning to go up to Sam's?"

"I don't know. It's almost 1:00 now. By the time I get into my green and gold clothes and drive up there, I won't see much of the game. I might just turn it on at home."

Leigh pulled out her phone and checked for messages. "We probably shouldn't have turned off our phones while we talked to Rita. I have several texts from Ed reminding me about the game."

"I have three missed calls from Sam," Nell said looking down at her phone.

"I guess he'll need to wait for another time to see you in your cheesehead. Talk to you soon."

After greeting the boys when she arrived home, Nell turned on the TV and found the game. She then gave Sam a call.

"Nell, I'm so glad you called. I was beginning to get worried when I couldn't reach you."

"I'm fine, Sam. Our coffee meeting with Rita lasted longer than I thought it would. She mentioned her husband has a fixation with red hair and she is a doll collector. She has both a Pippi Longstocking doll and a Midwest Annie."

"Are you saying you're back to thinking Phil is the killer?"

"Rita says he isn't. She went to their apartment to get the dolls to prove it. She couldn't find them, though."

"I think you may have found your murderer, Nell."

"Rita was visibly shaken and assured us that Phil must have moved the doll boxes," Nell sighed. "I hope she's right."

"When will you find out?"

"Rita said she'd talk to Phil by tomorrow. I think I'll go over there for lunch and see if I can speak with her."

"That's a good plan." Sam lowered his voice. "Are you coming up here?"

Nell glanced at the TV. "I see halftime is almost over. I think I'll watch the end of the game at home. However, I could be talked into coming up afterward."

"And might you be interested in having a bite to eat?"

"I'm looking forward to it," Nell laughed. "I'll probably be there around 5:00."

"Okay. See you then."

After watching a close 24-21 victory, Nell took George and Newman for a long walk. As they moved from one street to the next, her thoughts remained on Phil. His fixation with red hair and the disappearance of the dolls were too much of a coincidence for her. However, she could understand how Rita wouldn't want to believe her husband was a killer. She would never have believed that Drew was a murderer, no matter how much evidence was presented. How Nell hoped the dolls would be found! She just didn't have much confidence that that would be the outcome.

***

Nell opened the door to Sam's Slam and was shocked by the raucous laughter and rowdiness of the customers. She edged through the crowd searching for Sam. The age of the group was considerably younger than Sam's usual patrons. Reaching the bar, she saw him in a heated conversation with a young man. Sam was speaking very matter-of-fact, but the man was obviously annoyed.

"Everybody listen up!" The man turned from Sam with a sneer on his

155

face. "We're moving on to the next bar on our list. This place doesn't want our money." The revelers started to move to the door amid grumbling.

"Sam, what happened?" Nell asked as she moved closer to him. "Whatever it was, I have to say I'm glad that rowdy group is leaving."

"They just arrived, but had obviously been overserved. As a responsible bar owner I cannot sell them any more drinks. These days it's too much of a risk to serve someone who has already had too much alcohol."

"Good for you, Sam. Your regular clientele wouldn't appreciate all the noise that group was bringing in either." She glanced at the people sitting at the bar. The look of relief on their faces was evident.

Bud, one of Sam's frequent customers, ambled over to the window. "They're all going into The Speckled Goose across the street. I wonder if they'll get served over there."

"It's not my business whether or not they're served elsewhere." Sam ran a hand through his hair in agitation. "I just hope they all get home okay."

"Me, too," Nell said.

"Everything is under control here, Sam, if you want to go in and eat." Jeff, a second bartender, called to Sam.

"Nell, I don't think you've met Jeff. Jeff, this is my good friend, Nell."

Nell offered her hand and the two exchanged pleasantries and then Nell and Sam walked into the dining room.

They soon found a quiet table in a corner. Nell searched for the small picture of Vince Lombardi she had given Sam. She didn't have to look for long. It was strategically placed on a small shelf in the middle of the Packers' memorabilia.

Sam noticed where she was looking. "You wouldn't believe the number of people who comment on that photo. No one has seen it before. That was a great find and a thoughtful gift." Sam reached for her hand and whispered, "Thank you."

Nell smiled with a tilt of her head. "You are very welcome."

The waitress came by and they immediately ordered cheeseburgers and fries. Sam shared the ins and outs of his days since returning to Marinette. The food arrived as Sam finished his story about a delivery truck turning up that was meant for a nursing home. Then Nell told him all the information she had about the murder as they ate. She was anxious for his opinion and advice.

"You aren't going to like what I have to say." Sam shook his head as he looked in her eyes. "I think you have done enough. I know you don't want to, but take all your information to the police. Tell them everything. Then take a vacation. Go to Renae's in Minnesota or visit Kris in Traverse City. Just get out of town. I know if you stay in Bayshore the temptation will be too great to investigate. Maybe we could take a few days together somewhere."

"As tempting as that sounds, Sam, I can't do it. I have to see this case through to the end," Nell said, her voice firm.

"This is a safety issue. Phil could come after you when he hears what his wife has to say. I agree with you that the coincidence of his fondness for red hair and his wife owning those dolls is too much. It's very likely that Phil has something to do with the murder."

"That's what I'm going to find out. I'll talk to Rita tomorrow. I'll know more then." Nell looked at her watch. "I really need to be on my way. It was wonderful seeing you and being able to catch up. I've missed you, Sam."

They rose from the table and strolled toward the door. "I've missed you, too. I don't want to lose you, Nell. We could have a lot of happy years ahead of us. I'm looking forward to them. Please...be careful."

Nell smiled and whispered, "I will. Thanks for the cheeseburger and fries. It was perfect."

"You are more than welcome."

They stopped at the door where Sam engulfed her in a bear hug and then a loving kiss. Nell responded, but froze as she heard the customers clapping and whooping. Her face turned fifty shades of red, but Sam just laughed. "There are no secrets at Sam's Slam!"

Chapter 27.5

Getting caught was never part of the plan. Everything happened too fast. It's time to leave Bayshore, probably past time. Packed up some clothes, took some money. Phil will be upset, but that's just too bad. Miner's Fish House does a good business and makes plenty of money.

Where to go? Back to Escanaba? That was always a favorite. But in some ways it was too small a town. Word would filter back here. Can't have that. It better be farther away. Canada? California?

Bags are packed. The lie about going to Green Bay was brilliant. Everyone deserves a day off to get out of town. No one would have any idea about the real destination.

Chapter 28

Nell didn't have to work too hard to talk Elena into going with her to Miner's Fish House for lunch. She picked her up at home and headed toward the pub.

"Everyone I know wants me to stop trying to find the killer." Nell pulled her car into a space right in front. "I can't do that, Elena, I just can't."

"I know. But people are worried about you because they care. No one wants to see you get hurt or worse." Elena closed the passenger car door and headed for the entrance.

"At least we'll be able to enjoy a good lunch before we speak to Rita. I'm hungry."

Once inside, Nell noticed Curt was behind the bar. He left and went back toward the kitchen before they had a chance to even sit down.

"I hope he comes back soon," Elena announced. "I'm thirsty and thought a glass of beer would taste good today."

"That's not a bad idea. I think I'll order one, too."

Elena and Nell turned their heads as they saw Curt coming back, although he wasn't alone. A red-faced Phil was with him. Curt went back behind the bar, but Phil marched over to the table where they were sitting.

"I want you out of my restaurant," Phil barked as he towered over Nell. "Get up and leave quietly unless you want me to throw you out."

"I don't understand. Why are you ordering me to leave?" Nell held her ground.

Phil's eyes narrowed as he threatened, "You want every other customer here to know, too? That's fine with me. My wife came home in tears after meeting you yesterday. She couldn't sleep last night. You're filling her head with lies about me, but you still expect to be served lunch? Get out!"

"All you had to do was show her the dolls and she would have had a restful night." Nell countered. "Why didn't you just show her where her dolls are?"

"Because I don't know anything about any damn dolls!"

"I'd like to speak with Rita," Nell said, as calm as she could. Her nerves were frayed but she continued to stand her ground.

"She's too upset to be bothered. Do I need to call the police and have you removed? I'd do it myself, but you look like the type who would sue." Phil stood with his fisted hands on his hips and glared at them.

Nell and Elena walked out of the pub with their heads held high. "I'm sorry to have put you through that, Elena. I never dreamed he'd throw me out."

"I'm fine, but Miner's Fish House has lost a good customer. All of your friends should ban the place, too. He'll be sorry."

"I want to be able to go back," Nell complained. "I love the food there."

"After what he just did, you would still give him your business?" Elena looked at her with wide eyes, hands in the air. "I give up."

"Where else in town will I get pasty as good as it is here? And British style fish and chips? And the Sea Salty Caramel Guinness Brownie?" Nell released a large sigh. "My food obsession lives on."

"What just happened is another reason to stop your investigating. Maybe it's a sign."

"No, Elena. What just happened gives me more reason to investigate. Let's go to Bayshore Tap, have lunch, and discuss our options."

"One option for me is to make different friends," Elena grumbled.

"Come on. You know you've never had such excitement."

Sitting at a table at The Tap, they each ordered a glass of beer. The selection on the menu wasn't nearly as extensive as Miner's Fish House, but it would have to do. They each decided on a Reuben sandwich without fries.

"Tell me, Nell, how are you planning to pursue your investigation? You're not allowed back in your suspect's establishment. You can't talk to his wife. You have no way to get information from his bartenders or waitresses. Just what do you think you're going to do?"

"I have a couple really good friends who might want to carry on the investigation and report their findings back to me," Nell proposed. "What do you think, good friend?"

Elena sighed. "For heaven's sake, Nell, they all know Leigh and me there. If we start asking questions the bartender or waitress will run right back to Phil."

"Rats! You have a point," Nell conceded. "Even if I could go back, I bet their lips are sealed."

"The workers have probably been told not to speak to anyone about the murder or anything connected to it. At least that's what I'd tell Julie if something happened at my business."

"No doubt." Nell paused. "As I've been thinking about what just happened, I'm starting to have second thoughts about Phil. Leigh knows him from their shop and thinks he's a great guy. He appeared outraged and incredulous when asked about the dolls. Either he's a good actor or he's innocent."

"Now that you mention it, I agree. He was emotional, but he was trying to protect his wife." Elena took a sip of her beer. "If not Phil, then who?"

Nell's face paled as she looked over at her friend. "Rita. We haven't considered Rita."

160

Chapter 29

"What would make you suspect Rita?" Elena paused as the waitress set the sandwiches down. "You said she came back to the coffee shop yesterday in tears."

"For all I know she may think she's about to get caught." Nell removed the top slice of marble rye and spooned on some of the tangy dressing that was served on the side. Instead of sauerkraut that usually adorned a Reuben, the Tap loaded the heaping layers of corn beef and melty cheese with coleslaw. When Nell came to the Bayshore Tap, this sandwich was her favorite.

"I don't know if I can accept that a woman killed Ian. She'd have to be very strong, considering how he was killed."

"I don't think we can rule Rita out because she's a woman. I've read true crime books for years that have had female murderers. Look, Pippi Longstocking and Midwest Annie were her dolls. Maybe Phil has a wandering eye and she's jealous." Nell took a big bite, chewed and thought a moment. "Rita was the one who mentioned Phil liking red hair."

"She certainly would have access to the dolls. That part makes sense." Elena started in on her sandwich. "I guess a lot of it makes sense. Rita could have come down from upstairs to kill Ian as easy as anyone."

"I wonder if she was trying to frame Phil for the murder. Rita may have made up his fondness for red hair. The whole story about his cousin could be a lie." Nell took a gulp of her beer. "I have to find a way to speak to her again."

"Absolutely not!" Elena almost shouted, then glanced around her before glaring at Nell. "This is the last straw. If you try to talk to her I'm going right to the police. Do you even understand what it means to put yourself in danger?"

Nell gulped another drink of beer. *If it means finding the killer, then no.*

***

At loose ends, Nell paced through the house trying to decide on her next move. George and Newmie watched her from the loveseat. They were exhausted from the long walk they had just enjoyed, but Nell's nervous energy was boundless and completely out of character.

"Boys, I know I'm missing something. What can it be?" Two little faces looked at her in confusion. "I better call Leigh and warn her to watch out for Rita."

Nell picked up the phone, sat down between George and Newmie, and called Leigh's cell. "Do you have time to talk?"

"I'm downstairs in the shop, but I can chat for a minute."

"Are any customers there? I don't want to interfere with a sale."

"As a matter of fact, Phil is here. He's talking to Ed right now."

"Listen to me," rasped Nell. "I no longer think Phil is the killer."

"Good. I never thought he was. I'm glad you finally agree."

"I think it's his wife, Rita. Phil has no idea that she's a murderer. She may even have set him up to take the fall."

Leigh's voice became soft and deadly serious. "What do you want me to do?"

"Nothing. If Phil is at your place, then Rita is cooking. I'm going over there to confront her."

"No, Nell. She's not cooking. Phil had just come down here for a minute to ask Ed about making a decorative railing. He mentioned he's training three other workers to cook and that it's going well. He said soon he and Rita would be able to take a day off together. He's only been here for a few minutes."

"Maybe I could sneak in and go upstairs without anyone seeing me."

"Someone would see you. More importantly she's not upstairs either. Phil said he's doing double duty today as Rita had a rough day yesterday. She went into Green Bay to a spa for a facial and massage."

"It's probably just as well that she's gone. I haven't decided what to ask her anyway."

"Personally, I'm relieved you can't talk to her. If she is the killer as you think, she's dangerous. You need to be more careful, Nell."

Without conscious thought, Nell wandered into the kitchen and took a white box from the counter. After taking Elena home, Nell had gone downtown to The Mocha Chip and purchased half a dozen pecan pie bars. She had three left and knew they'd be gone before nightfall. So much for her being good about her diet.

The boys were immediately at her feet. "Yes, little ones, I'll save a bite for you."

The beauty of the bars was that they tasted just like pecan pie. The flaky crust and sweet filling topped with pecans melted in her mouth. She quickly gobbled down the sweet treat. George and Newman inhaled their bites.

Nell picked up the phone to let Annie know about Rita.

"Hello, Nell."

"Hi. How's everything going with you?"

"Great! Keith and I have renewed our relationship in a most positive way. The kids are happy again. He and I are making some serious decisions. Might even be wedding bells in the future for me."

Nell could hear Annie's happiness almost pulsing through the receiver. "That's wonderful news, Annie. I'm so glad for you. There hasn't been anything suspicious happening? No more dolls or anything?"

"No! Did Leigh get another doll?"

"Nothing like that." Nell took a deep breath. "I just wanted to tell you to watch out for Rita, Phil's wife. I think she may be Ian's killer."

"You're kidding. His wife? Are you sure?"

"I'm not positive. It's still speculation from what I know. Do you know what Rita looks like?"

"I remember her picture in the Reporter so I think I could recognize her."

"Good. And please don't mention it to anyone. I haven't gone to the police yet." Nell rubbed her left eyebrow in worry.

"Why not?"

"I've been warned by Chief Vance to stay out of his investigation."

"I'll be on the lookout for Rita. Thanks for letting me know. I won't tell anyone, but maybe it's time you take your information to the police anyway."

"So many people have made that suggestion I'm seriously considering it. Talk to you again soon."

Nell ended the connection and put her phone down. She realized the time had come to tell the police all she knew. Someone else's life might be in danger if she didn't. She mentally prepared herself for the reprimand she would receive from the chief. She probably deserved it, too. If she came clean now, maybe no charges would be filed against her.

She was still wearing her sweatsuit from the dog's walk, so she showered, and changed into a mauve top, navy dress pants, and clogs. She brushed her teeth and looked in the mirror to make sure she was presentable. She added a touch of lipstick, grabbed her purse, and headed toward the garage. She heard the doorbell and the sound of her boys flipping out. *Who could be at her front door now?*

Nell hurried to the door to take care of whoever it was. She wanted to be done with it so she didn't lose her resolve to go to the police station. She opened the door and an involuntary scream rose from her throat.

Rita?

Chapter 30

Nell quickly pulled herself together. "What are you doing here? I thought you went to Green Bay?"

"How on earth do you know that?" Nell would have enjoyed the look of surprise on Rita's face if she hadn't been so scared to see the woman.

"Your husband mentioned it to Ed Jackson when he was at Metallic Dreams today." George and Newmie were standing on each side of Nell. She wondered if she could count on them if Rita tried to pull something.

Rita glared at her. "Again, how do *you* know that?"

"I was in the store at the same time and heard him say so," Nell lied. "What happened to the facial and massage?"

"I'm glad Phil fell for my little white lie," Rita smirked. "I couldn't tell him what I was really doing."

Nell asked the next question, dreading to hear Rita's answer. "What *are* you really doing, Rita?"

"I had to come see you."

Nell's heart hit the floor as she tried to think of a way to protect herself. Did she have any heavy objects nearby?

"Why are you acting so nervous, Nell? We agreed at The Mocha Chip that we would talk today. I was crying when I told Phil about the dolls last night. I was so distraught he swore he wouldn't let you in our pub anymore." Rita bent over to let the dogs sniff her hand. "I had to come up with a good reason to take the car so I could come see you. I'm glad you're listed in the phone book."

Nell closed the front door and escorted her in to the living room and to a chair. She wasn't completely sold on her story, but wanted to hear the rest of it.

"My friend and I came to see you, but Phil kicked us out. I gathered you couldn't find the dolls."

"No. I asked Phil, but he didn't know anything about the whereabouts of Pippi and Midwest Annie. I know he didn't have anything to do with that murder. You have to believe me."

"What about you?"

"What *about* me? I told you. I believe my husband."

Nell took a deep breath. "Did *you* have anything to do with the murder?"

Rita's mouth dropped and her eyes bulged. "No! How could you even suggest such a thing?"

"I want to believe you, but considering the dolls are yours, the murder occurred at your pub with your fireplace poker and your darts on the body, you and your husband are the most logical suspects." Nell watched Rita closely.

"I don't know how to prove that we're innocent." Rita's shoulders drooped and she swallowed hard. "There are many others who live in our building and would have the same access to those items as we do."

Nell was beginning to believe Rita was innocent, too. If it wasn't Rita, who could it be? "As I said before, I want to believe you. Have any of your workers acted odd lately?"

"I don't think so, but I can't think right now."

"I'll be right back, Rita." Nell walked into the kitchen and came out with the remaining two pecan pie bars on separate plates. "Something sweet always helps me come up with a plan."

Chapter 30.5

Damn that car! I managed to sneak out most of my belongings during the early morning hours only to discover a flat tire. Then to find I don't have a jack. I'll have to borrow one from one of the other workers. I can't wake anyone up early. If that person helped me, my packed car would lead to all kinds of questions. I'll just have to say I can't leave because of the tire and work my early shift. Then I'll borrow a jack from someone who is working and won't have time to offer to help me. I'll have plenty of time to leave at the end of my shift. I can wait until four. No one has been suspicious of me yet. Just a few more hours and I'll be out of here.

Not before I pay a visit to that stupid old woman, though. Too bad there isn't such a thing as a Nosy Nellie doll. I'd tear it to pieces. Since I don't have a doll, I'll just have to take it out on her in person. *Your meddling days are over!*

Chapter 31

"What do you think of your employees, Rita? Have they all worked for you for a long time?"

"Most of them have." Rita nibbled at her pecan bar.

"Stay calm." Nell rose from her seat. "I think I just saw a head pop out of sight." Her heart was pounding like a hammer as she crept toward one of the windows.

"Did the murderer follow me here?" Rita whimpered.

George and Newman sensed Nell's unease and soon ran barking to the front door. Nell followed them and saw Annie coming to the porch and opened the door to her.

"Annie, were you just on my patio looking in a window?"

Annie nodded. "Are you okay?" Annie panted. "What's Rita Stewart doing here?"

"I'm now almost positive that Rita is innocent. How did you know she'd come to see me?"

"I was taking a walk down your street and Rita drove by. It's taken me several minutes to run down the street, but I was trying to make sure you weren't in harm's way. I had my cell phone out ready to call the police if it looked like you were in danger."

By this time Rita was at the door and heard the end of the conversation. "You really thought that I was the killer?"

"Not anymore," Nell said. "Come on in, Annie. We're putting our heads together to try to figure this out."

The three sat down and the boys jumped up on the loveseat with Nell. "Just to get the ball rolling here, I have a negative feeling about your bartender, Will."

"I'm surprised." Rita leaned forward. "Most of our customers like his friendliness and efficiency."

"His friendliness is the problem. He flirts too much," Nell countered.

Rita crossed her arms over her chest. "Has he flirted with you inappropriately?" she asked.

"Of course not!" Nell gasped.

"Is that the problem?" Annie laughed.

"Very funny." Nell shot her a look. "I don't remember you being such a wise guy when you were sitting in my classroom."

Annie grinned. "I can't help it."

"I guess that *was* funny." Nell gave Annie a wink. "What do *you* think of Will?"

"I think Will is a great bartender. He's part of the reason my friends and I like to go down to Miner's Fish House. He's quick with the drinks, laughs at our jokes, and teases us. I don't want him to change."

"And Will's a wonderful employee," Rita added. "He's considering staying in Bayshore and not going back to Escanaba. Phil and I are hoping he does."

"That's right," Nell said. "He told me he was married and had been looking for a place to rent. Then he added he might not stay in town. I didn't think to question him more about it at the time."

"He hasn't mentioned being unhappy with Bayshore to Phil or me. I wonder. I suppose if he goes, Curt would leave, too."

"Why?" Annie asked. "What does Will have to do with Curt?"

"He's married to Curt's sister."

"I didn't know Curt's sister was his wife." Nell turned to Rita. "What do you know about Curt?"

Rita thought for a minute. "I guess not as much as I'd like to know. He's friendly, but not as outgoing as Will. He's one of the few workers we didn't know very well before we hired him. Curt is from Escanaba, but he hadn't worked for us up there. The other bartender besides Will, who came here initially, quit after two days. Will vouched for his brother-in-law, so we gave him the job."

"The first time I saw him was the night of the murder," Annie said. Newmie jumped off the loveseat and went over to her as she bent down and wiggled her fingers. "He wasn't all that friendly that night. He didn't even introduce himself."

"That was the first night that Elena, Leigh, and I met him, too," added Nell.

"No," Annie disagreed. I'm fairly certain that Leigh met him before."

Nell's eyes widened. "Why?"

"That night when he brought our beer and popcorn, Leigh smiled and said 'Thank you, Curt.' I remember because I was going to ask her about it, but then we started talking about the flowers she had received."

"Now that you mention it, Annie, I remember, too. I knew there was something I was missing." Nell stood up to find her phone in the kitchen. "I'm going to call Leigh and have her tell me their connection." Nell made the call.

"Hi, Leigh, I have a quick question for you."

"Sure, what is it?"

"Had you ever met Curt, the bartender, who was bartending the night of the murder before that night?"

"Yes. I had a wonderful conversation with him in our shop several days before the murder. He made me laugh and was quite charming. He came in several more times looking at a large necklace I was working on. He was in here the day Ian was killed. So at the time of the murder, I still thought he was a pretty decent fellow."

"Did something happen to change your mind?" Nell prodded.

"The next day I noticed a set of the little decorative olive picks I make for drinks was missing. I looked for them, but never found them. I chalked it up to nerves because of the murder the night before. Then he came in again after I started putting my jewelry out. After he left, a pair of my handcrafted earrings had disappeared."

"That's horrible!"

"He came in another time, so I followed him around the shop talking to him and watching his every move. He left and hasn't been back since. Good riddance."

"So he's a shoplifter. Thanks, Leigh."

"Wait, Nell! Why did you want to know?"

"I no longer think Rita is the culprit." Nell glanced over at Rita, who rolled her eyes. "She's here at my house with Annie. We're discussing her employees."

"I'm done with work for the day. Mind if I join you?" Leigh asked.

"Not at all. Come on over."

Nell clicked off with one friend and punched in the number for the other.

Nell spoke into the phone, "I know you don't want any more to do with this case, Elena, but I think you'll regret it if you miss the finale."

"What are you talking about, Nell?" Elena sighed.

"Leigh is coming over to my place. Annie and Rita are already here. You're welcome to come and join us."

"Rita? I thought she was the killer."

"That conclusion was premature. She's over here helping us. We may have a lead on the murderer." Nell laughed. "You have a lot of catching up to do."

"It certainly sounds like it. Well, Sherlock, if the name of the murderer is within your grasp, Watson needs to be there."

***

When Elena and Leigh arrived, Nell broke out some tortilla chips and a jar of salsa she had on hand for unexpected company. She also offered an emergency six pack of Leinenkugel's Honey Weiss beer from the refrigerator in the garage. The boys were having a field day going from woman to woman with sad eyes and being rewarded with chips and petting.

"Have you noticed any missing supplies since Curt started working for you, Rita?" Nell scooped up some dried chile salsa on a chip.

"We were having a problem a couple weeks ago. Every day or two something would be missing. It ran the gamut from silverware to steaks. That's just from the kitchen. Phil didn't want to worry me, but I know beer and hard liquor were being stolen from the bar, too. Phil and I were looking into a security system. A hidden closed-circuit TV would flush out the thief."

"Did you have it installed?" Elena asked.

"No, not yet. We were still looking for the best deal when the stealing stopped. We'll still put it in, but it's not a priority right now. They're pretty expensive systems."

"The thief wasn't at it too long as you're new in the community," Leigh said.

Nell got up and walked to the kitchen, but called, "Are you sure it just started after Curt came?" She turned on the faucet and put more water in the doggie bowls.

"I think so, but Phil would know. He wrote everything down."

"Why don't you ask him when you go home?" Annie suggested. "Then we can get together again tomorrow and figure out what to do."

Nell made her way to the living room. "I say there's no time like the present. Let's go down there and ask him now."

"Is that the beer talking?" Leigh teased.

"One beer? Are you kidding me?"

Elena turned to Nell. "There's one small detail you seem to be forgetting. I was with you earlier today when Phil ordered you to leave in no uncertain terms."

"You just leave Phil to me." Rita rose from her chair. "Let's go."

Chapter 32

It was after 4:00 when Nell and the women piled out of Elena's new Subaru Forester and walked into Miner's Fish House. Will was behind the bar and had some trouble hiding his surprise at seeing Rita with the group.

"Go sit at a table and I'll go back and bring Phil out. He can answer our questions right now." Rita marched toward the kitchen.

They found a table for six and sat down. Will came over from behind the bar.

"Would you care for anything to drink?"

"I don't think so." Nell spoke for them all. "We're just here for some answers."

Rita and Phil came back from the kitchen and sat down. "I'm not happy about leaving my kitchen again with just the trainees back there. There better be a good reason." Phil scowled at each woman individually, and stopped at Rita.

"Knock it off, Phil. You're not intimidating anyone." Rita shook her head and poked his arm. "They want to know when all the stealing started here, and I do, too. It might have something to do with the murder."

"I'll be ecstatic when the cops solve that murder," Phil sighed deeply. "It's like an albatross around my neck."

"Yeah, yeah, yeah." Rita circled her hand to hurry him along. "When did you say supplies started disappearing?"

"About four days after we opened."

"So nothing was stolen before Curt starting working here?" Nell leaned over the table and spoke softly. "Do you think he's the thief?"

Phil knit his brows. "It's possible. Our other bartender quit after two days and Curt started on our fourth day. I thought of him, but someone else may have just waited a few days to get the lay of the land."

Rita motioned to Will. "Could you come over here for a second?"

Will approached the table. "Do you want a drink, Rita?"

"No, but I'd like to ask you about your brother-in-law."

"Curt?" Will's voice was barely above a whisper as he rubbed his hands down his pants.

"You've worked for us for a long time and you recommended Curt." The disappointment was evident in Phil's voice. "We have reason to believe he was the one stealing from us. Do you have anything to say?"

Will's face turned red and he looked from Rita to Phil. "I'm so sorry. My wife, Connie, begged me to get him a job here. I thought if I was watching him he wouldn't get into any trouble."

"Do you mean he'd been in trouble before?" Nell interjected.

"Yeah." Will's chin hit his throat, but he didn't meet her eyes. "I'm sorry."

"You knew alcohol was missing from the bar. Why the hell didn't you say something?" Phil's calm demeanor was gone.

"I spoke to Curt as soon as I realized what was going on. The stealing stopped. If I told you, I knew you'd fire him. He really needed the job." Will explained as his chin quivered.

"Well, we know who the thief is now, but that's a far cry from him being the murderer, too." Phil ran his hand through his hair. "I'll talk to you about this later, Will."

"We know Curt was friendly with Leigh. Now we need to find his connection with Annie." Nell rubbed her left eyebrow.

"And his connection to the dolls," Elena added.

"Right. Will, when exactly did you speak to Curt?" Nell asked.

"The night that Ian was murdered. Curt was working. I needed to fill my car with gas so I came down the stairs to go out and caught him in the act." Will edged over to the bar to see if anyone needed a drink.

"What did he take?" Phil's body was visibly shaking.

Will came back to the table and squatted down. "He was coming out of the closet with a box. I couldn't tell what was in it at first. He saw me and started apologizing so I knew he was stealing. We got into a big argument."

"Can you remember what you said to each other?" Nell leaned closer so she wouldn't miss a word.

"It was ugly. But we spoke quietly so we wouldn't be heard by customers." Will glanced at Rita and Phil. "I told Curt that I was going to Phil with the information and he deserved to be fired. He begged me not to tell. I told him I had to report him. He then said that I was too cozy with some of the women who came in the bar." He motioned to Annie. "He even mentioned you by name. He threatened to tell my wife."

"How did Curt ever see you with Annie and her friends?" Nell pressed. "When you're bartending, he's off work."

"There's not a lot to do in a room at night. Curt often came down for a couple drinks on nights that I worked."

"Bingo! That's the connection to Annie," Nell declared to Will. "He may have left the doll and then the note in an effort to scare her away from you."

"That's possible," Rita agreed, and met Will's eyes. "Were you afraid of his threats?"

"No. I explained to him that I was the same bartender I was in Escanaba. I have a good rapport with the customers. Connie had been in the R&P and knew how I could work a bar. She didn't have a problem with my friendliness. And believe me, we always found a place to use the tip money."

"Go on with your story," Phil growled.

"I could see Curt was getting all worked up. I didn't want to make a scene, so I told him if the stealing stopped for good I wouldn't say anything. As far as I know nothing more has been stolen."

"What time did this occur, and where is this closet where you had the argument?" Nell's mind had been in overdrive since listening to Will's story.

"It was after 8:00. The closet is across the hall from the game room, but we were standing right in front of the game room door when we argued."

That bit of news confirmed Nell's theory. "Ian was killed in the game room sometime after 8:30 that night. I only say 8:30 because Curt said he served him a drink at that time. He could easily be lying. Did you figure out what was in the box he was taking?"

"Yeah. When I turned to leave I noticed the flaps on the box were open and I looked. It was cooking utensils—big spoons, spatulas, that kind of thing."

"Were there any utensils with a long sharp blade?" Nell asked.

Will closed his eyes and arched his head back. "Curt would never kill someone. He didn't even know Ian." Will paused, brought his head down, and looked Nell in the eye. "But yes, there was a large knife with a long blade."

***

The group at the table sat in stunned silence as Will went back behind the bar.

"Nell, are you saying you think Curt gave me the doll, flowers, and note?" Leigh pressed her lips together and looked from Nell to Annie and back to Nell. "He left the doll and note for Annie, too?"

"That's where the clues are leading. I think he had a bit of a crush on Leigh. And saw Annie as a threat to his sister's marriage." Nell looked at Elena, Leigh, and Annie. "We sat at that table after receiving our beer and food quite oblivious to anyone else in the pub. Curt could easily have been gone for a large block of time."

"I'm getting to the bottom of this right now," Phil boomed. "I'm going upstairs to question him."

"I'd like to go with you, Phil," Nell said.

"That's fine, Nell. Rita, do you want to come, too?" Phil stood up. "I think the rest of you should wait here."

As Elena, Annie, and Leigh agreed, Phil, Rita, and Nell walked to the back hallway and up the stairs. At the top of the steps, the Stewarts' apartment was on the right. Turning left to go down the hall, Curt's room was the first one on the right. After giving the door several thunderous knocks, Phil pulled out his master key.

"Is it acceptable that you go into his room, Phil?" Nell questioned with raised eyebrows.

"Certainly. That was one of our stipulations with the workers. They stay here free of charge, but we can enter their rooms with good reason. I'd say this is a good reason."

The door opened to an empty room. It still had the bed, dresser, small table, chair, and night stand that were provided, but was glaringly bare of any personal items. Rita rushed over to the closet and found it empty.

"How the hell can that be?" Phil sputtered. "He was working here until 4:00 today. That was less than an hour ago."

Nell had been observing everything in Curt's room and made her way into the walk-in closet as Rita left. "Oh, my goodness! Rita, did you know about this hole?"

Phil and Rita both came over on the double. Nell stepped out so they could have a look. A hole had been drilled through the wall. Rita peered in. "That's our storage room, Phil! That's where I keep the dolls."

"I'm going to have another talk with Will. I want to know if he had any idea Curt was leaving." He turned to his wife. "Honey, I think it's time to call the police."

Rita pulled out her cell phone and made the call.

Back downstairs Will admitted that he had agreed to work Curt's shift for him today as he told Will he had to go to Green Bay. But he swore he had no idea that he was leaving for good. "Curt told me early this morning that he had a flat tire and decided to stay and work his early shift. I lent him my jack less than an hour ago."

"He might still be out back changing his tire," Phil called as he raced to the back door. The whole table followed him this time.

Officer Carson was coming in the front door as they were going out the other way. Leigh waved him over. "This way, Paul. He could still be here."

The officer ran down the hall and out the back door. "Stop! Police!" He yelled at Curt as they all saw him start to back out his car. They heard the siren and saw a squad car drive behind Curt's car and block his exit.

Curt opened his car door and stood up with his hands in the air. "What's going on here? Can't a guy drive his own car in his free time?"

Officer Carson looked in the back seat. "Looks like you're going away for the long haul. Just where are you going?"

"So now it's a crime to leave without giving notice," Curt sneered. "Okay, of that I'm guilty."

"I need to take some statements here." Officer Wunderlin took Phil aside and took notes as he listened to Phil report the theft of supplies.

Meanwhile Office Carson peppered Curt with questions. It was to no avail as Curt took full advantage of his rights and remained silent. Nell did notice a red permanent marker sticking out of his shirt pocket, though, and the glare Curt sent her way.

The officers took short statements from the women and then the suspect was loaded into the back of the squad car.

They lingered outside, dreading going back inside to tell Will that his brother-in-law was on his way to the police station.

"I understand Curt's connection to Leigh and Annie," Elena announced. "But how could Curt have laid his hands on Rita's dolls?"

"When we went upstairs to confront him, it was obvious Curt had packed up to leave," Rita explained. "Nell looked in the closet and noticed a hole. His room has a connecting wall to our apartment. He could look into the room and see all the items we had in storage. He might have watched me unpack the dolls and then put them away."

"We'll need to search that room to see if anything else is missing." Phil ran his hand through his hair. "I'm wondering how he was able to get in the apartment."

"Is Ringo walked at the same time each day?" Nell asked.

Phil and Rita looked at each other and nodded their heads.

"When there's only one of you in the apartment, do you lock the door when you leave?"

Again the couple looked at each other, but this time shook their heads in the negative.

"If Curt knew the items he wanted, it wouldn't take him long to slip into your apartment and take them when one of you was working and the other walking the dog, especially if the door was unlocked."

"What I don't understand is why any of this caused Curt to murder Ian," Annie admitted. "What am I missing?"

"His argument with Will happened in front of the game room door. Ian could have overheard that Curt had stolen those items. After Will left, he may have threatened Curt that he was going to report him. I think you mentioned, Annie, that Keith said Ian believed in always doing the right thing," Nell speculated. "Ian was in good physical shape and could have scared Curt. Will told us that Curt was getting agitated. Maybe he panicked and grabbed the knife from the box." Nell paused, then looked at Leigh and continued. "It's possible that the first night I saw Ian looking at Annie and Leigh, Curt was down in the bar, too. He may have thought Ian had an interest in Leigh. Jealousy has made murderers out of men before."

"That gives me a chill all the way up my spine." Leigh shivered at the thought.

"You think Curt stabbed Ian several times, moved him in the corner, and pushed in the fireplace poker?" Elena began. "Then placed darts in his wounds and covered him up with the rug?"

"As bizarre as all that sounds, yes, I do." Nell walked over to join Phil and Rita at the door. "Someone did all of those things. Do you have a different idea?"

Elena shook her head and headed to the door.

"It's time we tell Will what happened out here before he hears it from a customer." Phil opened the back door and they all trudged to the bar.

Phil and Rita took Will aside privately to give him the bad news. Nell, Elena, Leigh, and Annie walked out together to Elena's car. "Ed will be happy to hear the news that he is no longer a suspect." Leigh winked at Nell.

"That goes for Keith, too. Nell, you had us all on the defensive." Annie opened the back seat of the vehicle and moved over to the middle.

"I'm sorry about being suspicious, but that helped me rule people out." Nell got into the front with Elena. "Look at how many different people I considered!"

"Yes, just look," Elena gave her a lifted eyebrow. "It was almost like you were drawing names out of a hat."

Nell smiled, but was relieved the killer was caught. Perhaps she should say *alleged* killer.

She appreciated being dropped off at home and taking a long walk with the boys. Going over the events of the day as she walked, Nell realized she needed to put in some phone time. She planned to call Sam, Renae, Gary, Kris, Stacy, and Judson. The dolls just appeared a little more than two weeks ago. Her relatives and friends who lived far away would be surprised at how much had gone on since the last time they spoke. And she had done her part to help!

The leisurely stroll helped to clear her mind. Nell chuckled as every blade of grass seemed to either be sniffed or showered with pee. Sometimes both. The trio had just started their return home when a police car turned onto the street. Nell could see it was Chief Vance and her stomach dropped. She knew he didn't like her involvement and that he would confront her about it. The car came to a stop and Nell crept over, keeping control of the dogs.

"Nell Bailey." The chief's face was the color of a Door County cherry and Nell could almost see steam coming out of his ears.

"I'm sorry, Chief Vance. I couldn't help myself," Nell babbled. "It's just that I had an inside track to the information. I had to act on it."

"Are you telling me that you, a retired teacher, couldn't help yourself?" Vance mimicked. "How would that have flown in your classroom if you told a student not to do something and they did it anyway? Would 'I couldn't help myself' get the kid off the hook?"

Nell shook her head. "No. But this is different, I…"

The chief cut her off. "I'm not prepared to discuss this matter right now. Come down to the station tomorrow. Call first, though. I want to talk to you personally."

"You're not going to charge me with anything, are you?"

The squad car moved down the street as Nell stood there without an answer to her question.

***

Nell had originally planned to reveal her relationship with Sam to her son when she called him next. After sharing the events of the last two weeks with everyone, she chickened out—again. She was tired and couldn't handle any sort of confrontation. Instead, after she made quick calls to everyone sharing the news of solving the mystery, she had a low key night at home.

The next day Nell gathered up her nerve and called the police station at 1:00. She was asked to come down at 4:00. She had three hours to kill. The boys were snoozing on the couch after their walk. Nell was all showered and ready to go. She sat down and flipped through some cooking magazines, but her heart wasn't in it. *What if Chief Vance charged her? Orange may be the new black, but it didn't look good on her.*

The minutes passed slower for her than for a student waiting for recess. Finally she drove down to the station. She was directed into the chief's office.

Chief Vance sat at his desk paging through some papers. He acknowledged her with a nod of his head. Nell stood there waiting quietly.

"Take a seat, Nell." He motioned to the chair. "I've given this situation a lot of thought. You know I was concerned for your safety, don't you?"

"Yes, Chief," Nell murmured. "I know."

"You also brought in a bunch of other people. About six of you all together. What if the suspect had a gun and shot all of you when you were by his car? You got the others involved. What if they had been hurt?"

"I didn't consider that, Chief," she acknowledged. "I just wanted to find the killer."

"I have to admit, I believe you found the right man. Turner admitted the theft of supplies and even revealed the name of the man who bought the stuff. He's still not talking about the murder, but going through his car, we found a knife we already know was the instrument used on the victim. It was on the passenger seat. He may have intended to use it again soon. The blade was the right size and it still had a smidgeon of a dried substance on it that could be blood. It's at the lab. We also found several pads of yellow sticky notes in his luggage."

"Then why aren't you pleased that I led you to the right suspect?" Nell asked, curious.

"You should have given all the information you had acquired to us. Then there wouldn't have been any chance anyone else would've been hurt or worse." The chief took a hard look at Nell. "If I pressed charges against you, you'd have a record. That's not what I want. I've decided to let you off with a warning."

Nell was so relieved she wanted to give the chief a big hug, but restrained herself. "I don't know how to thank you, Chief." Nell smiled and stood up with wobbly legs.

"I do. Don't get involved again." He stood and walked Nell out of his office.

"Ah, Chief. What are the chances of another murder in Bayshore? I don't think that will happen any time soon."

"But if it does, I expect you to stay out of it." Chief Vance opened the outside door for Nell to leave the station. "If everyone thinks you're a private detective, it puts you in the eye of the storm. Just keep a low profile."

At that moment they saw Zane jump off his bike and come running over. "Mrs. Bailey, will you let me interview you? It'll be in the school newspaper and my mom knows the editor of the Bayshore Reporter, so he'll let me put it in there, too. Maybe the Green Bay Press-Gazette will pick up the story.

Who knows?"

"Of course, Zane."

Chief Vance walked back inside, shook his head, and Nell heard him mumble, "So much for keeping a low profile."

Chapter 33

The fire burned bright and hot at the fire pit in Nell's back yard. Even though there had been lots of joking about it, this was the first time Sam had sat on the wooden Adirondack chairs with her. The late October evening was cool, so the heat that the fire produced was appreciated.

Earlier, Sam had played ball with the boys, so now they were satisfied to snooze by the fire. Nell broke the silence. "You three look rather content."

"That's because we are. After so many hours at the bar, your place gives me peace." Sam reached for her hand. "You give me peace, Nell."

The sun was low in the sky, the fire crackling, and their wine glasses were full. Nell felt real contentment herself. Who knew what the rest of the night would bring?

The sound of her phone buzzing startled Nell. It was Jud. She had to tell him about Sam before their relationship could go any further. But this was such a perfect night. She didn't want to take a chance of ruining it. Sam gave her a questioning look as the phone continued to ring. But then again, she always had an excuse not to tell Jud about Sam.

Nell brought herself to her feet and spoke into the phone as she walked toward the house. "Hello, Jud. Something wonderful is happening and I want you to be a part of it."

The fire was just getting started.

Mediterranean Chicken Pasta

1 tablespoon olive oil

½ cup white wine

2 cubed boneless chicken breasts

2 tablespoons fresh basil

4 cloves minced garlic

½ cup sliced Kalamata olives

½ cup diced onion

crumbled feta cheese

1 can diced tomatoes with juice

1 teaspoon cayenne pepper

salt and pepper to taste

Saute chicken in olive oil over medium heat in a large skillet until golden. Remove from pan.

Put garlic, onion, and cayenne in the pan and sauté. Add tomatoes and bring to a boil. Lower the heat and add the wine and half of the basil that has been cut in ribbons. Simmer for 12 to 15 minutes.

Add the sliced olives, salt and pepper and return the chicken to the pan with the sauce. Let flavors meld for about five minutes.

Crumble feta cheese and the remaining ribbons of basil over the entire dish or each individual plate.

Judge the amount of cayenne by your family's own taste. This is delicious and healthy as long as you don't go overboard with the cheese!

Spicy Sausage Pizza

1 premade pizza crust

8 ounce can tomato sauce

2 tablespoons olive oil, divided

Italian seasonings

12 to 16 ounces of spicy Italian bulk sausage

Crushed red pepper flakes

2 cloves garlic

½ cup sliced ripe olives

½ cup sliced onion

8 ounces mozzarella cheese

Preheat oven to 450 degrees. Saute onions and garlic in 1 tablespoon olive oil in a skillet. Add Italian sausage and saute until browned. Drain off the fat.

Place pizza crust on pizza pan. Then pour remaining olive oil on the crust. With a paper towel make sure every spot of the crust is lightly covered with oil. Pour tomato sauce on the crust and sprinkle with Italian spices to your taste. Cover the sauce with sausage, onions, and garlic, then add the crushed red pepper flakes if you like a lot of spice.

The sliced ripe olives go over the sausage and the mozzarella cheese accents the top. Turn the oven down to 425 degrees and bake for 10 minutes. Let rest 2 minutes before cutting.

Making this pizza takes very little time and I like it so much more than the frozen kind. The premade crust makes it a cinch.

This is a scrumptious, but quite heavy pizza. I usually use only half of the sausage and freeze the other half to use another time. I also use only 4 ounces of the cheese as I don't like pizza too cheesy.

Black and Blue Burger

1 pound ground round

3 cloves chopped garlic, divided

crumbled blue cheese

1 tablespoon canola oil

8 ounces baby Portobello mushrooms

1 tablespoon butter

½ onion, sliced

½ cup red wine

salt and pepper to taste

Sauté onions and 2 cloves garlic in canola oil and butter in a frying pan. Add the chopped mushrooms and wine and continue until ingredients are tender. Remove from pan.

Shape the ground round into three patties blending in the last chunks of garlic. If necessary add more oil and butter to the pan. Fry the patties to whatever degree of doneness you prefer. When the burgers are almost ready, top with crumbled blue cheese and set a cover over the pan to melt the cheese.

A big pretzel bun goes nicely with this, but use whatever you like. Set the burger with cheese on the bun and add the mushrooms with onions and garlic to the top. Yum!

I add a sauce to this burger. It is a mixture of chipotle peppers and mayonnaise. I use it for tons of recipes. It's my favorite.

Chipotle Sauce

7 ounce can of chipotle peppers in adobo sauce

1 cup mayonnaise

>Put peppers and mayo in a blender. I use an immersion blender. I used to take a couple peppers out of the can and try to seed them and chop them. It can be done, but blending is a lot easier.

>That's the sauce. This keeps a long time in the refrigerator. (It's never been around long enough at my house to go bad, so I don't know how long it keeps.)

Corn Muffins with a Kick

corn muffin mix (probably needs milk and egg)

1 teaspoon chipotle pepper seasoning

1 chopped jalapeno pepper

½ cup orange marmalade

>Prepare corn muffin mix adding chipotle seasoning and chopped jalapeno pepper. (I used hot jalapeno nacho slices from a jar.) Fill muffin tins halfway then add a teaspoon or more of the orange marmalade. Top off the muffins with the rest of the batter. Bake just a little longer than the mix instructs.

>You can make these muffins as sweet or spicy as you like. It all depends on how much of the pepper and marmalade you add.

Elena's Wild Rice Soup

½ pound bacon

2 cans cream of celery soup

1 large onion

3 cans milk

½ cup long grain and wild rice

1 cup Velveeta cheese

2 cans cream of potato soup

salt and pepper to taste

sriracha sauce

Cut up and fry bacon with onion until brown, but not too crispy.

Cook the rice.

Heat the soups, milk and cheese together over medium heat. Then add bacon, onion, and rice.

I add the sriracha sauce to the individual bowl. Each person can then take responsibility for their own level of heat.

I received this recipe from my good friend, "Elena" although I added the sriracha sauce. It is comfort food at its best (and its worst.) I make it only rarely because I tend to eat too much and gain weight when I've made it in the past. If you're making it for a family where each person just gets one helping, (or you have some measure of control) this soup would be perfect!

Nell's Layered Lemon Love

12 ounce tub of Cool Whip, thawed

1 lime

2 jars of lemon curd

1 shortbread piecrust

Pour contents of one of the jars of lemon curd into a bowl. Blend until soft and can easily be stirred. Then spread into the piecrust. Pour the other jar of curd into the same bowl. Mix again until soft and then add ½ of the tub of Cool Whip. Continue stirring, but carefully so as not to break down the Cool Whip. When blended put on top of the lemon curd in the piecrust. Place the remaining Cool Whip on the top. Finally zest the lime and sprinkle as decoration. Refrigerate at least two hours.

I came up with this recipe after watching cooking shows and reading recipes. It's a mix of several ideas that really comes together well. It could also be done using a springform pan and making your own lemon curd and whipped cream. The taste is tart and fresh either way.

My guests have loved this "Lemon Love."

Dear Reader,

I hope you enjoyed **Death Knock**. Here is a sneak peek at the first chapter of **Death Nosh**, Nell's next adventure. To learn more about my culinary mystery series, visit my website at www.marygracemurphy.com. Thank you!

Mary Grace Murphy

Death Nosh

Chapter 1

Nell clutched the plastic tray of homemade cookies as she rushed from her car. It was late afternoon, but the street lights were twinkling and throwing a spotlight on the falling snow. She approached the large Victorian home where the previous evening she had been a guest. The outside still looked festive and inviting, except for the police car parked in the driveway. She rang the bell, uncertain as to who would answer it.

"Nell Bailey, what are you doing here?" Chief Vance, head of the Bayshore Police Department, stood tall in the doorway and did not step aside to allow her to enter.

"I want to pay my respects to Clayton's daughter and to offer some goodies so other visitors can have a bit of a nosh." Nell uncovered the tray and the aroma of the still warm cookies floated up. "Also, I attended the Christmas party here last night."

"I'll be damned." The chief shook his head. "How you are able to insinuate yourself into every case is beyond me. You've become Bay Shore's answer to Jessica Fletcher."

"Case? Are you saying Clayton Dunbar was murdered?"

Chief Vance stepped aside and gestured into the room. "That's not what I'm saying, but come on in. There's no point in having you stand out in the cold." He closed the door behind her, but kept her standing in the foyer.

Nell wiped her feet on the rug, then noticed Hazel Burton, Clayton's long time housekeeper, hovering in the background. She walked over to give her a hug. "Hazel, I'm so sorry for your loss. I know you worked for Clayton for years so he must have been like a member of your own family."

"He was, Nell. He was such a kind, gentle man. I can't believe he's gone." Hazel's frail body shook as she wiped at her eyes and said, "I know he was old, in his nineties, but he was so healthy. You saw him last night. He was

186

happy, bouncing around like a man twenty years younger." She took the tray Nell offered and trudged back to the kitchen. As she watched her, Nell realized that Hazel was just as fragile as Clayton. How had she been able to care for this magnificent home on her own? Shaking that thought off, Nell walked back to the chief.

"Are you suspecting foul play?"

"The cause of death has yet to be determined. How did you know him?"

"We taught a couple of years in the same building. He was finishing up his career and I was starting mine. Clayton helped me learn the ropes my first year. When he retired, my late husband and I used to run into his wife and him around town. Every year he always invited me to his Christmas party, just like last night. I was so pleased that he kept having the parties even after Bernice died."

"Do you think you could make a list of the guests who attended last night?"

"I could, but I wasn't here the entire time. It was an open house type of party." Nell absently stroked the soft green velvet on the back of the settee in the gigantic foyer. "His daughter, Emma, might be a better person to ask. I think she's been visiting for a few days."

"According to Hazel, Emma Dunbar Nyland said her goodbyes to her father last night. She headed back to Madison early this morning." The chief frowned and then studied Nell. "I guess I'm asking for your help."

"Yes, I'll definitely make a list. I probably can name all of the guests. They arrived at different times, but most everyone stayed until the end." Nell's blue eyes shone and her voice went into high gear. "There are tons of other ways I can help, too. I'll do anything. . ."

"Don't get ahead of yourself, Nell. I'm only asking for a list of guests." He looked toward the kitchen. "I probably could ask Hazel to make the list."

"No, I'll do it. I thought so much of Clayton that this will make me feel like I'm helping."

"Okay. Just bring it down to the station tomorrow morning." The chief opened the front door.

She took the hint and slipped outside.

***

Nell pulled her old tan Mercury into the garage saying a silent prayer in thanks that the thirteen year old Sable still ran just fine. She opened the door to the kitchen to the delight of her feisty Miniature Schnauzer, George, and mischievous Maltese, Newman. They were named during a time when Seinfeld was her favorite comedy show. Heck, it still was.

"Wanna go outside?" Nell walked to the sliding glass door in the living room and the three buddies ventured out onto the snowy patio. The boys trotted out to the yard to settle up some business. Newmie ran back to Nell, but George just stood there. She knew he was waiting for her to throw the ball. Nell almost always played fetch when she came out with them.

"I hate to break it to you, George, but winter has arrived. Soon there will be deep snow out here and most of our outdoor time will be on our w-a-l-k." Nell spelled it out as she didn't want to take them for a spin right now. She started toward the door with Newmie on her heels. "Come on, George. Time for a treat." He trotted toward her.

Once inside, Nell was true to her word and the treats were doled out. She then threw a few stuffed toys around in the living room to give the dogs a bit of exercise. She could only imagine what it would be like if she had two big dogs instead of little ones.

Soon Nell grabbed a notebook and plopped in her easy chair. Her boys settled down on the floor as she clicked on the TV. Thoughts of her conversation with Chief Vance were foremost on her mind. Why would the police still be in the home so long after the body was found? Could Clayton Dunbar have been murdered? Three hours ago that possibility hadn't even crossed her mind. Something must have made the chief suspicious. But what? Right now she had a little bit of an in with him. She needs to show him what an asset she can be. Police must need to bounce ideas off other people. Maybe their wives listen and offer opinions strictly off the record. But Chief Vance isn't married...

Just as she was beginning to mull that fact over in her mind, the phone rang. She looked over on the end table and saw that it was Sam Ryan. Sam, the wonderful man who Nell had been seeing for months. She felt a twinge of guilt.

"Hello, Sam."

"Ahh, Nell, how I look forward to our talks each day," Sam admitted in the deep sexy voice that made her melt on the spot.

"Me, too. I hope your day has been without incident?" Nell knew Sam was concerned about his restaurant and bar, Sam's Slam. One of his best waitresses had been having some personal problems that she'd brought into the bar.

"No more than usual. Just glad to go in my office for a bit and talk about something else."

"Oh. Then I guess we should." Nell lowered her voice to a whisper. "I may be involved in another murder."

"What?" bellowed Sam. "That's not welcome news. What are you talking about?"

Too late Nell realized her statement wouldn't be met with excitement. "I guess I'm overstating my involvement. Remember I went to a Christmas party last night at the home of a former colleague, Clayton Dunbar?"

"I do," Sam said with apprehension.

"This morning I saw on Facebook that he died. He was ninety-two, so I didn't think too much about it. I made some peanut butter cookies for his family and visitors. I just took them over a couple hours ago."

"Okay. Everything seems fine so far."

"The chief of police was over there examining the scene and he asked me to make a guest list from the party last night. He must be looking for suspects."

"Let me get this straight, Nell. The police were at the residence of someone who died at home. I believe that is proper procedure. I would imagine the police need to speak to those attending the event to ask if he was exhibiting signs of illness or distress. They would need a list of attendees. You've been asked to help. That sounds innocent to me. I don't see any reason to think there's been a murder." Sam gave a little chuckle. "I think you've exaggerated the situation this time, Nell."

"Maybe so." Nell heard a loud noise in the background. "What happened?"

"I don't know," he sighed, but I better go check it out. "Talk to you later."

Nell hung up her landline phone. Sam wasn't seeing Clayton's death and Chief Vance's request the way she did. Her explanation may have made Sam feel relief, but his reaction didn't please her. Nell walked to the kitchen.

She needed carbs.

If you enjoyed Death Knock, you may enjoy the following books by Helen Osterman and Annie Hansen...

The Emma Winberry Mysteries
Helen Osterman

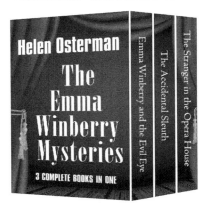

Emma Winberry and the Evil Eye

The first book in the Emma Winberry cozy mystery series, *Emma Winberry and the Evil Eye* combines mystery, suspense, humor, pathos and romance as the reader is introduced to amateur sleuth, Emma Winberry. When a world famous tenor, Marcantonio Speranza, a vendetta for a rival singer, and a boy named Angelo with a voice of an angel are all put together; it could be a plot for an opera. Emma's sixth sense tells her Speranza is in danger. To investigate she becomes a supernumerary (or extra) at the Midwest Opera Company. There she meets Nate Sandler, a fellow super, and they become romantically involved. But Emma has bizarre dreams and tries to warn the tenor he is in danger, but to no avail. In the exciting climax, during a performance of the opera, *A Masked Ball,* an unexpected sequence of events puts Emma in mortal danger as she tries to save Speranza's life. Will she succeed?

The Accidental Sleuth

Sixty-something Emma Winberry depends on her sixth sense and her Guardian Angel to get her through life. Nate Sandler, now her significant other, does his best to keep her out of trouble. *Most of the time.* When Emma leaves her house in the suburbs and moves into a posh condo in Chicago's lake front with Nate, she finds herself mixed up with a self-abusive, anorexic teenager, her cruel uncle, a couple of tough hoodlums who mistake Emma for someone else, and a cadre of homeless people. Emma feels the problems are somehow tied to the murder of an inventor found in a downtown alley. She calls on her Guardian Angel for help, but can her celestial guardian keep her out of harm's way as the complex puzzle unravels to a pulse-pounding climax involving treachery, deceit, and murder?

Stranger in the Opera House

Emma Winberry returns for another adventure in *The Stranger in the Opera House*. This time she and her significant other, Nate Sandler, are supernumeraries at the Midwest Opera for an upcoming production of *The Ghosts of Versailles*. This tile turns prophetic when the lead soprano screams that there is a strange man lurking in her dressing room. Although a police search turns up no evidence anyone was there, the cast and crew are left on edge. And nerves become more frayed as the 'stranger' is seen again and again, but never caught despite numerous attempts to apprehend him. Emma's sixth sense tells her he may be more than he seems. The rehearsals continue to be fraught with mishaps. When a large sum of money is stolen from the office and a guard seriously injured, everyone assumes it is the work of the mysterious 'stranger.' *Everyone except Emma.*

After finding an old trunk in a storeroom in the basement with documents dating back to the Underground Railroad, someone assaults the librarian in an attempt to steal them. The 'stranger' is again blamed, but Emma becomes convinced the apparition is a lost soul trapped between two worlds. Her Guardian Angel tells her she must help him cross over. But how? Adding to the mystery is a figure in black secretly leaving packages in a hidden niche. Can Emma solve this puzzle and release the 'stranger' at the same time? Determined to uncover the truth, Emma and friends are led on a life-threatening adventure that could very well be their last.

A Kelly Clark Mystery Series
Annie Hansen

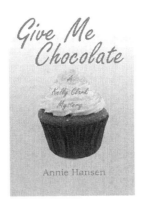 

Give Me Chocolate

In the quaint river town of Geneva, Illinois, Kelly Clark flees California and returns to her hometown to re-start her life after a horrific divorce from an abusive husband. She accepts her sister's generous offer to live in the apartment above Chocolate Love, her sister's specialty dessert shop in the Historic District of Geneva. Kelly's life starts to turn around when she reconnects with an old flame. Just when it looks like she is getting her life back on track, she stumbles over a dead body in the kitchen of Chocolate Love. The suspicious death of a Chocolate Love employee sends her hopes for a better future plummeting. Has her violent past and the danger she faced in California followed her home to Geneva?

Bean in Love

Rumors of a local ghost in small-town Geneva cause real distress for mystery novelist, Kelly Clark, at a time when her life is going great. She's moving on from her troubled past, her books are selling, and she's newly in love. But when a local dies across the street from Kelly's apartment in the Geneva History Museum under suspicious circumstances, Nikki, Kelly's sister, calls upon her to help figure out what happened. Despite Kelly's reluctance to get involved with the investigation, she and her sister team up to try and solve the mystery. Did a ghost really have a hand in the death, or are the sisters allowing a local legend of a haunting skew their judgment? Their paths divided, Nikki focuses on opening a new coffee shop as Kelly is haunted by nightmares and memories from her past. Things get even more complicated as the Clark sisters face an unexpected pregnancy, a surprise proposal, and a possible foreclosure. Her relationships crumbling, Kelly questions if she is really moving on with her life, or if she's just fooling herself. Can Kelly leave her past behind and focus on solving the mystery? Or will Kelly continue to be plagued with nightmares and run away from everything good in her life?

Acknowledgements

The greatest appreciation is extended to all my friends in the fictionalized city of Bayshore, Wisconsin. The citizens of this wonderful community welcomed my Noshes Up North Culinary Mystery series just as they welcomed me thirty-five years ago. Thank you for all of your support and for lending me this beautiful setting: Oconto–History on the Bay.

About the Author

Mary Grace Murphy grew up among the beautiful rolling hills of Southwest Wisconsin and moved to the woodsy Northeastern part of the state on the captivating shores of Green Bay where a teaching job awaited.

After a wonderful thirty plus years in a middle school classroom, Mary Grace finally took pen to paper (or fingers to keyboard) and did what she had dreamed of doing since childhood—wrote a book. Her first novel is *Death Nell*, a Noshes Up North Culinary Mystery. *Death Knock* is her second novel in the series.

The topic was easy—food, another constant theme in her life since the beginning. Family lore has it that Mary Grace's grandpa gave her a lick of his ice cream cone when she was six weeks old. After that taste, her head stretched and tongue came out as she reached for more. (Ice cream is still MG's favorite food.)

Widowed since 2002 and without a dog since 2010, Mary Grace loves to spend time reading books and magazines about food, watching TV and movies about food, collecting and revising recipes, cooking, and of course, eating! Readers can find more information about her books at marygracemurphy. com or on her Facebook page.

Made in the USA
Lexington, KY
20 March 2015